Praise for #1 *New* bestselling author Nora Roberts:

"Roberts weaves a story like no one else,
and if possible, she just gets better."
—*Rocky Mountain News*

"[Nora] Roberts...is at the top of her game."
—*People* magazine

"Her stories have fueled the dreams
of twenty-five million readers."
—*Entertainment Weekly*

"Nora Roberts has a talent for delivering the best."
—*Affaire de Coeur*

"With clear-eyed, concise vision and a sure pen,
Roberts nails her characters and settings
with awesome precision, drawing readers
into a vividly rendered world of family-centered warmth
and unquestioned magic."
—*Library Journal*

"A consistently entertaining writer."
—*USA TODAY*

"Roberts is indeed a word artist, painting her story
and her characters with vitality and verve."
—*Los Angeles Daily News*

"[Nora Roberts] is a storyteller
of immeasurable diversity and talent."
—*Publishers Weekly*

"You can't bottle wish fulfillment, but Nora Roberts
certainly knows how to put it on the page."
—*New York Times*

"Nora Roberts has been called 'a born storyteller'
and she lives up to that reputation."
—*Inside Books*

"Roberts has a warm feel for her characters
and an eye for the evocative detail."
—*Chicago Tribune*

"Nora Roberts just keeps getting better and better."
—*Milwaukee Journal Sentinel*

Dear Reader,

Here at Silhouette we are thrilled to offer readers the incomparable novels of Nora Roberts. *With Open Arms* is particularly special because both stories are among the very first romances Nora wrote for Silhouette Books back in the early 1980s.

Song of the West, first available in 1982 from Silhouette Romance, features a cocky rancher who tries to convince a city gal to take a chance on romance. Set in Wyoming, *Song* is one of the few books Nora wrote for Silhouette that features a Western setting. *Her Mother's Keeper,* another offering from Silhouette Romance, was first available in 1983. It focuses on a confident young woman who returns home to Louisiana and is drawn into the arms of her mother's handsome young boarder.

From the very first book Nora Roberts published to her bestseller status today, millions of readers across the country have agreed: there's no one like Nora. Here's what some of her fans have to say about her:

"Thank you for hundreds of hours of joy. It is such a pleasure to know every book will be a treasure when I pick it up to read." —Barbara Block, North Ft. Myers, Florida.

"If you ever wonder if your time and talent are appreciated—don't. Everybody loves Nora Roberts. I can only hope you derive as much satisfaction from your creations as we do." —Raphael Allred, Grand Junction, Colorado.

Happy reading!

The Editors
Silhouette Books

NORA ROBERTS

WITH OPEN ARMS

Silhouette® Books
Published by Silhouette Books
America's Publisher of Contemporary Romance

SILHOUETTE BOOKS

ISBN 0-373-28504-3

This edition published by arrangement with Harlequin Books S.A.

Visit Silhouette Books at www.eHarlequin.com

Printed in U.S.A.

CONTENTS

SONG OF THE WEST

Chapter 1

The land in southeast Wyoming is a magnificent paradox. Spreading plains and rolling hills coexist with rocky mountains and thick velvet pines. From the kitchen window, the view was astounding, and Samantha Evans halted in her duties for a moment to drink it in.

The Rockies dominated the vast curtain of sky, their peaks laced with snow, though it was late March.

Samantha wondered if she would still be in Wyoming the following winter. She dreamed of long walks with the air biting and sharp on her cheeks, or wild rides on a spirited mount with hooves kicking up a flurry of white. But none of that could happen until her sister was well enough to be left alone.

A frown creased her smooth brow. Sabrina was her reason for being in Wyoming, with its majestic mountains and quiet plains, rather than in the more familiar surroundings of Philadelphia's tall buildings and traffic-choked streets.

The two sisters had always been close, with that special, magical intimacy that twins share. They were not identical. Though they were the same in height and build, Samantha's eyes were a dark cornflower blue, widely set, with thick, spiky lashes, while Sabrina's eyes were a light gray. Both faces were oval set with small, straight noses and well-shaped mouths, but while Samantha's rich brown hair, with its highlights of gold, was shoulder length with a fringe of bangs, Sabrina's ash blonde was short, framing her face with delicate curls. The bond between them was strong and enduring. Even when Sabrina had married Dan Lomax and moved so many miles away to settle on his ranch in the Laramie Basin, their devotion had remained constant and unwavering.

They kept in touch by phone and letter, which helped to mitigate Samantha's aching loneliness. And she was happy in her sister's delight in the coming baby. The two women had laughed and planned together over the phone. But that was before Dan's call. Samantha had been aroused from a deep predawn sleep by the shrill ringing of the phone. She reached groggily for it, but was instantly alerted by the anxious tone of her brother-in-law's voice. "Sam," he said without any preamble, "Bree's been very ill. We did manage to save the baby, but she has to be very careful for a while now. She will have to stay in bed and have constant round-the-clock care. We are trying to find someone to—"

Samantha had only one thought—her sister, the person she loved best in the world. "Don't worry, Dan, I will come immediately."

She was on the plane to Wyoming less than twenty-four hours later....

The whistle of the kettle brought Samantha back to the present. She began to brew the herbal tea, placing delicate floral cups on a silver tray.

"Teatime," she called as she entered the living room. Sabrina was propped up with pillows and comforters on the long wood-edged sofa. Though her smile was warm, her cheeks still retained a delicate pallor.

"Just like the movies," Sabrina commented as her sister set a tray on the pine table. "But the role of Camille is getting to be a bore."

"I imagine so." Samantha poured the fragrant tea into cups. "But you may as well get used to it, Bree, you've got the part for a month's run.'' She transferred a large gray striped cat from Sabrina's lap to her own, offered Sabrina a steaming cup and sat on the rug. ''Has Shylock been keeping you company?''

''He's a terrible snob.'' With a wry smile, Sabrina sipped at her tea. ''He did graciously allow me to scratch his ears. I have to admit, I'm glad you brought him with you, he's my biggest entertainment.'' She sighed and lay back against the pillows, regarding her sister seriously. ''I'm ashamed to be lying here feeling sorry for myself. I'm lucky.'' She rested her hand on her stomach in a protective gesture. ''I shall have my baby, and I sit here moaning about your waiting on me.''

''You're entitled to moan a bit, Bree,'' said Samantha, immediately sympathetic. ''You're used to being active and busy.''

''I've no right to complain. You gave up your job and left home to come out here and take care of me.'' Another deep sigh escaped, and her gray eyes were dangerously moist. ''If Dan had told me what you were planning to do, I would never have allowed it.''

''You couldn't have stopped me.'' Samantha attempted to lighten the mood. ''That's what older sisters are for.''

''You never forget those seven minutes, do you?''

Sabrina's eyes cleared, and a reluctant smile curved her generous mouth.

''Nope, it gives me seniority.''

''But your job, Sam.''

''Don't worry.'' Samantha made another dismissive gesture. ''I'll get another job in the fall. There's more than one high school in the country, and they all have gym teachers. Besides, I needed a vacation.''

''Vacation!'' Sabrina exclaimed. ''Cleaning, cooking, caring for an invalid. You call that a vacation?''

''My dear Sabrina, have you ever tried to teach an overweight, totally uncoordinated teenager the intricacies of the parallel bars? Well, the stories I could tell you about vacations.''

''Sam, what a pair we are. You with your teenagers and me with my preadolescent Mozarts. Lord knows how many times I cleaned peanut butter off the keys of that old Wurlitzer before Dan came along and took me away from scales and infant prodigies. Do you think Mom expected us to come to this when she dragged us to all those lessons?''

''Ah, but we're well-rounded.'' Samantha's grin was faintly wicked. ''Aren't you grateful? She always told us we'd be grateful one day for the ballet and the piano lessons.''

"The voice lessons and the riding lessons," Sabrina continued, ticking them off on her fingers.

"Gymnastics and swimming lessons," Sabrina concluded with a giggle.

"Poor Mom." Samantha shifted Shylock to a more comfortable position. "I think she expected one of us to marry the president, and she wanted us to be prepared."

"We shouldn't make fun." Sabrina wiped her eyes with a tissue. "The lessons did give us our living."

"True. And I can still whip up a mean spinach soufflé.

"Ugh." Sabrina grimaced, and Samantha lifted her brows.

"Exactly."

"You have your medals," Sabrina reminded her. Her smile warmed with pride and a trace of awe.

"Yes, I have the medals and the memories. Sometimes, it feels like yesterday instead of nearly ten years ago."

Sabrina smiled. "I can still remember my terrified excitement when you first swung onto the uneven bars. Even though I'd watched the routine countless times, I couldn't quite believe it was you. When they put that first Olympic medal around your neck, it was one of the happiest moments of my life."

"I remember thinking just before that competition, after I'd botched the balance beam so badly, that I couldn't do it. My legs felt like petroleum jelly, and I was mortally afraid I was going to be sick and disgrace myself. Then I saw Mom in the stands, and it ran through my mind how much she'd sacrificed. Not the money. The bending of those rather strange values of hers to allow me those years of training and those few heady moments of competition. I had to prove it was justified, I had to pay her back with something, even though I knew she'd never be able to say she was proud of me.''

''You proved it was justified.'' Sabrina gave her twin a soft smile. ''Even if you hadn't won on the bars and the floor exercises, you'd proved it by just being there. And she was proud of you, even if she didn't say it.''

''You've always understood. So get over the idea I'm doing you a favor coming here. I want to be here. I *belong* here.''

''Sam.'' Sabrina held out a hand. ''I don't know what I'd do without you. I don't know what I *ever* would have done without you.''

''You'd manage,'' Samantha returned, giving the frail hand a squeeze. ''You have Dan.''

''Yeah, I do.'' The smile became soft. ''This is the time of day that I miss him most. He should be home soon.'' Her gaze wandered to the glass-domed anniversary clock on the mantel above the fire.

"He said something about checking fences today. I can't quite get away from the image of him chasing rustlers or fighting off renegade Indians."

With a light laugh, Sabrina settled back among the cushions. "City slicker. You know, Sam, sometimes I can't even remember what Philadelphia looks like. Jake Tanner was riding along with Dan today to make sure the boundary fences were in good repair."

"Jake Tanner?" Samantha's question was idle.

"Oh, that's right, you haven't met him yet. The northwest corner of the ranch borders his. Of course, the Lazy L would fit into one corner of his ranch. He owns half the county."

"Ah, a land baron," Samantha concluded.

"A very apt description," Sabrina agreed. "The Double T, his ranch, is the most impressive I've seen. He runs it like clockwork, super efficient. Dan says he's not only an incredible rancher, but a very crafty businessman."

"Sounds like a bore," Samantha commented, wrinkling her nose. "Steel-gray hair around a leathered face, a handlebar mustache drooping over his mouth and a generous belly hanging over his belt..."

Sabrina's laughter rang out, high and sweet.

"You're about as far off the mark as you can get. Jake Tanner is anything but a bore, and speaking from the safety of marital bliss, he's a fascinating man to look at. And, being rich, successful and unattached, all the females under forty buzz around him like bees around honey."

"Sounds like a good catch," Samantha said dryly. "Mom would love him."

"Absolutely," Sabrina agreed. "But Jake has eluded capture so far. Though from what Dan says, he does enjoy the chase."

"Now he sounds like a conceited bore." Samantha tickled Shylock's smooth belly.

"You can hardly blame him for taking what's offered." Sabrina defended the absent Jake Tanner with a vague movement of her shoulders. "I imagine he'll settle down soon. Lesley Marshall—her father's ranch borders the other side of the Double T—has her sights set on him. She's a very determined woman, as well as being more than a little spoiled, and dreadfully rich."

"Sounds like a perfect match."

"Mmm, maybe," Sabrina murmured. Her face creased in a small frown. "Lesley's nice enough when it suits her, and it's about time Jake had a wife and family. I'm fond of Jake. I'd like to see him set up with someone with more warmth."

"Listen to the old married woman." Samantha addressed a dozing and unconcerned Shylock. "A year of nuptial bliss, and she can't stand to see anyone unattached.''

''True. I'm going to start on you next.''

''Thanks for the warning.''

''Wyoming's full of good-looking cowboys and handsome ranchers.'' Sabrina continued to smile as her sister grimaced. ''You could find a worse place to settle down.''

''I have no objection to settling here, Bree. I've become quite attached to the wide open spaces. But—'' she paused significantly ''—cowboys and ranchers are not among my immediate plans for the future.'' She rose from the floor in a fluid motion. ''I've got to check on that roast. Here.'' She handed her sister the novel that rested on the table. ''Read your love stories, you incurable romantic.''

''You won't be so cynical when you fall in love,'' Sabrina predicted with the wisdom of experience.

''Sure.'' Samantha's grin was indulgent.

''There'll be bells ringing and fireworks shooting and trumpets blaring.'' She patted her sister's hand and strolled from the room, calling over her shoulder. ''Angels singing, flames leaping...''

''Just you wait,'' Sabrina shouted after her.

Samantha busied herself preparing vegetables for the evening meal, clucking her tongue at her sister's nonsense. *Love,* she sniffed derisively. Her only experience with that complex emotion had been fending off unwanted attentions from eager males. Not once had any man lit an answering spark in her. But whatever this love was, it worked for Bree. The younger twin had always been more delicate, softer and more dependent. And though Sabrina was trying to be brave and strong, her sister knew the fear of miscarriage still lurked in the back of her mind. She needed Dan's support and love, and right now, she needed to feel his arms around her.

Like the answer to a prayer, Samantha spotted two figures on horseback approaching from the lower pasture. Grabbing her heavy jacket from the hook by the back door, she scurried out of the kitchen and into the cold March air.

As Dan and his companion drew closer, Samantha greeted him with a smile and a wave. She had noticed, even at a distance, Dan's expression of concern. But a smile relaxed his features when he spotted Samantha.

''Sabrina's all right?'' he asked as he reined in next to her.

''She's fine,'' Samantha assured him. ''Just a trifle restless, and tremendously lonely for her husband.''

''Did she eat better today?''

Samantha's smile warmed, lighting her face with a quick flash of astonishing beauty.

''Her appetite was much better. She's trying very hard.'' Samantha lifted a hand to stroke the smooth flank of the gelding he rode. ''What she needs now is you.''

''I'll be in as soon as I stable my horse.''

''Oh, Dan, for heaven's sake. Let your hand do it, or I'll do it myself. Bree needs you.''

''But...''

'''S all right, boss,'' the other horseman interrupted, and Samantha spared him a brief glance. ''I'll tend to your horse. You go on and see the missus.''

Dan flashed his companion a wide grin and dismounted. ''Thanks,'' he said simply as he handed over the reins and turned to Samantha. ''Coming in?''

''No.'' She shook her head and hunched her shoulders in the confines of her jacket. ''You two could use some time alone, and I'd like some air.''

''Thanks, Sam.'' He pinched her cheek with brotherly affection and moved off toward the house.

Waiting until the door closed behind him, Samantha walked over and dropped wearily onto the stump used for splitting wood. Resting her back against the fence, she breathed deeply, devouring the brisk, cold air. The strain of caring for her sister in addition to running the house and cooking the meals, including, over his objection, Dan's predawn breakfast, had taken its toll.

"A few more days," she whipered as she closed her eyes. "A few more days and I'll have adjusted to the routine and feel more like myself." The heavy corded jacket insulated her from the bite of the cold, and she tilted back her head, allowing the air to play on her cheeks as her mind drifted on the edge of exhaustion.

"Funny place to take a nap."

Samantha sat up with a jerk, confused and disoriented by sleep. Her eyes traveled up to the speaker's face. It was a lean face, skin bronzed by the sun and stretched tightly over cheekbones, all lines and shadows, hollows and angles. The eyes were arresting, deep-set and heavily lashed. But it was their color, a deep, pure jade that caught and held her attention. His dusky gold hair curled from under a well-battered Stetson.

"Evening, ma'am." Though he touched the brim of his hat with due respect, his extraordinary eyes were faintly mocking.

"Good evening," she returned, struggling for dignity.

"Person could catch a bad chill sitting out too long after the sun's low. Wind's picking up, too." His speech was slow and thickly drawled. His weight was distributed evenly on both legs, hands deep in pockets. "Oughtn't to be out without a hat." His comment was accompanied by a fractional movement of his head toward her unadorned one. "Hat helps keep the heat in."

"I'm not cold." She feared for a moment her teeth would chatter and betray her. "I was...I was just getting some air."

"Yes, ma'am." He nodded in agreement, glancing behind her at the last, dying brilliance of sun as it slipped behind circling peaks. "Fine evening for setting out and watching the sunset."

Her eyes flashed at the teasing. She was embarrassed to have been caught sleeping. He smiled a slow, careless smile that crept unhurried across his face. The movement of his lips caused the hollows to deepen, the shadows to shift. Unable to resist, Samantha's lips curved in response.

"All right, I confess. You caught me napping. I don't suppose you'd believe I was just resting my eyes."

"No, ma'am." His answer was grave, with just a hint of apology.

"Well." She rose from her seat and was dismayed at how far she still had to look up to meet his eyes. "If you keep quiet about it, I'll see to it that you get a piece of the apple pie I baked for dinner."

"That's a mighty tempting offer." He considered it with a long-fingered hand reaching up to stroke his chin. "I'm partial to apple pie. Only one or two things I'm more partial to." His eyes roamed over her in a thorough and intense study that caused her heart to pound with unaccustomed speed.

There was something different about this man, she thought swiftly, something unique, a vitality at odds with lazy words and careless smiles. He pushed his hat back farther on his head, revealing more disorderly curls. "You've got yourself a deal." He held out his hand to confirm the agreement, and she placed her small hand in his.

"Thanks." The single word was breathless, as she found her speech hampered by the currents running up her arm. Abruptly, she pulled her hand away, wondering what it was about him which disturbed her equilibrium. "I'm sorry if I was short before, about Dan's horse." She spoke now in a rush, to conceal a reaction she could not understand.

"No need to apologize," he assured her, and the new soft texture in his tone both warmed and unnerved her. "We're all fond of Mrs. Lomax."

"Yes, well, I..." she stammered, suddenly needing to put a safe distance between herself and this slow-talking man. "I'd better go inside. Dan must be hungry." She looked past him and spotted his horse, still saddled, waiting patiently. "You didn't stable your horse. Aren't you finished for the day?'' Hearing the concern in her own voice, she marveled at it. Really, she thought, annoyed, why should I care?

''Oh, yes, ma'am, I'm finished.'' There was laughter in his voice now, but Samantha failed to notice. She began to study the mount with care.

It was a magnificent animal, dark, gleaming chestnut, at least sixteen hands, she estimated, classic lines, fully flowing mane and proud, dished face. Arabian. Samantha knew horses and she recognized a full-blooded Arabian stallion when she saw one. What in the world…? ''Than's an Arabian.'' Her words interrupted her thoughts.

''Yes, ma'am,'' he agreed easily, entirely too easily. Her eyes narrowed with suspicion as she turned to him.

''No ranch hand is going to be riding around on a horse that's worth six months' pay.'' She stared at him and he returned the steady survey with a bland, poker face. ''Who are you?''

''Jake Tanner, ma'am.'' The slow grin appeared again, widening, deepening, then settling as he lifted the brim of his hat at the introduction. ''Pleased to meet you.''

The land baron with the women at his feet, Samantha's brain flashed. Anger darkened her eyes.

''Why didn't you say so?''

''Just did,'' he pointed out.

"Oh." She tossed back her thick fall of hair. "You know very well what I mean. I thought you were one of Dan's men."

"Yes, ma'am." He nodded.

"Stop *ma'aming* me," she commanded. "What a mean trick! All you had to do was open your mouth and say who you were. I would have stabled Dan's horse myself."

"I didn't mind." His expression became annoyingly agreeable. "It wasn't any trouble, and you had a nice rest."

"Well, Mr. Tanner, you had a fine laugh at my expense. I hope you enjoyed it," she said coldly.

"Yes, ma'am." The grin widened without seeming to move at all. "I did."

"I told you to stop…" She halted, biting her lip with frustration. "Oh, forget it." Tossing her head, she took a few steps toward the house, then turned back crossly. "I notice your accent has modified quite a bit, Mr. Tanner."

He did not reply, but continued to stand negligently, his hands in his pockets, his face darkened by the late-afternoon shadows. Samantha spun back around and stomped toward the house.

"Hey," he called out, and she turned toward him before she could halt the reflex. "Do I still get that pie?"

She answered his question with a glare. His laughter, deep and rich, followed her into the house.

Chapter 2

The sound of the slamming door reverberated through the ranch house as Samantha struggled out of her jacket and marched into the living room. At the sight of her sister's face Sabrina slipped down into the pillows, picked up the novel lying on her lap and buried her nose in its pages. Dan, however, did not recognize the storm warning in his sister-in-law's blue eyes and flushed cheeks. He greeted her with a friendly, ingenuous smile.

"Where's Jake?" His gaze slid past her. "Don't tell me he went home without a cup of coffee?"

"He can go straight to the devil without his coffee."

"I expect he wanted to get home before dark," Dan concluded. His nod was sober, but his eyes were brilliant with merriment.

"Don't play innocent with me, Dan Lomax." Samantha advanced on him. "That was a rotten trick, letting me think he was one of your hands, and..." A giggle escaped from behind the paperback. "I'm glad you think it's amusing that your sister's been made a fool of."

"Oh, Sam, I'm sorry." Warily, Sabrina lowered the book. "It's just hard to believe anyone could mistake Jake Tanner for a ranch hand." She burst out laughing, and Samantha was torn between the pleasure of seeing her sister laugh and irritation at being the brunt of the joke.

"Well, really, what makes him so special?" she demanded. "He dresses like every other cowboy I've seen around here, and that hat of his has certainly seen better days." But, she remembered, there *had* been something special about him that she had not quite been able to define. She firmly dismissed this disquieting thought. "The nerve of him." She rounded on Don again. "Calling you boss, and ma'aming me in that exaggerated drawl."

"Reckon he was just being polite," Dan suggested. His smile was amiable and pure. Samantha sent him the look that terrified her students.

"Men." Raising her eyes, she searched the ceiling in hopes of finding the answer there. "You're all alike, and you all stick together." She bent and scooped up the sleeping Shylock and marched into the kitchen.

Time at the ranch passed quickly. Though her days were full and busy, Samantha fretted for some of the physical outlet that had so long been part of her life. At times, the confinement of the house was suffocating. Years of training and discipline had left her with an inherent need for activity.

Unconsciously, she separated her life into three categories: the pre-Olympic years, the Olympic years and the post-Olympic years.

The pre-Olympic years were a blur of lessons, piano teachers, dance instructors, her mother's gentle but inescapable admonishments to "be a lady." Then, the first time she had gripped the lower bar of the unevens, the new chapter had begun.

By the time she was twelve years old, she had remarkable promise. The gymnastics instructor had informed her mother, who was more distressed than pleased at the praise. Though her mother had objected to more intense training, Samantha had ultimately prevailed.

The hours of training became months, county meets became state meets, and national competitions became international competitions. When Samantha was picked for the Olympic team, it was just another step down a road she was determined to follow. Weariness and aching muscles were accepted without hesitation.

Then it was over, and at fifteen she had found it necessary to alter what had become a way of life. College had to be considered, and earning a living. The years passed into the post-Olympic period, and she remembered her days of athletic competitions as a dream. Now her life was shifting again, though she was unsure as to the direction. The mountains and plains were calling to her, inviting her to explore, but she buried her desires, remaining indoors to see to her sister's needs. Dan is a busy man, she thought as she prepared lunch, and Bree needs someone within calling distance during this critical period. When she's better, there will be plenty of time to see the country.

She arched her back and rubbed a small spot of tension at the base of her neck. The kitchen door opened and Dan burst in, accompanied by Jake Tanner. Samantha met the amused green eyes levelly, though once more she felt treacherously at a disadvantage.

Her hair had been carelessly scooped on the top of her head that morning, and now, with their usual abandonment, stray locks were beginning to escape confinement. She was dressed in a black ribbed sweater that had seen too many washings and ancient jeans, splattered, faded, patched and too tight. She resisted the urge to raise her hand to her tumbling hair, forced a smile and turned to her brother-in-law.

"Hello, Dan. What are you doing home this time of day?" Purposefully, she ignored the tall figure beside him.

"Wasn't too far out," Dan explained. Slipping off his jacket and hat, he tossed both over the hooks provided. "Jake was giving me a hand, so I figured it was only neighborly to bring him back for lunch."

"Hope I'm not imposing, ma'am." The slow smile spread, once more rearranging the angles of his face.

"No imposition, Mr. Tanner. But you'll have to settle for potluck."

"My favorite dish—" he paused, giving her a cheeky wink "—next to apple pie."

Samantha sent him a withering glance and turned away to warm the previous evening's stew.

"I'll just go tell Sabrina I'm home," Dan announced to the room in general, and strode away. Samantha did her best to ignore Jake's disturbing presence. She stirred the stew busily.

"Smells good." Jake moved over to the stove and lounged against it. Samantha went to the cupboard to get the bowls.

When she turned back to place them on the round kitchen table, she noticed that he had shed his outdoor clothing. The slim-fitting jeans, snug and low on narrow hips, accentuated his leanness. His flannel shirt fitted over his broad shoulders and hard chest before tapering down to a narrow waist. The athlete in her immediately responded to the firm, well-proportioned body; there was not an ounce of spare flesh on him.

"Don't talk much, do you?" The drawl was there again, the exaggerated twang of the previous evening. Samantha turned her head, prepared to freeze him with her eyes.

His face was barely inches from hers as he slouched by the stove. For a moment, her mind ceased to function.

"I really have nothing to say to you, Mr. Tanner." She struggled to keep her voice cold and detached, but she could feel the blood rush to her face.

"Well, now, we'll have to see if we can change that." He spoke with easy confidence as he straightened to his full height. "We're not much on formalities around here. Just make it Jake." Though his words were spoken with his usual lazy delivery, there was an undertone of command. Samantha's chin rose in defense.

"Maybe I prefer to keep things formal between us, Mr. Tanner."

His lips were curved in his careless smile, but in his eyes she now recognized that special something that separated him from an ordinary ranch hand. *Power.* She wondered how she had missed it at their first meeting.

"I don't think there's much chance of that." He paused and tugged at a loose lock of his hair before adding with irritating emphasis, "Ma'am. Nope, I don't think there's much chance of that at all."

Samantha was saved from coming up with a suitable rebuttal by Dan's reappearance. She began to spoon the stew into ceramic bowls, noting to her dismay that her hands were not altogether steady. This man was infuriating her with his arrogantly lazy confidence. I have never met a more irritating male, she thought. He thinks he can switch on that rugged cowboy charm and women will drop in droves at his feet. Well, maybe some do, but not this one.

"Okay, Sam?" Dan's voice shattered the electric silence.

"What? I'm sorry, I wasn't listening."

"You'll keep Jake company over lunch, won't you? I'll have mine in the living room with Sabrina."

She swore silently. "Of course," she answered with an impersonal smile.

Within a short time, Samantha found herself sitting across from the man she wanted most to avoid.

''You've a fine hand with dumplings, Sam.'' Her brows rose involuntarily at his easy use of her nickname, but she kept her voice even.

''Thank you, Mr. Tanner. It's just one of my many talents.''

''I'm sure it is,'' he agreed with an inclination of his head.

''You haven't changed much from the girl in the picture in Sabrina's parlor.'' Samantha was astonished.

''You'd have been about fifteen,'' he continued. ''A bit skinnier than you are now, but your hair was the same, not quite willing to stay bundled on top of your head.'' Samantha's blank expression had turned to a frown at the word skinnier. She remembered the photo clearly.

''You'd just finished winning your second medal.'' She had indeed been fifteen. The picture had been snapped at the moment she had completed her floor routine. It had captured the look of stunned triumph, for she had known in that instant that a medal was hers.

''Sabrina's just about as proud of you as you are worried about her.'' Samantha said nothing, only staring into the lean, handsome features. His brows rose ever so slightly, a movement that would have gone unnoticed had she not been so intent on his face. For a moment, she forgot the thread of the conversation, caught up suddenly in a series of small, irrelevant details: the curling gold which spilled over his brow, the tiny white scar on his jawline, the thickness of his long lashes. Confused, she dropped her eyes to her bowl and struggled to bring her thoughts to order.

"I'd forgotten Bree had that picture," she said. "It was a long time ago."

"So now you teach. You don't look like any gym teacher I ever knew."

"Oh, really?"

"No, ma'am." He shook his head slowly and considered her through another mouthful of stew. "Don't look strong enough or old enough."

"I assure you, Jake, I'm both strong enough and old enough for my profession."

"What made you become a gym teacher?" His sudden question caught her off balance, and she stared at him.

"Well, I..." Her shoulders moved restlessly. "Our mother was a fanatic on lessons when Bree and I were growing up." She smiled in spite of herself. "We took lessons in everything, Mom's theory on being well-rounded. Anyway, Bree found her talent in music and I developed a knack for the physical. For a while, I focused on gymnastics, then, when the time came to work, it seemed natural. Bree taught little people to play the classics, and I teach bigger people to tumble.''

''Do you like your work? Are you happy with it?''

''As a matter of fact, I do,'' she retorted. ''I like the activity, I like being involved in a physical type of work. It can be frustrating at times, of course. Some of the girls I teach would rather be flirting with their boyfriends than learning gymnastics, I suspect.''

''And you yourself are more interested in calisthenics than men?'' The question was delivered with a broad masculine smile.

''That's hardly relevant,'' she snapped, annoyed that she had lowered her guard.

''You don't think so?''

Samantha scraped back her chair and moved to the stove. ''Coffee?''

''Yes, ma'am, black.'' It was unnecessary to turn around; she felt the slow grin crease his face as clearly as if she had witnessed it with her eyes. She set the cup down on the table with a bang. Before she could spin back to pour her own, her hand was captured in a firm grip. There was nothing soft about the hand. It was hard and masculine.

Completely outmatched in the short battle that ensued, Samantha discovered that under the lean, lanky exterior lay an amazing strength. Deciding that it was undignified to grapple in her sister's kitchen, she allowed her hand to rest quietly in his, meeting his laughing eyes with a resentful glare. Her heart began to pound uncomfortably against her ribs.

"What do you want?" Her voice came out in a husky whisper. His eyes left hers to travel slowly down to the generous curve of her mouth, lingering until she could taste the heat on her lips, as real as a kiss. Taking his time, he moved his gaze back to her eyes.

"You're jumpy." His observation was laconic, as if none of the heat had touched him, though she herself was beginning to suffocate. "Powerful strong for such a little bit of a thing."

"I'm not little," she retorted. "You're just so big." She began to tug at her hand again, feeling a near desperate urgency to shake off the contact that was infusing her with an unexplained weakness around the knees.

"Your eyes are fabulous when you're angry, Sam." His tone was conversational. "Temper agrees with you. You grow beautiful with it." He laughed and pulled her closer.

"You're insufferable," she said, still struggling to escape his grasp.

"For telling you you're beautiful? I was just stating the obvious. I'm sure it's been mentioned to you once for twice before."

"You men are all the same." She ceased her struggles long enough to aim a lethal glare. "Always grabbing and groping."

"I don't grope, Samantha." His drawl was feather-soft. For an instant, the cocky cowboy vanished, and she glimpsed the man, shrewd and ruthless, beneath. Here was a man who not only expected to have his own way, but would. "And the next time I grab you, it won't only be to hold your hand." Releasing her, he leaned back in his chair. "You have been warned."

Later, as Sabrina napped and the house grew still around her, Samantha found herself staring blankly at the pages of a novel. Scowling, she tossed it aside and rose from the sofa to pace to the window. What an infuriating man. Obviously, he considers himself irresistible. She began to wander the room, attempting to block out the effect his blatant virility had had on her.

It was too bad, she decided on her fourth circle, that all those good looks, all that strength and appeal, had to belong to such a rude, arrogant man.

Deciding that a brisk walk was just what she needed to get Jake Tanner out of her mind, she stopped her pacing and grabbed a warm jacket. Moments later she was out the door, gazing around her in delight at the beauty of the starlit Wyoming night. Her breath puffed out in thin white mists as she moved. The air, tinged with frost, carried the aroma of pine, and she drank it in greedily, enjoying the mixed scent of hay and horses and aged wood. She could hear the lonely sound of a coyote calling to the full silver moon. And suddenly she realized that she had fallen in love with Wyoming. The spell of the mountains and plains was on her, and she was inexplicably glad she had come.

"Goodness, you were out a long time," her sister commented as Samantha plopped down in a wing-backed chair in front of the fire a few minutes later. "You must be frozen."

"No." Samantha stretched out her legs and sighed. "I love it out there. It's fantastic! I never realized how big the sky was before, and I don't think I'll ever get used to the space, the openness."

She turned her attention to the powerfully built man sitting next to her sister on her sofa. "I wonder if you appreciate it, Dan, living here all of your life. Even your letters, Bree, didn't do justice to that world out there." Running her fingers through her hair, she made a small sound of pleasure. "To someone used to traffic-choked streets and huge buildings, all this..." Her hands moved in an inadequate gesture.

"You haven't had much of a chance to see anything since you've been here," Dan observed. "You've been with us a month and you haven't gone a quarter mile away from the house. And that's been mostly to fetch the mail in the mornings."

"I'll have plenty of time to explore later. I'll be around through the summer."

"Just the same, we're not having you tied to the house while you're here, Sam," Dan announced, and sat back against the cushions. "Even the most devoted sister is entitled to a day off."

"Don't be silly. You make it sound as though I were slaving from dawn to dusk. Half the time I'm not doing anything."

"We know how hard you're working, Sam," Sabrina said quietly, glancing up at Dan before returning her gaze to her twin. "And I know the lack of activity is harder on you than the work. I also know how you disrupted your life to come out here and take care of me."

"Oh, Bree, for heaven's sake," Samantha began, shifting uncomfortably. "I never would have found out how much I love Wyoming if I hadn't come."

"Don't try to shrug if off, Sam." Dan grinned at the embarrassed motion of her shoulders. "We're grateful, and you'll just have to get used to us telling you so. But tomorrow, we're going to show we're grateful instead of just talking about it. We're kicking you out for the day.''

''Huh?'' Blankly, Sam blinked at the bland smile before shifting her gaze to Sabrina's serene one.

''That's right.'' His grin widened as she drew her brows together. ''Tomorrow's Sunday, and I'm staying home with my wife. And you...'' He pointed a warning finger at his sister-in-law. ''You're going to have your pick of the horses and take off.''

Samantha sprung up from her slouched position. ''Do you mean it?'' Her face was glowing with pleasure, and Dan's smile warmed with affection.

''Yes, little sister, I mean it. It should be more.''

''The dapple-gray gelding,'' she began in a rush, ignoring the last part of his comment. ''Can I take him?''

''Already inspected the stock, and it appears you know your horses.'' Dan chuckled and shook his head. ''Spook's a good mount. A little frisky, but from what Sabrina's told me, you can handle him.''

''Oh, I can, and I promise I'll be careful with him.'' She sprang from her chair and crossed the room, flinging her arms around his neck. ''Thanks, Dan. You are absolutely my favorite brother-in-law, bar none.''

''I think she likes the idea, Sabrina,'' Dan commented as he met his wife's eyes over Samantha's head. "In fact, I'd say she's downright pleased about it."

"And I thought I hid my emotions so effectively." She gave his cheek a loud, smacking kiss.

"You be ready to start out about nine." He patted Samantha's slim shoulder. "Jake'll be around, then."

"Jake?" Samantha repeated. Her smile froze.

"Yeah, he'll be riding out with you. Actually," Dan continued, "he suggested the idea this afternoon. He thought it would do you good to get out of the house for a while." He sighed and scratched his dark head, managing to appear sheepish, for all his size. "I'm ashamed I didn't think of it first. I guess I've been a bit preoccupied and didn't notice you were looking a littled tired and hemmed in."

"I'm not tired," she denied automatically.

"Hemmed in?" Sabrina offered with a knowing smile.

"A little, maybe, but I'm hardly in the last stages of cabin fever. I'm sure it's very kind of Mr. Tanner to be so concerned about my welfare." She managed to say his name in a normal voice. "But there's certainly no need for him to go with me. I know he has hundreds of more important things to do with his Sunday."

"Well, now, he didn't seem to think so," Dan

said. ‘‘It was his suggestion, and he seemed keen on the idea, too.’’

‘‘I don’t know why he would be,’’ she muttered. ‘‘Besides, I don’t want to impose on him. We’re practically strangers. I can just go by myself.’’

‘‘Nonsense.’’ Dan’s refusal was good-natured but firm. ‘‘I couldn’t possibly let you ride out by yourself just yet, no matter how good you are on a horse. You don’t know the country, and it’s easy to get lost. There’s always the possibility of an accident. Besides,’’ he added, and his grin was expansive, ‘‘you’re part of the family, and I grew up with Jake, so you’re not strangers. If anyone knows his way around this part of Wyoming, he does.’’ He shrugged and rested his back against the cushions. ‘‘He owns half of it, anyway.’’ Samantha glanced at her sister for help. Sabrina, however, appeared to be engrossed in her needlepoint.

Frowning at the lack of support, Samantha stewed over her predicament. If she refused Jake’s company, she would not only forfeit the opportunity to ride the Wyoming countryside, but she would spoil Sabrina’s and Dan’s plans for a day alone together. She shrugged in resignation and offered a smile.

‘‘I’ll be ready at nine.’’ She added to herself, If Jake Tanner can stand a day in my company, I guess I can stand a day in his.

Chapter 3

Sunday dawned with a sky as cold and clear as sapphire. The sun offered thin light and little warmth. To her annoyance, Samantha had overslept. Hurriedly, she showered and dressed in forest-green cords and a chunky beige pullover.

Her riding boots clattered on the parquet floor as she hurried from her room and down the hall to the kitchen. She frowned as she reached the doorway. Jake was sitting at the table, enjoying a cup of coffee with the air of one very much at home.

He was, she noted with illogical irritation, every bit as attractive as she remembered.

''Oh, you're here.'' Her greeting was hardly welcoming, but he returned it with his slow smile.

‘‘Morning, ma’am.’’

‘‘Don’t start ma’aming me again,’’ she said.

He remained silent as she clattered the cups in the cupboard and filled one with the steaming liquid from the pot on the stove.

‘‘Sorry.’’ She popped a piece of bread in the toaster and turned to offer a peace-offering smile. ‘‘My! I overslept. I hope you haven’t been waiting long.’’

‘‘I’ve got all day,’’ he answered, leaning back in his chair as if to emphasize his words.

She drew a slab of bacon and a carton of eggs from the refrigerator. ‘‘Have you eaten?’’ she asked in invitation.

‘‘Yeah, thanks.’’ He rose, poured himself another cup of coffee and resumed his position at the table. ‘‘Dan’s already seen to breakfast for himself and Sabrina. They’re having it in their room.’’

‘‘Oh.’’ She replaced the items and pulled out the butter.

‘‘Aren’t you going to eat?’’

‘‘Toast and coffee. I’m not much on breakfast.’’

‘‘If you always eat like that,’’ he observed over the rim of his cup, ‘‘it’s no wonder you never grew any bigger.’’

‘‘For goodness’ sake.’’ She whirled around, brandishing the butter knife. ‘‘I’m hardly a midget. I’m five-four, that’s tall enough for anybody.’’

He held up his hands in mock surrender. "I never argue with an armed woman."

"Ready?" He rose when she had finished both the toast and another cup of coffee.

When she mumbled her assent, he plucked her jacket from its hook, holding it out so that she had no choice but to allow him to help her into it. She stiffened as his hands touched her shoulders and turned her to face him. Her pulses responded immediately. As if he were aware of her reaction, he began to do up her leather buttons with slow care. She jerked back, but his hold on the front of her coat prevented her from a clean escape.

"You're a pretty little thing," he drawled, completing his task with his eyes directly on hers. "Can't have you catching cold." He reached out and plucked Sabrina's dark wide-brimmed hat from a peg and placed it neatly on her head. "This'll keep your head warm."

"Thanks." She pushed the hat firmly in place.

"Anytime, Sam." His face was unperturbed as he pulled his own sheepskin jacket over his flannel shirt and jeans.

On the way to the stables, Samantha increased her pace to a trot to keep up with Jake's long, careless stride. Despite herself, she admired the confident, loose-limbed grace of his movement. He took his time, she noted, deciding he probably did nothing quickly, and more than likely still finished ahead of everyone else.

The dapple gray had been saddled and led outside by a smiling ranch hand.

"Howdy, ma'am. Dan said to have Spook ready for you."

"Thanks." She returned his friendly smile and patted the gelding's neck. "But I could have done it. I don't like to give you extra work."

"No trouble, ma'am. Dan said you weren't to do a lick of work today. You just go and have yourself a good time, and I'll rub old Spook down when you get back."

Samantha vaulted easily onto the horse's back, happy to feel a mount beneath her again. Riding was an old pleasure, to be enjoyed only when finances allowed.

"Now, you take good care of Miss Evans, Jake," the cowboy admonished with a conspirator's wink Samantha failed to catch. "Dan sets great store by this little lady."

Little again, Samantha thought.

"Don't you worry about Miss Evans, Lon." Jake mounted his stallion with a fluid motion. Again Samantha noticed that he wasted no time on superfluous movement. "I intend to keep a close eye on her."

Samantha acknowledged Jake's statement with a

wrinkled nose, then, following the direction his hand indicated, set off in a brisk canter.

As the neat cluster of ranch buildings was left behind, her irritation vanished. The rushing air was exciting, filling her lungs and whipping roses into her cheeks. She had almost forgotten the sense of liberation riding gave her. It was the same sensation that she had experienced many times when flying from top to bottom or springing high in a double twist.

They rode in silence for a quarter of an hour. Jake allowed her to fill her being with the thrill of movement and the beauty of the countryside. Wild peaks jutted arrogantly into the sky. The rolling plains below were yellow-green with winter. They rode by Herefords, white-faced and sleek, who noted their passing with a lazy turn of the head before resuming their grazing.

A shape darted across an open field, and Samantha slowed her horse to a walk and pointed. ''What's that?''

''Antelope,'' Jake answered, narrowing his eyes against the sun.

''Oh!'' She halted her mount and watched the animal's graceful, bounding progress until it streaked over a hill and out of her view. ''It must be marvelous to run like that, graceful and free.'' She turned her unguarded face to the man beside her and found him regarding her intently. His eyes held an expression she did not understand. A strange tingling raced along her spine, like warm fingers on cold skin. The tingling increased, the sensation spreading to settle somewhere in her stomach. Suddenly, his expression changed. The shadows of his face shifted as his lips moved into a smile.

"Someday you will be caught, little antelope."

She blinked at him, totally disoriented, trying to remember what they had been talking about. His grin increased. He pointed to a large, bare-limbed tree a quarter of a mile away.

"Race you." There was challenge under the lazy dare.

Her eyes brightened with excitement. "Fine chance I'd have against a horse like that. What handicap do I get?"

Jake pushed his hat back as if to view her more completely. "From the look of you, I'd say you've got a good fifty-pound advantage. That should balance the odds some."

"No head start?"

"No, ma'am."

She pouted for a moment, then grinned. "All right, Jake Tanner, I'll give you a run for your money."

"Whenever you say, Sam." He pulled the brim of his hat low over his forehead.

''Now!''

She met the gelding's sides with her heels and spurted forward in a gallop. The quiet morning air vibrated with the thunder of hooves. Samantha, her hair flowing behind her, gave herself over to the thrill of the race. She reached the finish just ahead of her competitor and reined in, filling the morning with dusty, breathless laughter.

''Oh, that was wonderful, absolutely wonderful.''

''Any time you want to give up teaching, Sam, you can work for me. I can use a hand who rides like you.''

''I'll keep that in mind, even though I know you let me beat you.''

''Now what makes you think that?'' He leaned his arm on the horn of his saddle and watched her thoughtfully.

''I'm not stupid.'' Her grin was good-natured and friendly. ''I couldn't beat that Arabian in a million years. You, maybe,'' she added with a touch of arrogance, ''but not that horse.''

''Pretty sharp, aren't you?'' he returned, answering her grin.

''As a tack,'' she agreed. ''And,'' she continued, brushing her hair from her shoulders, ''I am not a weak female who needs to be placated. With my background, I know how to compete, I know how to lose, and—'' she grinned and lifted her brows ''—I know how to win.''

''Point taken.'' He tilted his head as if to view her from a different angle. ''From now on, Sam, we play head-to-head.'' He smiled, and she was no longer sure they were talking about the same thing. ''I know how to win, too,'' he added slowly. They continued at a leisurely pace for a time, crossing a narrow branch of the Medicine Bow River. They paused there for the horses to quench their thirst in the icy water that forced its way over shining rocks with hisses and whispers. At Samantha's request, Jake began to identify the surrounding mountains.

Pointing to the long fingers of peaks at the south, the Laramie Range, he told her they extended from eastern Colorado. The middle section was the Medicine Bow Range, and the Sierra Madre loomed to the west. The vast ranges were separated by broad tongues of the Wyoming Basin. Silver-blue, they gleamed in the sunlight, lacings of snow trembling from their summits.

She had reined in without being aware of her action. ''I can never look at them long enough. I suppose you're used to them.''

''No.'' There was no laughter or mockery in his tone. ''You never get used to them.''

She smiled a bit uncertainly, not at all sure she could deal with this side of him.

''Are there bears up there?'' she asked.

He glanced up at the mountains, smiled, then looked back at her. ''Black bear and grizzly,'' he informed her. ''Elk, coyotes, mountain lions...''

''Mountain lions?'' she repeated, a little nervously.

''You're not likely to run into one down here,'' he returned with an indulgent smile.

She ignored the mockery in his voice and looked around her, again awed by the miles of open space. ''I wonder if this looked the same a century ago.''

''Some of it. Those don't change much.'' He indicated the Rockies with an inclination of his head. ''The Indians are gone,'' he continued, as if thinking aloud. ''There were Arapaho, Sioux, Cheyenne, Crow, Shoshone, all roaming free over the state before the first white man set foot here. Then trappers came, trading with Indians, dressing like them, living like them, and the beaver was nearly driven into extinction.'' He turned back to her, as if suddenly remembering she was there. ''You're the teacher.'' His smile appeared. ''You should be telling me.''

Samantha shook her head in mock despair. ''My knowledge of Wyoming's history is limited to late-night westerns.'' They were walking their horses slowly, side by side. She had completely forgotten her aversion to the man beside her. ''It's impossible to believe the killing and cruelty that must have gone on here. It's so serene, and so vast. It seems there would have been room enough for everyone.''

This time it was Jake who shook his head. ''In 1841 more than a hundred and fifty thousand people crossed the South Pass going west, and a few years later, fifty thousand more came through on their way to California looking for gold. This was Indian land, had been Indian land for generations. Game disappeared, and when people get hungry, they fight. Treaties were signed, promises made by both sides, broken by both sides.'' He shrugged.

''In the 1860s, they tried to open the Bozeman Pass from Fort Laramie to Montana, and open war broke out. The trail ran through the Sioux hunting ground. The fighting was of the worst kind, massacres, indiscriminate killing of women and children, butcheries by both white and Indian. More treaties were signed, more misunderstandings, more killing, until the whites outnumbered the Indians, drove them away or put them on reservations.''

''It doesn't seem fair,'' Samantha whispered, feeling a wave of sadness wash over her.

''No, it doesn't.'' He heard the wistful note in her voice and turned to regard her. ''Life isn't always fair, though, is it, Samantha?''

''I suppose not.'' She sighed. ''You seem to know

quite a bit about what happened here. You must have had a good history teacher.''

''I did.'' He held her curious look with a teasing half-smile on his lips. ''My great-grandmother lived to be ninety-eight. She was Sioux.''

Samantha lifted her brows in surprised interest. ''Oh, I'd love to have met her. The things she must have seen, the changes in nearly a century of living.''

''She was quite a woman.'' His smile faded a moment. ''She taught me a lot. Among other things, she told me that the land goes on no matter who walks on it, that life moves on whether you fight against it or flow with it, that when you want something, you go after it until it's yours.''

Suddenly, she felt he was leading her out of her depth, reaching for something she was not sure she possessed. She turned from the directness of his eyes to search the land.

''I'd like to have seen all this before there were any fences, before there was any fighting.''

Jake pointed skyward. Glancing up, Samantha watched the graceful flight of an eagle. For a timeless moment, he soared overhead, the undisputed sovereign of the skies. They moved off again, in companionable silence. ''I hope you're getting some fun out of this trip, some compensation for taking care of your sister,'' Jake said at last.

"I don't need any compensation for taking care of Bree, she's my sister, my..."

"Responsibility?"

"Well...yes. I've always looked out for Bree, she's more delicate, more...dependent than I am." She shrugged and felt uncomfortable without knowing why. "Dad always joked that I took my share of strength and half of Bree's while we were still in the womb. She needs me," she added, feeling compelled to defend what she had always taken for granted.

"She has Dan," Jake reminded her. "And she's a grown woman now—just as you are. Did it ever occur to you that you have your own life to lead now that Sabrina has a husband to care for her?"

"I'm not trying to take over for Dan," she said quickly. "Perhaps you can figure out how he could see to her needs and tend to the house and the ranch all at the same time, but I can't." She glared at him, half in anger, half in exasperation. "What do you expect me to do? Sit up in Philadelphia teaching kids to jump on a tramp while my sister needs help?"

"No, Samantha." He met her eyes with a quiet patience that was more disturbing than angry words and shouts. "What you're doing is very kind and unselfish."

"There's nothing kind or unselfish about it," she

interrupted, shrugging the words away. ''We're sisters. More than that, we're twins. We shared life from its beginning. You can't understand the kind of bond that creates. I'd give up a hundred jobs to help Bree if she needed me.''

''No one's condemning your loyalty, Samantha. It's an admirable trait.'' He gave her a long, level look. ''Just a word of advice. Don't become so involved that you forget who Samantha Evans is, and that she just might have the right to her own woman's life.''

Samantha drew herself up to her full height in the saddle. ''I hardly need your advice on how to run my life. I've been managing nicely for some time now.''

His face creased in a lazy smile. ''Yes, ma'am, I'm sure you have.''

Chapter 4

Samantha had been riding the dapple gray in stubborn silence for nearly thirty minutes when she noticed more cattle. Her guide seemed unperturbed by her silence and slowed his Arabian's gait to the gelding's meandering walk. She would never have admitted to the man at her side that his words had disturbed her peace of mind.

What business was it of his how she chose to run her life? What gave Jake Tanner the right to question her relationship with Sabrina? No one asked him for his advice. And why in heaven's name should anything he said matter in the first place?

They were approaching a large ranch house. A redwood porch skirted the building's front, graced by evergreen shrubs. A gray wisp of smoke rose in a welcoming spire from the chimney. Ranch buildings sat neat and unobtrusive in the background.

"Welcome to the Double T, ma'am."

Jake drew her eyes with the uncharacteristic formality in his tone. She turned to see him smile and touch the brim of his well-worn Stetson.

"Thank you, Mr. Tanner. I can honestly say your ranch is spectacular. But what, may I ask, are we doing here?"

"Well, now..." Jake shifted in the saddle to face her directly. "I don't know about you, but nearly three hours in the saddle gives me a powerful appetite. I figured here we might do a bit better than beef jerky."

"Three hours?" Samantha repeated, and pushed Sabrina's hat from her head so it lay against her back. "Has it really been that long?"

The angles of his face moved slowly with his grin, and she found herself once more intrigued by the process. "I'll take that to mean you were so delighted with my company, time stood still."

She answered with a toss of her head. "I hate to tread on your ego, Jake, but the credit goes to Wyoming."

"Close enough for now." Reaching over, he

plopped the brimmed hat back in place on Samantha's head and urged his mount into a canter.

Samantha stared after him in exasperation, watching the confidence with which he rode the Arabian. They moved like one form rather than horse and man. Scowling, she pressed her heels to the gelding's side and raced forward to join him.

As she reached his side, he skirted the ranch house and rode toward the buildings in the rear, following the left fork on a long, hard-packed road. A large, sleepy-eyed Saint Bernard rose from his siesta and romped forward to greet them. A deep, hoarse bark emitted from his throat. Jake halted in front of the stables. He slid off the Arabian's back, running his hand through the dog's thick fur as he hit the ground.

''Wolfgang's harmless.'' He acknowledged the loving, wet kisses with another brief caress and moved to the gelding's side. ''He's just a puppy.''

''A puppy,'' Samantha repeated. ''You don't see many hundred-and-fifty-pound puppies.'' Tilting her head, she gave the overgrown baby a thorough examination before she brought her leg over the saddle to dismount.

Jake gripped her waist as she made her descent, holding her off the ground a moment as if she were weightless. As her boots touched earth, she was turned around and drawn against a hard chest. She tilted her head to inform him that his assistance was unnecessary, but saw only a brief blur of his face before his lips captured hers.

Her mind whirled with the touch and scent of him. She felt as though she were falling into a deep well and her heart began to beat a mad tempo against her ribs. She clutched at his jacket in defense. Perhaps the kiss was brief. It could have lasted no more than a portion of a minute, but it felt like forever. She knew his mouth was warm and sure on hers while decades flew into centuries.

The strange sensations of timelessness and loss of control frightened her. She stiffened and began to struggle against his grasp. He released her immediately, staring down at her clouded blue eyes with a satisfied smile. The smile transformed terror into fury.

"How dare you?"

"Just testing, ma'am." His answer was complacent, as though the kiss had been no more than that, a traditional touching of lips.

"Testing?" she repeated, running an agitated hand through her hair. "Testing what?"

"I've always wanted to kiss a teacher." Grinning, he gave her a friendly pat on the cheek. "I think there're some holes in your education."

"I'll show you holes, you conceited, high-handed—" her mind searched for something appropriately derogatory and settled on a generality "*—man*. If I didn't consider that kiss so insignificant, you'd be lying on your back checking out the sky."

He surveyed her as she trembled with a mixture of fury and wounded pride. He rubbed his chin thoughtfully. "You know, Sam, I almost believe you could do it."

"You can bank on it," she confirmed with an arrogant toss of her head. "And the next time you..." Feeling her arm sharply pulled, she glanced down to see the sleeve of her jacket captured in the awesome jaws of the Saint Bernard. "What'd you do, teach him to eat unwilling females?"

"He just wants to make your acquaintance," Jake laughed, as he led the horses to the stable to turn them over to one of his men.

Samantha was not normally timid, and her pride refused to allow her to call Jake to untangle her from the teeth of his puppy. She swallowed and spoke to her canine captor.

"Hello...Wolfgang, wasn't it?" she muttered. "I'm Sam. You, ah, wouldn't consider letting go of my jacket, would you?" The dog continued to stare with droopy, innocent eyes. "Well, that's all right," she said, trying out magnanimity. "It's just an old one, anyway. I'm very fond of dogs, you know." Tentatively, she brought her free hand up to touch the fur on his huge head. "Well, actually, I have a cat,'' she admitted in apology, ''but I have absolutely no prejudices.''

Though his expression did not alter, she decided it was prudent to give him time for consideration. Her patience was rewarded when he released her sleeve and bathed her hand with his enormous tongue.

''Well, I see you two have made friends,'' Jake drawled, coming up behind her.

''No thanks to you,'' she said. ''He might have eaten me alive.''

''Not you, Sam,'' Jake disagreed, taking her hand and striding toward the house. ''Too tough for Wolfgang's taste.''

Jake led her to the back entrance through a paneled, tiled-floor mudroom and into the kitchen. A large square room, it was bright and cheery with tangerine curtains framing the wide windows. The pleasant-looking woman who stood by the sink smiled at Samantha. ''Jake, you scoundrel, have you had this poor little lady out in the cold all this time?'' Samantha met the warm brown eyes with a returning smile.

Jake grinned, unabashed. ''Samantha Evans, meet Annie Holloway, my cook, housekeeper and best girl.''

''Don't you try soft soaping me, you young devil.'' She brushed off his words with indulgent affection, but pleased color rose to her pudgy cheeks. ''Thinks he can get around me with sweet talk. Pleased to meet you, Miss Evans.'' Samantha found her hand enclosed in a firm grip.

''Hello, Miss Holloway, I hope I'm not putting you out.''

''Putting me out?'' Annie let out a rich, full laugh, her ample bust heaving with the sound. ''Isn't she the sweet one? Don't you be silly, now, and you just call me Annie like everyone else.''

''Thank you, Annie.'' Samantha's smile warmed. ''Everyone calls me Sam.''

''Now that's a pretty thing,'' Annie commented, peering candidly into Samantha's face. ''Yes, sir, a right pretty thing. You two run along,'' she commanded with an attempt at sternness. ''Out of my kitchen. Lunch will be along, and I'll bring you in some tea to warm you up. Not you,'' she said with a scowl as Jake grimaced. ''For the little lady. You don't need any warming up.''

''Annie runs things,'' Jake explained as he led Samantha down a wide hall into the living room.

''I can see she does, even when she's securely wrapped around your little finger.''

For a moment, his smile was so boyish and full of mischief, she nearly gave in to the urge to brush the curls from his forehead.

The paneling in the living room was light. The

expanse of wood was broken by a large stone fireplace and wide windows framed with cinnamon-colored sheers. The dark gleaming furniture had been upholstered in gold, burnt sienna and rich browns. There was a comfortable hodgepodge of Hepplewhites and Chippendales with piecrust tilt-top tables and Pembrokes, ladder-back chairs and candlestands. In the center of the hardwood floor lay a wide rug of Indian design, so obviously old and handworked, that Samantha wondered if it had been his great-grandmother's fingers that had hooked it perhaps nearly a century ago. The room reflected a quiet, understated wealth, a wealth she somehow did not associate with the rangy, brash cowboy side of Jake.

A Charles Russell painting caught her eye. She turned to study it, attempting to sort out her new impressions of this complex man. Turning back, she found him watching her reaction with unconcealed amusement.

"I have a feeling you were expecting bearskins and oilcloth."

Samantha focused her attention on the inviting fire. "I never know what to expect from you," she muttered.

"No?" He dropped his lanky form into a wing-backed chair and pulled out a long, thin cigar. "I thought you were pretty bright."

Samantha seated herself in the chair across from him, keeping the warmth and hiss of the fire between them. "This is a lovely room, very appealing and very warm."

"I'm glad you like it." If he noticed her blatant change of subject, he gave no sign. Lighting his cigar, he stretched out his legs and looked totally relaxed and content.

"I have a weakness for antiques," she continued, deciding the topic was safe and impersonal.

He smiled, the smoke curling lazily above his head. "There's a piece in one of the bedrooms you might like to see. A blanket chest in walnut that was brought over from the East in the 1860s."

"I'd like that very much." She returned his smile and settled back as Annie wheeled a small tea cart into the room.

"I brought you coffee," she said to Jake, and passed him a cup. "I know you won't take tea unless you douse it with bourbon. Something not quite decent about doing that to a good cup of tea."

"Tea is an old ladies' drink," he stated, ignoring her rapidly clucking tongue.

"How do you think Sabrina looks?" Samantha asked him when Annie had bustled back to the kitchen.

"I think you worry too much about her."

She bristled instinctively before replying. "Perhaps you're right,'' she surprised herself by admitting. ''Our mother always said Bree and I were mirror images, meaning, I discovered after a while, opposites.''

''Right down to Sabrina being right-handed, and you being left.''

''Why, yes.'' She looked at him in faint surprise. ''You don't miss much, do you?'' He merely shook his head and gave her an enigmatic smile. ''Well,'' she plunged on, not sure she liked his expression, a bit like a cat who already had the mouse between his paws. ''I suppose the summary of my discrepancies was that I could never keep the hem in my white organdy party dress. You'd have to know my mother to understand that. She would have Bree and me all decked out in these frilly white organdy dresses and send us off to a party. Bree would come back spotless, pure and angelic. I'd come back with dirt on my frills, bloody knees and a trailing hem.''

During her story, Jake's smile had widened. The coffee in his cup cooled, unattended as he watched her. ''There're doers and there're watchers, Samantha. I imagine you had fun scraping up your knees.''

As ridiculous as it seemed, she felt she'd just been complimented, and was both pleased and faintly embarrassed.

''I suppose you're a doer, too.'' She dropped her eyes. ''You couldn't run a ranch like this and not be. Cattle ranching sounds romantic, but I imagine it's long hours, hot summers and cold winters. I don't suppose it's really all that different from the way it used to be a hundred years ago.''

''The range isn't open anymore,'' he corrected. ''You don't find cowboys going off to Texas to punch cattle with a ten-dollar horse and a forty-dollar saddle.'' He shrugged and set his empty cup on the table beside him. ''But some change slow, and I'm one who likes to take my time.''

She was frowning into his smile when Annie announced lunch. It was not until they were settled in the dining room that she spoke directly to him again, pressing him for more details on how the ranch was run.

He explained how roundups, which had once been accomplished on the vast open range with only men and horses, were now aided by fences and technology. But it was still men and ponies who moved the cattle into corrals. Over a few states there were still strongholds of riders and ropers, men who cultivated the old technique and blended it with the new. On the Double T, Jake employed the best of both.

''If roundups aren't what they once were, they still accomplish the same end. Getting the cattle together and branding them.''

''Branding?'' Samantha interrupted, and shuddered.

"Your Philadelphia's showing, Sam." He grinned. "Take my word for it, branding is a good deal more unpleasant for the branders than the brandees."

She decided to ignore his comments and changed the subject abruptly. "Bree told me your ranch borders Dan's. This place must be huge for it to have taken us three hours to get here."

Jake's deep, rich laughter filled the room, and she decided unwillingly that she liked the sound very much. "It's a pretty big spread, Sam, but if you take the straight road north for the Lazy L, you can be here in twenty minutes on horseback. I took you on a big circle today," he explained. "Just a small taste of our part of the Laramie Basin."

They lingered over coffee, relaxed in each other's company.

"We'd better get started back," Jake said after a while. He rose and extended his hand. Her own slipped without hesitation into it as he pulled her to her feet. When she looked up at him, her smile was warm and spontaneous.

"Annie was right, that's a pretty thing." He lifted his hand and traced his fingers over the curve of her mouth. She started. "Now don't go skittish on me, Sam, I'm not going to use spurs and a whip."

His mouth lowered, gentle and persuasive. One hand held hers while the other circled the back of her neck to soothe with coaxing fingers. She had only to sway forward to feel his body against hers, had only to lift her hand to bring his mouth firmer and warmer on hers. Before the choice could be made, he drew her away and the decision was taken out of her hands.

"Sam." He shook his head as if exasperated and lightly amused. "You're enough to try a man's patience."

With this, he pulled her through to the kitchen.

"Well, so you're off again." Annie wiped one hand on her apron and wagged the other at Jake. "And don't be keeping her out in that cold too long."

"No, ma'am," Jake returned with suspicious respect.

"Thank you, Annie," Samantha broke in. "Lunch was wonderful."

"Well, now, that's fine, then." She gave Samantha a friendly pat on the cheek. "You just come back real soon, and you say hi to Sabrina for me, and that young rascal Dan, too. As soon as she's fit again, I'll be coming by to see her. Oh, Jake, I clean forgot." Annie turned to him and sighed at her absentmindedness. "Lesley Marshall called earlier, something about dinner tonight. I told her you'd give her a call, then it went straight out of my mind."

"No problem," Jake said easily. "I'll get back to her later. Ready, Sam?"

"Yes, I'm ready." She kept her smile in place, though a large black cloud seemed to have suddenly smothered the sunshine.

Lesley Marshall, she mused, automatically going through the motions of securing her hat and coat. That was the woman Bree had predicted would marry Jake when he decided to settle down. Why should it matter to me? She straightened her spine and accompanied Jake to the waiting horses. I have absolutely no interest in Jake Tanner's affairs.

He's probably had dozens of girlfriends. Well, it's no concern of mine. Vaulting into the saddle, she followed as he set off down the hard-packed road.

They spoke little on the return journey. Samantha pretended an engrossment with the scenery that she was far from feeling. Unhappily, she realized Wyoming's magic was not quite enough to lift her flagging spirits. Snow-capped peaks glistened just as brightly in the late afternoon sun, and the land still spread and beckoned, but as she surveyed them now she felt strangely depressed.

It had been an unusual day, she concluded. Jake had annoyed her, charmed her, angered her and delighted her, all in a handful of hours. His kiss had aroused excitement and a deeper feeling she could not explain.

The knowledge that he was dining with another woman that evening depressed her beyond belief. She stole a sidelong look at his lean, tanned features.

He was undeniably attractive, she admitted, pulling her eyes away from him before he could sense her study. There was a powerful aura of virility about him, which alternately intrigued her and made her wary. Perhaps it would be wise to avoid his company. He confused her, and Samantha liked to know precisely where she stood with a man. She wanted to call the shots, and she realized that this man would never allow anyone to call the shots but himself.

She would keep her distance from now on. Let him spread his charm over this Lesley Marshall, or any of the other women who were undoubtedly thirsting for his attention. Samantha Evans could get along very easily without him. As the Lazy L grew closer, she resolved to be polite and casually friendly to her escort. After all, she reflected, there was no reason to be rude. He was perfectly free to dine with whomever he chose; his life was most assuredly his own. Besides, she added to herself, if she had anything to say about it, they would be seeing very little of each other in the future.

When they reached the ranch, she dismounted, handing Spook's reins to a waiting cowboy. "I had a wonderful time, Jake." Samantha's smile was faultless in its social politeness as he walked her toward the ranch house, leading his stallion behind him. "I appreciate your time and hospitality."

Jake's mouth lifted at one corner. "It was my pleasure, ma'am."

If there was a mockery in his tone, Samantha chose to ignore it. Reaching the back door, she turned to smile at him again as he stood, tall and lean, beside the gleaming chestnut.

"Would you like some coffee before you go?" she invited, determined to be polite.

"No, thanks, Sam." He continued to watch her, his eyes shaded by the brim of his hat. "I'd best be getting along."

"Well." She breathed a small sigh of relief when her hand touched the doorknob and safety was in easy reach. "Thanks again."

"Sure." He nodded briefly and turned to his horse, paused and turned back to look at her with a penetrating intensity that turned her legs to water. When he spoke, it was soft and final. "I mean to have you, you know."

Several moments of silence passed before she could summon up an answer.

"D-Do you?" Her voice was a shaky whisper, unlike the coolly flippant tone she would have wished for.

"Yes, ma'am." He vaulted onto the chestnut's

back and pushed the Stetson back on his head so that she had a disturbingly clear view of his eyes. "I do," he confirmed, turning his mount and galloping away.

Chapter 5

Often over the next few days, Samantha told herself that her reaction to Jake's kiss had been merely a passing physical attraction. She was a normal woman, wasn't she? So why feel guilty about it?

Jake Tanner *was* a very attractive man. *Too attractive,* she added to herself. And he knew too much about charming women. The fact that Jake was abrasive, smug and irritating had nothing to do with the way she had acted. It had just been a passing fancy. *And would certainly not occur again.*

Finally Sabrina was allowed up from the confinement of her bed. Samantha decided it was safe to leave her sister for a few hours. With a light heart, she saddled Spook and set off from the ranch at a brisk canter. For a while she enjoyed the feeling of Spook's hooves pounding the hard road. The sky hung low above her, and heavy, leaden gray clouds draped the distant mountains in mysterious gloom. There was a stillness, a waiting in the air, unnoticed by Samantha in her eagerness to escape the close confines of the house.

She rode swiftly past the bored, white-faced cattle and the stretches of barbed wire, eager to explore new territory, tasting the joy of motion and freedom. The mountains, grim sentinels above her, stood stone-gray under the unbroken sky. Remembering Dan's instructions, Samantha took care to mark her route, choosing a clump of rocks, a cottonwood tree with a broken limb, and a gnarled stump as landmarks for her return trip.

She led her mount to a crest of a hill, watching as a jackrabbit, startled by her intrusion, darted across the road and out of sight.

Nearly an hour passed before the first flakes began to drift lazily from sky to earth. She stopped and watched their progress in fascination. The snow fell slowly. Lifting her face, she let it caress her cheeks and closed lids. The air was moist, coming to life around her, and she stirred herself out of her dream.

"Well, Spook, this is my first Wyoming snow.

I'd like to stay here all day and watch it fall, but duty calls. We'd better head back.'' Patting the horse's neck, she turned back toward the ranch.

They rode slowly. Samantha was enchanted with the fairyland that was forming around her. Cottonwoods and aspens were draped in white, their branches a stark contrast to the brilliant etchings of snow. The ground was cloaked quickly. Though the beauty was breathtaking, Samantha began to feel uncomfortably alone.

She took Spook into a canter. The sound of his hooves was soft and muffled. The quiet surrounding her was unearthly, almost as though the world had ceased to breathe. She shivered, suddenly cold in the warm confines of her jacket. To her annoyance, she saw that in her preoccupation with the landscape she had taken a wrong turn, and she began to backtrack, berating herself for carelessness.

The snow increased, plunging down from a sky she could no longer see. She cursed herself for having come so far, fighting down a sudden surge of panic. ''Don't be silly, Sam,'' she spoke aloud, wanting the reassurance of her own voice. ''A little snow won't hurt you.''

The cold became more intense, piercing the layers of her skin. Samantha tried to concentrate on steaming coffee and a blazing fire as she looked around for a familiar landmark. Nothing was the same as it had been. She clamped her lips tight to still the chattering of her teeth, telling herself that it was impossible that she could be lost. But it was a lie. The trees and hills around her were strangers blanketed in white.

The snow fell thickly, a blinding white wall blocking her vision. A wind had sprung up, breaking the silence with its moans and tossing snow, hard and bitter, into her face. She was forced to slow the gelding to a walk, afraid of tangling with the sharp teeth of barbed wire she was unable to see. Her teeth savaged her lips in an effort to control a growing terror.

It's so cold, she thought as she began to shiver convulsively, so unbelievably cold.

The snow had soaked through the wool of her slacks and slipped mercilessly down the neck of her coat. She hunched her shoulders against the driving wind. Snow was everywhere, blocking her in and seeping into her clothing.

She let the reins hang limp, praying that the horse's instinct would guide him back to the warm shelter of his stables. They trudged on, the vortex of white that had begun so innocently now whirling around her. Time and direction had lost all meaning, and though she tried calling out, her voice was soundless against the fierce breath of the wind.

Now she felt the cold. Her body was numbed into

submission. Her mind was following suit. The swirling snow was hypnotic, and a growing lethargy was creeping over her. In a small part of her mind, she knew her survival depended on remaining alert.

Horse and rider plodded on. There was no time, no world beyond the unbroken curtain of white. Samantha felt her eyelids growing heavy, but she willed them open with all her strength. The snow piled onto her back, weighing her down until she slumped onto the gelding's mane and clung to him. Staring down at the gelding's front hoof, she began to count each drudging step that Spook took as he continued his slow progress through the blinding storm.

Samantha's concentration on the horse's halting steps began to fade.

If I close my eyes, she thought dimly, I won't see all that white and I can sleep. Oh, how I want to sleep....

The snow was talking, she mused deliriously. Well, why not? It's alive. Why should it sound like Jake? Helplessly, she began to giggle. Well, why shouldn't it? *They both play to win.*

"Samantha!" The snow was shouting at her. "Open your eyes. Stop that insane laughing and open your eyes!"

Wearily, she forced herself to obey the command. Dimly she saw the blur of Jake's features through the flurries of snow. "You would be the last thing

I see before I die.'' With a moan, she closed her eyes again and sought the silence.

''Tell Dan we've found her,'' Jake shouted against the howl of the wind. ''I'm taking her back to the Double T.''

The darkness was comforting. Samantha gave herself over to it, feeling herself falling slowly into a hole with no bottom. She burrowed deeper into it. Her consciousness swam to the surface.

Bemused, she looked around a dimly lit room. The snow that pooled around her was not snow at all, but a bed with a thick, warm quilt. She allowed her heavy lids to close again.

''Oh, no, you don't.'' The lids opened fractionally, and Samantha saw Jake standing in the open doorway.

''Hello.''

His mouth thinned as he advanced to the bed to tower over her. It seeped through the misty reaches of her brain that he was angry. She stared at him with lazy fascination.

''What in heaven's name were you doing out in such a storm? I've seen some dumb stunts, but taking a joyride in the middle of a blizzard tops them all.''

She wanted to ask him to stop shouting at her,

but lacked the energy. ''Where am I?'' was all she could find to say.

Sitting on the edge of the bed, he drew her head from the pillow, then held a cup to her lips. ''Here, drink this first, then we'll talk.''

The brandy was warm and strong, and she sputtered and gasped as he poured it down her throat. Its power spread through her, pushing back the mists of unconsciousness.

''Now, to answer your question, you're at the Double T.'' Jake set the empty cup aside, and laid her head back on the mound of pillows.

''Oh.''

''Is that all you can say?'' He was shouting again. He took her shoulders as if to shake her. ''Just 'Oh'? What in heaven's name were you doing out there?''

''It seems so long ago.'' She frowned in concentration, closing her eyes with the effort. ''It wasn't snowing when I left,'' she said in weak defense.

''Wasn't snowing?'' Jake repeated, incredulous. ''Samantha, didn't you see the sky? Where are your brains?''

''There's no excuse for insults,'' she retorted with a small flash of spirit.

''No excuse for insults? Are you stark raving mad? Do you realize what nearly happened to you?'' His hands retreated to his pockets, as though he could barely prevent them from throttling her.

"Out here in the middle of a blizzard, half-frozen and helplessly lost! It was a miracle we found you. A little longer, and you'd be lying somewhere buried in it, and no one would have found what was left until spring. Dan was half out of his mind when he got through to me and told me you'd gone out in this."

"Bree?"

"Knew nothing." He whirled to face her again. "She was taking a nap. It never occurred to her that you had gone out with a storm brewing." He laughed harshly.

The memory of the snow and the terror washed over her, and she began to shake. "I'm sorry," she managed through the tears that threatened to flow. With a brief oath, Jake ran a hand through his hair. He closed the distance between them and gathered her in his arms. "Samantha," he murmured against her hair. "What hell you put us all through."

"I'm sorry," she repeated, and she began to sob in earnest. "I was so scared, so cold."

He rocked and murmured words she could not understand, his lips brushing through her hair and over her damp cheeks until they met hers. The kiss mingled with the salt of her tears. "I've gotten your shirt all wet," she murmured after a while.

He let out a deep breath. She saw his smile begin to spread before he rested his brow against hers.

"That is without doubt the worst calamity of the day."

"It's dark," she said with sudden realization. "How long…?"

"Too long. What you need now is rest."

"Spook?" she began as he lay her down on the pillows.

"Is sleeping off his adventure in the stables. He looks a lot better than you, I might add."

"I want to thank you for everything." Samantha reached for his hand. In that instant, she discovered there was nothing covering her save sheets and blankets. "M-My clothes," she stammered, drawing the quilt higher in a purely feminine gesture that caused Jake's mouth to twitch.

"Soaked through, Sam." Rising, he stood, rocking gently on his heels. "It was necessary to get you warm and dry."

"Did Annie?" she managed a smile at the thought of the matronly presence of Jake's housekeeper. "I seem to have put everyone to a lot of trouble. Will you thank her for me?"

"Well, Sam, I'd like to oblige you, but Annie left yesterday for Colorado to spend a week with her nephew." Jake's grin broadened.

"Then who—?" The question caught in her throat, and her eyes became round and impossibly dark. ''Oh, no,'' she whispered, closing her eyes in humiliation.

''No need to be embarrassed, Sam, you have a beautiful body.''

''Oh, no.'' With a moan, she squeezed her eyes tighter.

''Now, don't you fret.'' His tone took on the light insolence of the cowboy she'd met a month before in the cold March sunset. ''When I took off your clothes and rubbed you down, it was strictly medical. I'd do as much for any stray.'' He patted her hand, and her eyes opened warily at his touch.

''Yes, of course.'' Moistening her lips, she attempted to see the practical side. ''I, well...thank you.''

'''S all right, don't give it a thought.'' He moved toward the door, then paused and turned back. ''Now, the next time I get your clothes off, my purposes'll be completely different.''

He strolled casually from the room, leaving a speechless Samantha.

Chapter 6

Samantha looked around her. She remembered with a shock that she was in Jake's house—and, worse yet, *naked* in bed. She was debating the wisdom of wrapping the quilt around her and searching for more appropriate attire when footsteps sounded down the hall outside her room. She pulled the covers to her chin as Jake strode through the open door.

"So, you're awake. How do you feel?"

"Fine." Her respiratory system behaved erratically as he continued toward her and dropped onto the bed. "I'm just fine," she repeated, then added unnecessarily, "It's still snowing."

"So it is," he agreed without taking his eyes from her face. "Slowing down, though."

"Is it?" She forced herself to look out the window.

"The worst'll be over by midday." He reached up and pried one of her hands loose from the death grip on the blanket. "Calm down, Sam, I'm not going to ravish you, I'm going to check your pulse."

"I'm fine," she repeated again.

"Far from fine, Samantha," he corrected. His fingers brushed against her cheek, as if to test its substance. "The first thing is to get some food into you." Rising, he held out a large flannel robe that he had dropped at the foot of the bed. "You'd probably feel better if you had something on." His smile was gently mocking. "Can you manage to get into this by yourself?"

"Of course." Plucking it from him, she kept a cautious grip on the blankets. "I'm not an invalid."

"You best think like one. Put that on, then get back in bed. I'll bring you some breakfast."

"I don't..."

"Don't argue." The two words were swift and final. He was gone before she could say another word.

He had shut the door, however, and grateful for the concession, Samantha tossed back the covers and slipped her arm into the robe. When she stood, the room swayed and spun around her. She sank back onto the bed and slipped her other arm into its sleeve, pulling the robe around her before attempting to stand again. Her limbs felt heavy and weak, and she noted with puzzlement that her ankle was throbbing lightly. Gripping one poster of the bed until the room steadied, she rolled up the sleeves of the robe several times until her hands became visible, then moved to the bathroom to study herself in the mirror.

The sight of her own face caught at her breath. Her skin seemed nearly transparent, her eyes darker and larger in contrast. The breath of color that resulted when she pinched her cheeks faded instantly. She ran a hand through her hair falling on the shoulders of the dark green robe.

It must be his, she realized, looking down at the sleeves, which swallowed her arms, and the hem, which fell nearly to her ankles. A strange sensation flowed over her as she felt the material on her skin. Turning away from the mirror, she studied the bed.

"I'm not getting in there again," she muttered, and with a small gesture of defiance belted the robe more securely. "I can eat at the table like a normal person."

After a moment, her progress down the hall seemed more of a crawl than a walk. Her legs were heavy with a weakness which infuriated her. The stillness of the house vibrated around her, playing havoc with her nerves, and the need to hear the natural, everyday movements of another human being became increasingly important. She cursed the waves of giddiness that swam around in her head, forcing her to stop time after time to rest her hand against the wall.

"This is ridiculous."

"You're right."

The harsh agreement came from behind as Jake's hands gripped her shoulders.

"What are you doing out of bed?"

"I'm all right." She swayed against his chest. He gripped her waist to support her, and she rested her hands on his arms.

"I'm just a bit wobbly, and I'm having some trouble with my ankle."

He let his gaze travel down to rest on her bare feet. "Probably turned it when you fell off the horse."

"I fell off Spook?" Her expression was incredulous.

"You were unconscious at the time. Now, get back in bed and stay there." Effortlessly, he swept her into his arms, and she laid her head against his shoulder.

"Jake, don't make me go back to bed. It's so

quiet in there, and I don't feel like being alone now.''

He bent and brushed lips that parted in confusion. ''If you think you can sit in a chair without sliding on your face, you can come in the kitchen.''

She nodded, sighed and closed her eyes. ''I hate being so much trouble.''

She felt him shift her in his arms before he began the journey down the hall. ''I knew you were trouble the minute I set eyes on you.''

''Don't tease, Jake, I'm trying to thank you.''

''What for?''

She lifted a hand to his cheek, turning his face so that he would look at her. ''For my life.''

''Then take better care of it in the future,'' he suggested.

''Jake, please, I'm serious. I owe you...''

''Nothing, you owe me nothing.'' His voice had hardened with annoyance. ''I don't want your gratitude.'' They had reached the kitchen, and he placed her in a chair at the table. ''Which ankle did you hurt?'' He crouched down by her feet.

''The left one. Jake, I— Ouch!''

''Sorry.'' He grinned up at her, then rested his hand with friendly ease on her knee. ''It's not swollen.''

''It still hurts,'' she said stubbornly.

"Keep off it, then," he advised with simple logic, and turned away to finish breakfast.

"You've got some bedside manners, Dr. Tanner," she observed sharply.

"Yes, ma'am, so I've been told." When he turned to face her, his smile was bland. "Tell me, Sam, does Sabrina have a mole on her left hip, too?"

Color flooded her face. "You...you..." she faltered, and clutched the robe tight at her throat.

"Around here, we call that locking the barn door after the cow's got loose. Have some coffee," he invited with sudden graciousness, pouring a cup and setting it on the table. "Start on this bacon," he ordered, sliding a plate in front of her. "That color didn't last long, you're pale as a ghost again. When did you eat last?"

"I...at breakfast yesterday, I guess."

"Toast and coffee, I imagine," he said disgustedly. "It's a wonder you can manage to sit up at all. Eat." He plucked a piece of bacon from the plate and held it out to her. "I'll have some eggs ready in a minute."

Obediently, she accepted the bacon and took a bite. "Are you going to have something?"

"In a minute," he answered absently, involved with breaking and beating eggs in a bowl.

With the first bite of bacon, Samantha realized she was ravenous. Through her preoccupation with food, she watched Jake cook with a deftness that amused and surprised her.

In a moment, he sat across from her, his plate piled high. She wondered how he could eat with such abandon and remain hard and lean.

She watched him under the cover of her lashes, and the thought came unbidden into her mind that never before had she shared the breakfast table with a man. The intimacy of their situation washed over her; the scent of bacon and coffee drifting through the air, the house quiet and empty around them, the soft flannel of his robe against her skin, the faint masculine scent of him clinging to it. It was as if they were lovers, she thought suddenly, as if they had shared the night, and now they were sharing the morning. Her face grew warm.

"I don't know what thought put roses back in those cheeks, Sam, but keep it up."

Her eyes lifted to his, and she had the uncomfortable feeling that he knew very well what road her thoughts had taken. She dropped her eyes to her plate. "I should call Bree and let her know I'm all right."

"Phones are out," he said simply, and her eyes flew back to his.

"The phones are out?" she repeated.

No telephone, her mind said again. Without a telephone, they might as well be on an island a thousand miles from anyone. Their isolation was complete, and the snow was still falling as though it would never stop.

"With a storm like this, it's not surprising to lose the phones. Power's out, too. We're on generator. Don't worry about Sabrina, she knows you're with me." His words did nothing to erase her tension.

"When...when do you think I'll be able to get back?"

"Couple of days," he returned with an easy shrug, and sipped his coffee. "The roads'll have to be cleared after the storm lets up, and you're not in any shape to travel through a mess like that yet. In a day or two, you'll be more up to it."

"A couple of days?"

He leaned back comfortably in his chair, his voice smooth as a quiet river. "Of course, by then you'll be hopelessly compromised, not a scrap of your sterling reputation left. Alone with me for two or three days, without Annie to add a thread of decency to the situation." His eyes traveled down her slim figure. "Wearing my bathrobe, too." He shook his head. "Not too many years back, I'd have had to marry you."

"Thank goodness for progress," she retorted smartly.

"Oh, I don't know, Sam." His sigh was convincing. "I'm an old-fashioned sort of man."

"It's only a matter of circumstance that we're alone here in the first place." With great dignity, she folded her arms. "And I've hardly been compromised, as you so quaintly put it."

"No?" He watched her through lazily narrowed eyes. "So far, I've undressed you, tucked you in and fixed your breakfast. Who knows what that might lead to?"

His smile might have been lazy, but it was full of meaning. Suddenly Samantha found it difficult to swallow.

"Relax, Sam." His laugh was full of arrogant enjoyment. "I told you I mean to have you, but it's not in my plans to take on a pale child who barely has the strength to stand." He paused, lit one of his long, thin cigars and blew smoke at the ceiling. "When I make love to you, I want you to have your wits about you. I don't want you passing out in my arms."

The man's arrogance was amazing! "You conceited mule," she began. "How dare you sit there and tell me you're going to make love to me? You seem to think you're irresistible! Well, you have another thing coming—"

"I'm going to remind you of that one day, Sam," Jake said mildly as he crushed out his cigar. "Now, I think you better lie down again. You're not quite up to sparring with me yet."

"I do not have to lie down. And I certainly don't need you carting me around. I can manage." She stood up, then was forced to grasp the table as the room revolved around her.

"You don't look ready to turn cartwheels, teacher," Jake observed as he took her arm.

"I'm all right." Her hand, which she had lifted to push him away, lay weakly on his chest for support. He tilted her chin, and he was no longer smiling. "Samantha, sometimes you have to be strong enough to let someone else take care of things. You're going to have to hand over the reins to me for a couple of days. If you fight it, you're only going to make it harder on yourself."

With a sigh, she allowed her head to fall against his chest, not protesting as his arms encircled her. "Do I have to like it?"

"Not necessarily." He gave a short laugh and lifted her easily and carried her back to bed.

Her small spurt of energy deserted her. With an odd feeling of contentment, she settled down under the covers. She was asleep even before his lips had lightly touched her forehead in a farewell kiss...

"I was beginning to think you'd sleep through the night."

She turned her head quickly. Jake was sitting across the room, the smoke of his cigar spiraling upward, the flickering lights from the fire shooting specks of gold into his eyes. Samantha brushed the tousled hair from her face and struggled into a sitting position.

"It's dark," she said. "What time is it?"

He glanced at the gold watch on his wrist and took a slow drag from his cigar. "It's a bit past six."

"Six? I've slept for hours. I feel as if I've slept for weeks."

"You needed it." Tossing the stub of his cigar into the mouth of the fire, Jake rose and moved toward her. His concerned eyes roamed over her sleep-flushed cheeks and heavy eyes. Gradually, his expression lightened, the angles of his face moving into a satisfied smile. "Your color's coming back." He took her wrist, and her eyes dropped from his to study the dancing flames of the fire. "Pulse's a bit jumpy." The smile reflected in his voice. "Strong though. Hungry?"

"I shouldn't be." She forced her eyes to meet his. "I've done nothing but lie around all day, but I'm starved."

He smiled again, lifting her without comment. She felt small and vulnerable in his arms, a sensation that was both pleasant and disturbing. She found it difficult to resist the impulse to rest her head against the strong curve of his shoulder. Instead, she concentrated on the sharp, clean lines of his profile.

"I'm sure I can walk. I really feel fine."

"I doubt it." She could feel his warm breath on her face. "Besides, you seem to fit in my arms pretty well."

Finding no quick comeback to this comment, she took the journey to the kitchen in silence.

Leaning back in her chair, replete and content, Samantha sipped the cool white wine in her glass and gave Jake a nod of approval.

"You're going to make some woman a terrific husband. You're an outstanding cook."

"I think so." He nodded smugly. "My wife wouldn't have to be a gourmet cook," he added with casual consideration. "I'd demand other qualities."

"Adoration," Samantha suggested. "Obedience, unswerving loyalty, solicitude."

"That's all right for a start."

"Poor woman."

"Of course, I don't want her to be a doormat. Let's say I like a woman who knows how to think, one who doesn't pretend to be anything but who she is. Of course," he added, finishing off his wine, "I'm also partial to good looks."

"Well, so far it doesn't sound as though you're asking for much," Samantha giggled. "Just perfection."

"The woman I have in mind can handle it." He

smiled broadly as he rose to pour coffee. Samantha stared at his back, feeling as though her heart had been dropped into a deep hole. *Lesley Marshall.* Her mind flashed the name like a neon sign in bright red letters.

Jake squelched her offer to do the dishes and swooped her from her chair and deposited her on the living room sofa.

"I feel useless," she muttered, helplessly cocooned by blankets and pillows. "I'm not made for lying around. I'm never sick." She gave Jake a sulky glare as if the entire matter was his fault. "I don't know how Bree coped with this sort of thing for a month."

"Could be you got her share of strength, and she got your share of patience," he considered, then shrugged. "Of course, I could be wrong." She heard his chuckle and the quiet click of his lighter as he lit a cigar.

Well, Samantha, she chided herself, you've really done it this time. Not only are you isolated with a man who constantly confuses you, but you can't even stand on your own feet. They say people learn about each other quickly when they live together, but I think it's going to take much more than one day to learn what this man is all about. *Living together,* she repeated, finding herself more amused than embarrassed. If Momma could see me now, we'd need a gallon of smelling salts.

Chapter 7

Dawn was breaking. Pink and gold streaks split the hazy blue of the sky, and light tumbled through to rest on Samantha's closed lids.

Morning? Sitting up with a start, she shook her head vigorously to dispel the last remnants of sleep. Pulling on the borrowed robe, she set her feet on the floor, took three deep breaths and stood. When both the room and her head remained stable, she let out a long sigh of relief. Her legs were weak, but they no longer felt as if they would melt from under her, and the stiffness in her ankle had disappeared.

Mobility, she thought with arrogant glee. I've never truly appreciated it until now. Coffee. One thought followed swiftly on the trail of the other, and she deserted the room with the intention of making fantasy fact. A door opened as she passed it, and with a cry of surprise, she fell against the opposite wall.

Jake stood in the doorway, rubbing a towel briskly through his damp hair, a terry-cloth robe tied loosely around his waist. ''Morning, ma'am.''

''You startled me.'' She swallowed, overpowered by the lean, bronzed maleness that the terry cloth did little to hide. He took a step toward her, and her breath caught instinctively. ''I—I'm much better.'' She began to babble, unconsciously cowering against the smooth paneling. ''I can actually walk a straight line.''

Her voice died to a whisper as he stood directly in front of her. Her eyes were on a line with the tanned column of throat revealed by the open neck of the robe. His hand lifted her chin, and she trembled.

''Relax, Sam.'' His laughter sounded deep in his throat. ''I just want to look you over. You must have the constitution of an elephant,'' he concluded with unflattering candor. ''You look as though you've been on vacation instead of battling blizzards. One day's rest after nearly freezing to death. Most women would have been stretched out for a week.''

''I'm not most women.'' She pushed his hand

away from her face. "I'm not fragile and delicate, and I'm not going back to bed. I'm going to fix breakfast." She nudged him out of her path and started down the hall.

"Coffee's already on," he called after her.

Samantha had breakfast under way by the time Jake joined her. Clad in the less disturbing attire of corded jeans and flannel shirt, he watched her prepare the meal as he silently sipped at the coffee at the kitchen table.

"I'm getting used to having a pretty face across from me at breakfast," he commented when she sat down to join him.

"I'm sure I'm not the first," she commented with studied indifference. Nor, she added to herself, will I be the last.

"Nope," he agreed easily, "but there's something to be said for big blue eyes first thing in the morning."

"Blue eyes are common enough," she muttered, and lowered them to the contents of her plate. "Besides, this is hardly a long-term arrangement." He did not speak for a moment, and her fork moved restlessly among her eggs.

"We should have the road clear enough sometime tomorrow."

"Tomorrow?" she repeated. A hollow feeling spread through her stomach.

"There's a lot of snow out there, some of the drifts are small mountains. It's going to take a little time to move it."

"I see."

"Do you think you could manage on your own for a while today?"

"What? Oh, sure, I'll be fine."

"There's a lot I should see to. My foreman was in charge yesterday, but the men need all the help they can get." He was frowning. "Cattle need hay brought out to them. They haven't the sense to dig through to the grass. They'll just stand there and starve to death."

"I suppose the storm did a lot of damage."

"It's only minor from the reports I've gotten. We were hit worse a couple years ago."

"Reports?"

"One of my men came by yesterday afternoon to fill me in." Pouring more coffee in his cup, he reached for the cream. "You were asleep."

"Oh." Strange, she thought, there had been a ripple in their isolation and she had been totally unaware of it.

Lifting his cup, he studied her over the rim. "I don't like leaving you alone, especially with the phones out."

Her shoulders moved. "Don't worry about me,

I'll be fine.'' Glancing up, she met his speculative gaze.

''I don't know how long I'll be gone.''

''Jake, stop fussing. I feel fine.''

He tilted his head to the side, his eyes still narrowed. ''Stand up. I want to see how you feel for myself.''

Before she realized his intent, his arms were around her, and his mouth was on hers. Her legs buckled.

His mouth was light, teasing, his teeth nibbling at the fullness of her bottom lip until she moaned from the exquisite agony. She gripped his shoulders as a dim light of control seeped into the darkness. Pulling away she shook her head in refusal.

''Now, Sam...'' His voice was soft and persuasive, but the hands that descended to her hips were firm. ''You wouldn't send a man out in the cold without something warm to remember, would you?''

Insistently, he brought her closer, molding her hips, exploring the soft roundness until she was pressed against him with exciting intimacy. His mouth closed over her protest, his tongue moving with slow devastation to tease hers until she felt the room spinning as wildly as it had the day before. Slowly, his hands ascended, his thumbs circling the side of her breasts while his mouth and tongue destroyed all resistance. She was straining against him, moving against him, reason forgotten. Her body heated urgently at his touch. Her sigh was a moan as his mouth descended to her throat. His lips tasted, lingered, traveled to new territories, the tip of his tongue moist and warm against her skin, erotic and devastating against her ear, until her mouth was desperate for its return to hers.

Her mouth was to go unsatisfied. He pulled her away with the same arrogance as he had pulled her to him. Dazed and limp, she could do no more than stare up at him as her body throbbed with a myriad of newly discovered desires.

''You're learning fast, Sam. That was enough to keep any man moving through a six-foot snowdrift.''

Furious, and humiliated by her own response, she drew back her hand.

''Now, Sam.'' He caught her wrist easily, holding it aloft, ignoring her efforts to escape. ''You're not strong enough yet for wrestling. Give yourself a couple more days.'' Turning her hand over, his lips brushed her palm, causing her struggles to cease abruptly. ''I'm going to bring in Wolfgang to keep an eye on you. Take it easy today, and try to remember, you're not as tough as you'd like to think.''

Ruffling her hair as though she were a child, he disappeared into the adjoing mudroom.

* * *

Later Samantha indulged in a hot, steaming shower, attempting to forget, as she soaped her skin, the feel of Jake's hands running over her. In the bedroom, she noticed her clothes piled neatly on the spoon-back chair. She slipped them on and wandered through the house in aimless exploration, the Saint Bernard lumbering at her heels.

The house abounded in small, delightful treasures, an oak rolltop desk, a wall box with Friesian carving, a Windsor cradle. With a small sigh, she wondered if the latter had rocked the baby Jake. Opening yet another door, she found Jake's library.

It smelled of leather and age, and her fingers ran over volume after volume. She pulled out a small volume of love poetry and opened the cover. Light, feminine handwriting adorned the top corner, and her mouth turned down at the inscription.

Darling Jake… To remind you.

Love, Lesley

Shutting the book with a snap, Samantha held it for one heat-blinded movement over the wastebasket, then, grinding her teeth, stuck it firmly back in place.

"It makes no difference to me," she informed Wolfgang. "She can give him a hundred books of poetry, she can give him a thousand books of poetry. It's her privilege."

She nudged the big dog with her toe. "Come on, Wolfgang, let's get moving."

She returned to the living room and built up the fire, which had burned down to a hissing pile of embers. She curled up beside it.

One hour slipped into two, two slipped into three. Surely, Jake should be home by now, she told the silent clock as the hands crept past six. It was getting dark. Rising, Samantha stared out into the diminishing light.

What if something had happened to Jake? Her throat went dry, fear creeping along her skin. Nothing could happen to him, she told herself, running her hands over her arms to combat the sudden chill. He's strong and self-reliant.

But why am I so worried about him?

"Because," she said aloud, slowly, *"I love him. I've lost my mind and fallen in love with him."* Her hands lifted to cover her eyes as the weight of the knowledge crushed down on her. "Oh, how could I be so stupid? Of all the men in the world, I had to fall in love with this one."

A man, she remembered, *who had chosen Lesley Marshall to be his wife.* Is that why I've felt pulled in two? Is that why I responded to him when I've never responded to anyone else? Looking out into the darkness, she shuddered. I might as well admit that I don't care about anything except his getting home....

When finally the sound of the outside door slamming reached her ears, she ran into the mudroom and threw herself at an astonished, snow-covered Jake.

"Sam, what's going on?" He tried to pull her away from his cold, wet jacket.

"I was afraid something had happened to you." Her voice was muffled against his chest, her cheek oblivious to the frigid dampness.

"Nothing's happened, except I'm half-frozen and soaked to the skin." Firmly now, he took her shoulders, disentangling himself from her arms. "You're getting covered with snow." His grip was gentle. She stared up at him with huge, swimming eyes. "I'm sorry I was gone so long, but things were piled up, and it's slow working in a mess like this."

Embarrassed by her outburst, she backed away. "You must be exhausted. I'm sorry, it was stupid to go on like that. It must come from being alone in the house all day." As she babbled, she was backing purposefully toward the door. "You probably want a shower and something hot to drink. I—I've got dinner on."

"Something smells good," he commented. His

eyes roamed over her flushed face, and a smile spread over his features.

''S-Spaghetti,'' she stammered and despised herself. ''I'll go finish it up.''

Retreating into the kitchen, Samantha kept her back toward him when he emerged and announced casually that he would have a hot shower before dinner. She mumbled a vague reply, pretending a complete involvement with her dinner preparation. Listening to his receding footsteps, she let out a long, pent-up breath.

''Oh, idiot that I am,'' she sighed, and pushed her hair from her face in an angry gesture. The type of behavior she had displayed in the mudroom would only lead to trouble. She took a solemn oath to keep her emotions on a tight leash as long as Jake Tanner was around.

Tomorrow, she remembered, with a mixture of relief and disappointment, she would be back with her sister, and avoiding Jake would be a great deal easier. She had only to get through one more evening without making a fool of herself, and then she would sort out her thinking.

She was setting the table when Jake returned.

''If that tastes as good as it smells, I'll die a happy man.'' He lifted the lid on the pot and gave a sigh of approval. Grinning, he disappeared for a moment, then returned with a bottle of wine just as she was placing the pot on the table.

"A nice burgundy," he said, opening the bottle and setting out two glasses.

"Samantha, this is fantastic." He broke off eating long enough to give her a smile. "Where'd you learn to cook like this?"

"More of my mother's famous lessons."

"What else can you do?"

"Well, let's see. I do a rather superb swan dive, a very graceful arabesque, I can walk on my hands as easily as some walk on their feet, whip up an incredible quiche, and waltz without counting the time."

"I am suitably impressed. How did a woman of your talents spend the day?"

She sighed and grimaced and began to toy with her spaghetti. "Sleeping, mostly."

"Hmm." His cough did not quite cover his laugh.

After dinner, Samantha insisted on seeing to the washing up herself. She wanted to avoid the intimacy of working side by side with him in the confines of the kitchen.

When the last signs of the man had vanished, she walked down the hall to the living room. Jake was adding another log to the low, shifting blaze. As she entered, he turned to smile at her. "Want some brandy?"

''No, no, thank you.'' She took a deep breath and willed her legs to carry her to the sofa.

''Not in training, are you?'' He moved from the hearth to join her on the sofa.

Smiling, she shook her head. ''The fire's wonderful.'' Grasping the first topic that came to mind, she riveted her eyes on the flames. ''I always wanted one in my apartment. We had one at home, and Bree and I used to pop corn over it. We'd always burn it, and...''

The rest of her rush of words was lost as Jake placed his finger under her chin and turned her face to his. His face moved closer, and when she jerked back in defense, his brow lifted in amusement. He bent toward her again, and again she started.

''I'm only going to kiss you, Samantha.'' His grip tightened on her chin. Sliding from her chin, his hand framed her face as his lips moved over hers, soft as a whisper. In spite of herself, she relaxed against him. Her lips parted, inviting him to explore, begging him to take.

''Samantha.'' Her name was a sigh.

''Kiss me again,'' she whispered slowly as she lifted her mouth to his.

With a low groan, he brought his lips down on hers. She clung to him, her body throbbing with heat, her heart desperate against his, while a part of her looked on, aghast, as she answered his kiss.

Her mouth clung, avid and sweet, to his. Dormant passion exploded into life until there remained only man and woman and the need, older than time, to love and be loved, to possess and be possessed.

He opened her shirt and claimed her breast. The first desperation mellowed into slow exploration as his fingers trailed lightly, drugging her with a new, delirious languor. His mouth moved to sample the taste of her neck, his face buried in the spreading lushness of her hair. She pressed against the rippling muscles of his back as his mouth and tongue and hands raged fire over her.

She felt rather than heard him say her name against her mouth, sensed rather than felt the tension enter his body before her lips were set free. Dimly, she heard the strident insistence of bells ringing as she groped to bring heaven back within reach.

''Hell of a time for them to fix the phones.'' She opened her eyes, dark as sapphires, and stared without comprehension. ''There's nothing I'd like more than to ignore it, Samantha, but it might be important.'' Her lids fluttered in confusion. She could feel the warm raggedness of his breath against her cheek. ''The phones have been out for two days, and there's a lot of damage out there.''

His body left hers and took the warmth with it. She struggled to sit up, pulling her shirt closed. The hands that worked at the buttons were unsteady and, rising on weak legs, she sought the warmth of the fire. Pushing at tumbled hair, she wrapped her arms around her body and closed her eyes.

What had she done, losing herself that way? Tossing away pride like damaged goods! What if the phone hadn't rung? Her arms closed tighter. Does love always hurt? Does it always make a fool of you?

"Samantha." She whirled at the sound of her name, her arms still tight in protection. "It's Sabrina." Dropping her eyes from his, she moved into the hall.

Samantha picked up the phone and swallowed. "Hi, Bree." Her voice sounded strangely high-pitched to her ears, and her fingers gripped hard on the receiver.

"Sam, how are you?"

Taking a deep breath, she answered. "Fine. How *you* are is more important."

"Stronger every minute. I'm so glad you had the sense to head for the Double T when the snow started. The thought of you getting caught in that blizzard makes my blood turn cold."

"That's me, a steady head in a crisis." Samantha nearly choked on a gurgle of hysterical laughter.

"Are you sure you're all right? You sound strange. You aren't coming down with a cold, are you?"

"It's probably the connection."

"I thought they'd never get the phones fixed! I guess I just couldn't really relax until I'd talked to you and made sure you were safe! Of course, I know Jake would take care of you, but it's not the same as hearing your voice. I won't keep you, Sam, we'll see you tomorrow. By the way, I think Shylock misses you."

"Probably indigestion. Tell him I'll see him tomorrow." After replacing the receiver, she stared at it for a full minute.

"Samantha." She whirled again at Jake's voice, finding him watching her from the living room archway.

"I...ah...Bree seems fine." She avoided his eyes and toyed with the ink pot by the phone. She took a step backward as Jake advanced. "She said she thought Shylock misses me. That's quite an accomplishment, he's so self-sufficient and aloof."

"Samantha. Come, sit down." He held out his hand for hers. She knew if he touched her, she would be lost.

"No, no, I think I'll go to bed, I'm still not quite myself." Her color had ebbed again, leaving pale cheeks and darkened eyes.

"Still running, Sam?" The anger in his tone was well controlled.

"No, no, I..."

''All right, then, for the moment we seem to be at a stalemate.'' He captured her chin before she could avoid the gesture. ''But we haven't finished by a long shot. Do you understand?''

She nodded, then broke away to flee to the sanctuary of her room.

Chapter 8

As each day passed, Sabrina became more cheerful. Her features took on a roundness that gave her a contented appearance. And as Samantha watched her, she wondered if Sabrina possessed more strength than she had ever given her credit for. It was a sobering experience to see her usually dreamy sister grabbing life with determination and purpose while she herself couldn't seem to stop daydreaming. Jake Tanner, she had to admit, was disturbing her days and sneaking into her dreams.

Stuffing her hands in her pockets, she scowled and continued her morning trudge to the mailbox. He meant to have her, did he? Well, Samantha

Evans had no intention of being had by anyone, especially some annoying cowboy with too much charm for his own good…and fascinating green eyes, and that beautiful mouth….

Now the days began to lengthen. The sun grew in strength. Spring began to drift over the basin greening the grass and teasing the crocuses to push their heads from the earth.

Scurrying down the hall as the doorbell interrupted her latest project—painting the nursery—Samantha wiped a few streaks of canary yellow on her jeans and opened the door.

The woman in the doorway smiled, her almond-shaped dark eyes making a thorough survey. "Hello, you must be Samantha. I'm Lesley Marshall."

The introduction was unnecessary, for with an instinct she had been unaware of possessing, Samantha had recognized the woman instantly. "Please, come in. It's still rather cold, isn't it?" She smiled, refusing to acknowledge the effort it cost her, and shut the nippy May air outside.

"I'm so glad to meet you at last." The dark eyes swept down, then up Samantha briefly. "I've heard so much about you." There was light amusement in her voice.

"Oh, really? I'm afraid I can't say the same."

Her smile was faintly apologetic. "But, of course, I've been rather busy."

"I would have been by sooner, but I wanted to wait until Sabrina was more up to company."

"Bree's feeling much better these days. I'm sure she'll be glad to see you. Let me take your coat." Samantha hung the soft fur in the hall closet. Turning back to her visitor, she needed all her willpower to keep the social smile in place. The oatmeal slacks accentuated Lesley's sleekness; the trim cerise blouse set off her delicately feathered ebony hair and the perfect ivory of her skin. Desperately, Samantha wished a miracle would transform her navy sweatshirt with its Wilson High School banner and her paint-streaked jeans into something smart and sophisticated. As usual, her hair was escaping from its pins. She resisted the urge to bring her hand up to it and jam them in tightly.

"Bree's in the living room," she announced, knowing the pale gray eyes had studied her and found her wanting. "I was just about to make some tea."

Sabrina appeared at that moment, and Samantha gladly relinquished the role of hostess and escaped to the kitchen.

"So, she's beautiful," she grumbled to an unconcerned Shylock as she set the kettle on to boil. "So, she's smooth and sophisticated and makes me feel like a pile of dirty laundry.'' Turning, she lowered her face to his and scowled. ''Who cares?'' Shylock scowled back and went to sleep. Her thoughts wandered on. ''I don't imagine he's ever laughed at her and patted her head as though she were a slow-witted child,'' she muttered as she gathered up the tea tray.

''Sabrina, you look wonderful,'' Lesley commented sometime later, sipping from a dainty china cup. ''I'm sure having your sister with you must be very good for you. I don't have to tell you how concerned everyone has been.''

''No, and I appreciate it. Sam's made everything so easy. I didn't have anything to do but sit and heal.'' She shot her sister an affectionate glance. ''I don't know what we would have done without her these past two months.''

Lesley followed her gaze. ''Jake was telling me that you're a gym teacher, Samantha,'' she purred, managing to make this sound faintly disgusting.

''Physical education instructor,'' Samantha corrected, slipping into a vague southern drawl.

''And you were in the Olympics, as well. I'm sure it must have been fascinating. You don't look the sturdy, athletic type.'' The shrug of her shoulders was elegant, as was the small gesture of her hand. ''I suppose one can never tell.'' Samantha gritted her teeth against a biting retort and was vastly relieved when, glancing at a slender gold watch, Lesley suddenly rose from her chair. ''I must run now, Sabrina, I have a dinner engagement.'' Turning to Samantha, she offered a small smile. ''So happy to have met you. I'm sure we'll be seeing each other again soon.''

She left amidst a swirl of fur and the drifting scent of roses. Samantha sat back in the cushioned chair, relaxing for the first time in more than an hour.

''Well, what did you think of Lesley?'' Sabrina questioned, shifting into a more comfortable position on the sofa.

''Very sophisticated.''

''Come on, Sam.'' Sabrina grinned, her hands folding across the mound of her belly. ''This is Bree.''

''I don't know why I should have to comment, since you seem to be reading me so well. But—'' her mouth curved into a rueful smile ''—I suppose she's a bit smooth for my taste, and I didn't much care for the way she looked down that aristocratic nose at me.''

''Actually, you really don't appear very sturdy.'' The observation was made with wide-eyed innocence. Samantha grimaced, pulling pins from her hair with a sharp tug until a cascade of golden brown tumbled in confusion about her shoulders.

"She'd have gotten her own back on that one if you hadn't sent me that 'Don't make a scene' look."

"Oh, well, Lesley can be nice enough when it suits her. Her father spoils her dreadfully. Her mother died when she was barely into her teens, and he transferred all his attention to Lesley. An overabundance of clothes, the best horses, and, as she grew older, cars and European tours and so on. Whatever Lesley wants, Lesley gets."

"Poor thing." The sarcasm caused her to feel spiteful and unjust. She sighed. "I suppose too much is as bad as too little. It was nice of her to come and see how you were getting along."

Sabrina's laughter floated through the room. "Sam, darling, I've never known you to be so slow." At her sister's puzzled expression, she continued. "Lesley didn't come to see me, she came to get a look at you."

"At me?" Finely etched brows disappeared under a fringe of bangs. "What for? I wouldn't think a lowly gym teacher from Philadelphia would interest Lesley Marshall."

"Any teacher who caught Jake Tanner's attention the way you have would interest Lesley. He wouldn't have gone out of his way to show just anyone around the ranch, you know."

A light color rose in Samantha's cheeks. "I think Miss Marshall's mind was put to rest after she got a good look.'' Her hand moved expressively down her sweatshirt and jeans. ''She'd hardly see any danger here.''

''Don't underestimate yourself, Sam.''

''No false modesty.'' Samantha's sigh came from nowhere. ''If a man's attracted to silk and champagne, cotton and beer are no competition. I'm cotton and beer, Bree,'' she murmured. Her voice trailed away with her thoughts. ''I couldn't be anything else if I wanted to.''

The following day, Samantha's continuing battle with her paints and brushes was interrupted by a more welcome visitor. Annie Holloway arrived at the ranch's kitchen door with a beaming smile and a chocolate cake.

''Hi.'' Samantha opened the door wide in welcome. ''It's nice to see you again, and bearing gifts, too.''

''Never like to come empty-handed,'' Annie announced, handing the thickly frosted cake to Samantha. ''Dan always had a partiality for chocolate cake.''

''Me, too.'' She eyed the cake hungrily. ''He's not here right now, and I was just going to make some coffee. Do you suppose we could start without him?''

''Good idea.'' Setting herself comfortably in a

chair, Annie waved a wide-palmed hand. "I reckon it wouldn't hurt for us to have a slice or two."

"Bree's taking a nap," Samantha explained as she put down the mugs of steaming coffee. "The doctor says she still has to lie down every day, but she's beginning to grumble about it a bit. Very quietly, of course."

"You're keeping an eye on her." Annie nodded and added two generous spoons of sugar to her coffee. "Dan says she's up to company now."

"Oh, yes, people have been dropping by now and again. Ah…" Samantha added cream to her own cup. "Lesley Marshall was by yesterday."

"I wondered how long it would be before Lesley hauled herself over to get a look at you."

"You sound like Bree." Sipping her coffee, Samantha shook her head. "I don't know why Lesley Marshall would want to meet me."

"Easy. Lesley's a mite stingy with her possessions, and she'd like to group Jake among them. She hasn't figured out yet that Jake is his own man, and all her daddy's money can't buy him for her. When my Jake picks his woman, he'll decide the time and place. He's always been an independent rascal. He was barely twenty when he lost his folks, you know." Samantha lifted her eyes to the warm brown ones. "It wasn't an easy time for him, they'd been close. They were a pair, Jake's folks, always squabbling and loving. You're a bit like her when she was a young thing.'' Annie smiled, her head tilting with it as Samantha remained silent. ''Nobody's going to ride roughshod over you, at least not for long. I saw that straight off. She was stubborn as a mule with two heads, and there's times, though it's been better than ten years, I still miss her.''

''It must have been hard on Jake, losing his parents and having all the responsibility of the ranch when he was still so young,'' Samantha murmured.

''Seemed to change from boy to man overnight, just out of college and still green. 'Course,'' she continued, ''he'd been in the saddle since childhood and what he hadn't learned about ranching from his father and that fancy college, he learned from doing. He picked up the reins of that ranch with both hands. There's not a man who works for him wouldn't wrestle a long-horned bull if he asked them to. He can fool you with that easygoing way of his, but nobody gets the better of Jake Tanner. He runs the ranch like his life, and Lesley's going to find him a hard steer to rope and brand.''

''Maybe it's more the other way around,'' Samantha suggested. Annie's response was prevented by the appearance at the kitchen door of the man in question.

He entered with the easy familiarity of an old friend.

''Howdy, ma'am.'' He broke the silence with a cocky smile, removed his battered Stetson and glanced at her attire. ''Been painting?''

''Obvious, isn't it?'' Samantha said sharply.

''Nice colors.'' He helped himself to a cup of coffee. ''Are you going to part with another piece of that cake?''

''Jake Tanner!'' Annie exclaimed in disgust. ''You should be ashamed, gobbling Dan's cake when you've got a perfectly good one of your own at home.''

''Somebody else's always tastes better, Annie.'' He slipped off his jacket, tossing it over a hook, and grinned boyishly. ''He won't miss it, anyway. I brought you and the cake over, didn't I? You're not going to begrudge me one little piece?''

''Don't waste those eyes on me, you young devil.'' Annie attempted to sniff and look indignant. ''I'm not one of your fillies.''

Jake's appearance had successfully shattered Samantha's peace of mind. After a reasonable period of politeness, she excused herself to Annie and Jake and went back to her job in the nursery.

Samantha's artistic talent was decidedly impressionistic. The floor, protected by plastic, was splotched and splattered, but the walls were coming to life with a joy of brilliant colors. Of the four walls, two were yellow and two were white, and each was trimmed with its opposite's color. On the one wall that was unbroken by door or windows, she had begun the construction of a wide, arching rainbow, carefully merging blues into pinks into greens.

Time passed, and in the quiet concentration of her work she forgot her preoccupation with Jake. Sitting on the ladder's top step, she paused, brushing the back of her hand across her cheek absently as she viewed the results.

"That's a mighty pretty sight."

She jolted, dropping the brush with a clatter, and would have fallen from the ladder had Jake's arms not gripped her waist and prevented the tumble.

"Sure spook easy," Jake commented, removing the dangerously sloshing paint bucket from her hand.

"You shouldn't come up behind a person like that," she complained. "I might have broken my neck." She wiped her hands on the legs of her jeans. "Where's Annie?"

"With your sister. She wanted to show Annie some things she's made for the baby." He set the bucket on the floor and straightened. "I didn't think they needed me."

"No, I'm sure they didn't. I need that paint, though, and the brush you made me drop." She glanced down, but his eyes remained on hers.

"I like the blue, especially that spot on your cheek," Jake said.

She rubbed at the offending area in annoyance. "If you'd just hand those things back to me, I could finish up."

"Green's nice, too," he said conversationally, and ran a finger over a long streak on her thigh. "Wilson High." His eyes lowered to the letters on her shirt. "Is that where you taught back east?"

"Yes." She shifted, uncomfortable that the name was prominent over her breasts. "Are you going to hand me my things?"

"What are your plans for tonight?" he countered easily, ignoring her request. She stared, completely thrown off balance by his unexpected question.

"I, ah, I have a lot of things to do." She searched her mind for something vital in her schedule.

"Things?" he prompted. His smile grew as his finger began to twist through a stray curl that had escaped its confines.

"Yes, things," she retorted, abandoning the attempt to elaborate. "I'm going to be very busy, and I really want to finish this room."

"I suppose I could let you get by with that, even though we both know better. Well." He smiled and shrugged. "Come down and kiss me goodbye, then. I've got to get back to work."

"I will not kiss you goodbye…." she began, the

words trailing off as he gripped her waist. Her hands automatically went to his arms, and he plucked her from her perch.

He lowered her slowly, his eyes never leaving hers, and her mouth was roughly claimed before her feet could reach the floor. His hands slipped under her shirt to roam the smooth skin of her back, pressing her closer as her body betrayed her and dissolved against his. Slowly he explored her soft, firm breasts, subtly rounded hips, lean thighs.

Every time, every time, her mind murmured. Every time he kisses me, I go under deeper, and one day I'll never find my way back. His teeth moved to nip at her ear and neck, searching and finding new vulnerabilities before returning to ravage her mouth again. Without will, without choice, she rested in his arms, surrendering to forces she could never defeat.

He drew her away, breaking the intimacy, but his mouth returned to hers to linger briefly before he spoke. ''About tonight, Samantha.''

''What?'' she murmured as his tongue traced the softness of her lips.

''I want to see you tonight.''

Jerking herself back into reality, she pressed her hands against his chest, but did not manage to break away. ''No, no, I'm busy. I told you.''

"So you did," he acknowledged, and his eyes narrowed in speculation.

His words were cut off by the sound of Sabrina's laughter drifting down the hall. Samantha wiggled against Jake's hold. "Let me go, will you?"

"Why?" He was grinning now, enjoying the flood of color in her cheeks.

"Because..."

"Don't ever play poker, Sam." The warning was curt. "You'd lose your shirt."

"I...I..."

"Sabrina's due in September, right?"

The sudden question caused her to blink in confusion. "Well, yes, she..."

"That gives you a little breathing space, Samantha." He leaned down, and his kiss was hard and brief and to the point. "After that, don't expect to get away so lightly."

"I don't know what..."

"You know exactly what I mean," he said interrupting. "I told you I meant to have you, and I always get what I want."

Her eyes flashed. "If you think I'm going to let you make love to me just because you say so, then you..."

The suggestion she would have made died as his mouth took hers again. She went rigid telling herself she would not amuse him with a response this time.

As she told herself she would not, her arms circled his neck. Her body became pliant, her lips parted with the hunger she had lived with all through the past month. As he took, she offered more; as he demanded, she gave. Her own mouth was mobile, her own hands seeking, until it seemed the month of fasting had never been.

"I want you, I don't have to tell you that, do I?"

She shook her head, trying to steady her breathing as his eyes alone caused her pulse to triple its rate.

"We'll settle this in September, unless you decide to come to me sooner." She began to shake her head again, but the fingers on the back of her neck halted the movement. "If you don't come to me, I'll wait until after the baby's born and you've got that much off your mind. I'm a patient man, Sam, but..." He stopped talking as Annie and Sabrina stepped into the room.

"Well." Annie shook her head at the two of them. "I can see he's been giving you a hard time." She turned to Sabrina with a half-exasperated shrug. "He's always been fresh as a new-laid egg. This is going to be a beautiful room, Sam." She glanced around at Samantha's handiwork, nodding in approval. "Let go of the little lady now, Jake, and take me back home, I've got dinner to fix."

"Sure. I've already said what I came to say." He released Samantha with a last, penetrating look and strode from the room, calling a goodbye over his shoulder.

"Fresh as a new-laid egg," Annie reiterated, and echoing his goodbye, followed him.

When the guests had departed, Samantha began to gather up paint buckets and brushes.

"Sam." Walking over, Sabrina placed a hand on her sister's arm. "I had no idea."

"No idea about what?" Bending, she banged the lid securely on rose pink.

"That you were in love with Jake." The truth she had avoided for so long was out in the open now: She had fallen hopelessly, irrevocably in love with Jake Tanner! Standing, Samantha searched in vain for words of denial.

"We know each other too well, Sam," Sabrina said before she could answer. "How bad is it?"

Samantha lifted her hands and let them fall to her sides. "Terminal."

"Well, what are you going to do about it?"

"Do about it?" Samantha repeated. "What can I do about it? After the baby comes, I'll go back east and try to forget about him."

"I've never known you to give up without a fight," Sabrina spoke sharply. At the unexpected tone, Samantha's brows rose.

"I'd fight for something that belonged to me, Bree, but I don't move in on someone else's territory."

"Jake's not engaged to Lesley Marshall. Nothing's official."

"I'm not interested in semantics." Samantha began to fiddle with the paint cans. "Jake wants an affair with me, but he'll marry Lesley Marshall."

"Are you afraid to compete with Lesley?" Bree asked.

Samantha whirled around, eyes flashing. "I'm not afraid of anyone," she stormed. Sabrina's lips curved in a smug smile. "Don't try your psychology on me, Sabrina! Lesley Marshall and I don't belong in the same league, but I'm not afraid of her. I *am* afraid of getting hurt, though." Her voice wavered and Sabrina's arm slipped over her shoulder.

"All right, Sam, we won't talk about it any more right now. Leave those brushes, I'll wash them out. Go take a ride. You know the only way to clear your head is to go off by yourself."

"I'm beginning to think you know me too well." With a wry smile, Samantha wiped her hands on her jeans.

"I know you, all right, Samantha." Sabrina patted her cheek and urged her from the room. "I just haven't always known what to do about you."

Chapter 9

During the months since their first meeting, Samantha had grown to know Jake Tanner, and to realize that when he wanted something, he made certain he got it. And she knew he wanted her.

If, when she rode out on horseback, she kept closer to the ranch than had been her habit, she told herself it was not fear of encountering Jake that prompted the action, but simply her desire to spend more of her free time with Sabrina. Now Sabrina was growing cumbersome in her pregnancy, there was a grain of truth to this, so Samantha found it easy to accept the half-truth.

Every day she fell more under the spell of Wyoming. Bare branches were now fully cloaked in green. The cattle grew sleek and fat. The land was fully awakened and rich.

"I think you may just have twins in there, Bree," Samantha commented as the two sisters took advantage of golden sun and fragrant warmth. Sabrina glanced down to where Samantha sat cross-legged on the wide front porch. "Dr. Gates thinks not." She patted the mound in question. "He says there's only one, and I'm just getting fat. One of us should have twins, though."

"I'm afraid that's going to be up to you, Bree. I think I'll revive the tradition of old-maid school teachers."

Sabrina was sensitive to the wistfulness in the words. "Oh, no, you'll have to get married, Sam. You can't let all those lessons go to waste."

This brought the light laugh it had intended. "I'm perfectly serious. Remember what Madame Dubois always said: 'Von must reach for ze stars.'"

"Oh, yes, Madame Dubois." Samantha smiled at the memory of their former ballet teacher. "You know, of course, that accent was a phony. She came from New Jersey."

"I'm suitably crushed. She did think she had a genuine protégé in you."

"Yes, I was magnificent." Samantha sighed with exaggerated pride.

"Let's see a few of your famous leaps now, Sam."

"Not on your life!"

"Come on, cutoffs are as good as a tutu any day. I'd join you in a pas de deux, but it would actually be a pas de trois."

Samantha rose reluctantly from her seat on the porch. "All right, I don't mind showing off a little."

With quiet dignity, Sabrina began to hum a movement from *Swan Lake,* and Samantha lowered into a purposefully dramatic body sweep before exploding with an energetic series of grand jetés, stage leaps and cabrioles. She concluded the performance with a group of pirouettes, ended by dropping in a dizzy heap on the grass.

"That's what you get," she said, closing her eyes and shaking her head at the giddiness, "when you forget to spot focus."

"Is this show open to the public?"

Samantha glanced sharply toward the sound of the all-too-familiar voice.

"Dan!" Sabrina exclaimed. "I didn't expect you back so early."

"Ran into Lesley and Jake out on the north boundary," he explained, striding over and planting a firm kiss. "I thought you and Sam might like some company."

"Hello, Lesley, Jake." Sabrina included them

both in her smile. ''Have a seat, I'll bring out something cool.''

Samantha had been sitting, praying without result for the ground to open up and swallow her. ''I'll do it, Bree.'' She jumped at the opportunity to escape. ''Don't get up.''

''I'm up,'' Sabrina pointed out, disappearing inside before Samantha could argue.

''Do you teach ballet, as well, Samantha?'' Lesley asked. She surveyed Samantha's outfit of semi-ragged cutoffs and T-shirt with dark, mocking eyes.

''No, no,'' Samantha muttered, feeling once more desperately at a disadvantage next to the slim woman in elegantly tailored breeches and silk shirt.

''I thought it was real nice,'' Dan commented, innocently turning the knife.

''Samantha's just full of surprises,'' Jake said.

Now that he had spoken again, Samantha was forced to give Jake a portion of her attention. He looked devastatingly male, the denim shirt rolled past his elbows to expose bronzed, corded arms, the low-slung belt in his jeans accentuating his leanness. She concentrated on a spot approximately six inches to the left of his face, in order to avoid the smile that had already mastered his face.

''Yeah,'' she returned. ''I'm just a bushel of surprises.''

''Anything you can't do, Sam?''

"A few things." She attempted a cool sophistication.

"You're so energetic," Lesley commented, slipping her hand through Jake's arm. "You must be horribly strong and full of bulging muscles."

For one heady moment, Samantha considered flight. She was opening her mouth to make her excuses when Dan effectively cut off all hope.

"Sit down, Sam, I want to talk over a little idea with you and Sabrina." Sinking down on the porch steps, Samantha avoided any glimpse of Jake's face. "Do you think Sabrina's up to a little party?" Samantha looked up at Dan's question and attempted to marshal her thoughts.

"A party?" she repeated, drawing her brows together in concentration. "I suppose so. Dr. Gates says she's doing very well, but you could always ask to be sure. Did you want to go to a party?"

"I was thinking of having one," he corrected with a grin. "There're these twins I know who have this birthday in a couple of weeks." Bending over, he tugged at Samantha's loosened locks. "Seems like a good excuse for having a party."

"Oh, our birthday." Samantha's response was vague. The impending anniversary had slipped her mind.

"Did I hear someone say party?" Sabrina

emerged through the screen door with a tray of iced tea.

Samantha sipped the cool, sweet tea her sister handed her and watched Sabrina's face light up with anticipation.

"A birthday party, Sam." She turned to her sister, eyes shining with excitement. "When's the last time we had one?"

"When we were twelve and Billy Darcy got sick all over Mom's new carpet." Leaning back against the porch rail, Samantha unwittingly lifted her face to Jake's.

"Well, then, it's high time for another," Dan said. "What do you say, Sam? I know it means extra work for you."

"Huh." Tearing her eyes from Jake's smile, she endeavored to pick up the threads of the conversation. "What? Oh, no, it's no trouble. It'll be fun." Concentrating on Dan's face, she blocked out the sight of Lesley lounging intimately against Jake. "How many people did you have in mind?"

"Just neighbors and friends." He reached up to rub his chin. "About thirty or forty, I'd say. What do you think, Lesley?"

The full mouth pouted a moment in thought. "If you want to keep it small, Dan," she agreed after a short deliberation. Samantha's eyes grew wide.

These people definitely had a different idea of small than she did.

"Oh, Lesley, come take a look at this punch bowl I've got, see if you think we should use it." Rising, Sabrina took Dan's hand. "Come, get it down for me, Dan." Throwing her sister an innocent smile, Sabrina disappeared inside and left her alone with Jake.

"How's the painting coming?" Jake stretched both arms over the back of the swing.

"Painting? Oh, the nursery. It's finished."

That, she recalled with a frown, was just one of many times he had come upon her in a ridiculous situation. Sleeping on stumps, covered with paint, and now leaping across the lawn like some crazed ballerina. Samantha, she told herself, you have class.

"What do you want for your birthday, Sam?" He prodded her with the toes of his boot and earned a scowl.

Blowing a wisp of hair from her eyes, she moved her shoulders. "Fur, diamonds."

"No, you're not the type for furs." Taking out a cigar, he lit it and blew a lazy stream of smoke. "You'd be thinking about all the little minks that were scalped to make it. And diamonds wouldn't suit you."

''I suppose I'm more the quartz type.'' She rose, irritated.

''No, I was thinking more of sapphires.'' He caught her wrist. ''To go with your eyes, or maybe rubies to go with your temper.''

''I'll be sure to put both on my list. Now, if you'll excuse me.'' She glanced at her captured hand, then back at him. ''I've got to go feed my cat.'' She gestured to where Shylock lay on the far side of the porch.

''He doesn't look very hungry.''

''He's pretending to be dead,'' she muttered. ''Shylock, let's eat.''

Amber eyes opened and blinked. Then, to her pleasure, Shylock rose and padded toward her. However, upon reaching his mistress, he gave her a disinterested stare, leaped into Jake's lap and began to purr with wicked enjoyment.

''No, ma'am.'' Jake glanced down at the contented cat. ''He doesn't look hungry at all.''

With a final glare, Samantha turned, stalked to the door and slammed the screen smartly behind her.

The sun shone warm and friendly on the morning of the twins' birthday. Samantha carried a large parcel into the kitchen. Dumping her burden on the table where her sister was enjoying a cup of tea, she nudged Shylock away with her foot. She had not yet decided to forgive him for his treacherous advances to Jake.

"This just came, it's from the folks."

"Open it, Sam." Sabrina poked an experimental finger at the package. "Dan refuses to give me my present yet, and I've searched everywhere I can think of."

"I bet it's six books on child rearing for you, and six on etiquette for me."

"A present's a present," Sabrina stated, and tore the mailing paper from the box.

"Here's a note." After breaking the seal, Samantha produced a sheet of paper and read aloud.

"To Samantha and Sabrina:

A very happy birthday and our love to you both. Sabrina, I do hope you are taking good care of yourself. As you know, proper diet and rest are essential. I'm sure having Samantha with you during the last weeks of your confinement is a great comfort. Samantha, do look after your sister and see that she takes the necessary precautions. However, I hope you're not overlooking your own social life. As your mother, it is my duty to remind you that you are long past the marriageable age. Your father and I are looking forward to seeing you and our first grandchild in a few weeks. We will be in Wyoming the first part of September, if Dad's schedule holds true.

With love,
Mom and Dad

"There's a postscript for you, Bree.

"Sabrina, doesn't Daniel know any suitable men for your sister?"

With a sigh, Samantha folded the letter and dropped it on the table. "She never changes." Dipping into the box, Samantha plucked out a smaller one with Sabrina's name on it and handed it to her. "Marriageable age," she muttered, and shook her head.

"Did you peek in here before?" Sabrina accused, dumping out volumes on infant and child care.

"No," Samantha denied with a superior smirk. "I just know Mom." Drawing out her own package, she ripped off the concealing paper. "Good grief." She let the box drop to the table and held up a brief black lace negligee.

"I thought I knew Mom." Both sisters burst into laughter. "She must be getting desperate," Samantha concluded, holding the negligee in front of her.

"Now that's a pretty thing," Jake observed as he and Dan entered the kitchen. "But it's even prettier with something in it." Samantha bundled the garment behind her and flushed scarlet.

"Presents from Mom and Dad," Sabrina explained, indicating her stack of books.

"Very suitable." Dan grinned as he glanced through the volumes.

"Doesn't look like Sam feels the same about hers." Jake smiled. Samantha felt her already alarming color deepen. "Let's see it again."

"Don't tease, Jake." Sabrina turned to her husband. "Mom says they'll be here the first part of September."

"I'll put this stuff away." Samantha tossed the gown into the box and began to bury it under books.

"Leave that till later." Dan took her hand and pulled her away. "I need you outside for a minute."

She went willingly. Escape was escape. Imagining it had something to do with Sabrina's gift, she was surprised when Dan slowed his pace and allowed his wife to join them in their walk toward the ranch buildings. He kept her involved in a running conversation about the party until they came to a halt at the paddock fence.

"Happy birthday, Sam." Sabrina kissed her sister's cheek as Samantha's eyes focused on the golden Arabian mare.

"Oh." She could manage no more.

"She's from a good line," Dan informed her, his arm slipping around Sabrina's shoulders. "She's out of the Double T stock, no finer in Wyoming."

"But I..." Words faltered, and she swallowed and tried to begin again.

“What do you give someone who packs their own life away for six months without hesitation, without asking for anything in return?” Dan’s free arm slipped around Samantha and pulled her to his side.

“We figured if you insisted on going back east, we’d always have a hold on you. You’d have to come visit us to ride your mare.”

“I don’t know how to thank you.”

“Then don’t,” Dan ordered. “Go try her out.”

“Now?”

“Now’s as good a time as any.” Not needing a second urging, Samantha was over the fence, stroking the mare and murmuring.

“We may convince her to stay yet,” Dan commented, watching as she slipped into the saddle and took the mare around the paddock. “I could have a word with Jake.”

Sabrina shook her head. “No, Sam would be furious if we interfered. She’d bolt back to Philadelphia before we could take a breath. For now, we’d better keep out of it.” She lowered her voice as a beaming Samantha trotted around to them and slipped off the little mare.

“She’s a real beauty,” she sighed. “I don’t know how I can ever bear to leave her…”

Sabrina’s eyes met her husband’s in silent satisfaction. Perhaps it will not be necessary, their unspoken message said.

"Come, little sister," Dan said. "If you can tear yourself away from your new friend, I sure could use a cup of coffee now."

As the trio trooped back toward the house, Jake swung through the back door. "Delivery just came. It's in the living room."

"Oh," Dan murmured, looking entirely too innocent. "Come on, Sabrina, we'd best see what it is."

"Is it the piano?" Sam asked Jake, and Dan and Sabrina disappeared inside.

"Looked like one to me. I guess that's another present that'll go over big. Walk to the truck with me," Jake commanded, and captured her hand before she could protest.

"Really, Jake, I have a million things to do." She trotted to keep pace with his loose, lanky stride.

"I know, you're indispensable." Stopping by his truck, he reached in the cab and produced a package. "But this seems to be the time for gift giving. I thought I'd let you have your present now."

"You didn't have to get me anything."

"Samantha." His drawl was lazy, but his eyes narrowed in annoyance. "I never do anything unless I want to." Taking her hand from behind her back, he placed the box in it. "Open it."

Lifting the statue from its tissue bedding, she examined it in silent amazement. The alabaster was smooth and cool in her hands, carved into the shape of a horse and rider in full gallop. The artist had captured the fluid grace, the freedom of motion. She ran a hesitant finger over the delicate features.

"It looks like me." She lifted her eyes to Jake's.

"And so it should," he answered easily. "It's supposed to be you."

"But how?" She shook her head, torn between pleasure and confusion.

"A man I know does this kind of thing. I described you to him."

For the second time that day, Samantha found herself at a loss for words.

"Why?" The question was out before she could swallow it.

Slowly, a smile drifted across his face. He pushed back his hat. "Because it suits you better than furs and diamonds."

She braced herself to meet his eyes again. "Thank you."

He nodded, his face solemn. He took the box from her hands and placed it on the hood of the truck. "I think a birthday kiss is traditional."

Swallowing, she took an instinctive step in retreat, but he gripped her arms and held her still. She offered her cheek, and his laughter broke out, full and rich on the summer air. "Sam," he turned her face to his, and his eyes sparkled with humor, "you're incredible."

His lips met hers. His hand moved from her arms to her hips, drawing her firmly against the hard lines of his body. She submitted to the embrace, as long as his arms held her, as long as they were mouth to mouth, as long as the heat from his body infused hers, he owned her, and she could not run.

Finally he drew her away, bringing his hands to her shoulders while hers rested on his chest for support.

"Happy birthday, Sam."

"Thank you," she managed, still breathless from the impact of his embrace.

He lifted the box from the hood of the truck and placed it in her hands before sliding into the cab. "See you tonight." With a salute, he started the engine. The truck moved down the road, leaving her staring after it.

Chapter 10

Party sounds filled the house. Laughter and voices and music mingled and drifted through open windows to float on the night air.

On this evening, the twins were dramatically different in their appearance. Sabrina's pale blue gown floated around her, cunningly disguising her pregnancy. Her hair was a glinting halo around rose-tinted cheeks. Samantha's black-striped satin clung to her body, her halter neckline plunging deep to a wide, gathered waist. Her hair was free and thick around her shoulders.

As she moved and mingled with the crowd, Samantha searched for a tall, lanky form, noting with increasing despair and a gnawing jealousy that a slim, dark woman had also as yet failed to put in an appearance.

Cornered by an enthusiastic young cowboy, Samantha was feeling her attention begin to wander from a detailed account of horse breeding when her eyes met dark jade across the room.

He was standing with two men she did not recognize, and Lesley Marshall stood beside him. She was elegant in an oyster-white gown. Her fine-boned ivory hand was placed from time to time on Jake's arm, as if, Samantha thought grimly, she were flaunting her possession.

Furious with the sudden feeling of inadequacy, Samantha turned to her companion with a dazzling smile. He stammered over his lecture, his words grinding to a halt. She tucked her arm in his and used her eyes without shame.

"Howdy, Tim." Jake appeared from nowhere and placed a hand on the young man's shoulder. "I'm going to steal this little lady for a moment." He paused and smiled easily into Samantha's mutinous face. "There's a couple of people she hasn't met yet."

Without waiting for an assent, he had her unwilling hand in his, propelling her through the crowd. "Tim won't be the same for weeks," he whispered close to her ear. "A woman could get run out of town for using her eyes that way on susceptible young boys,'' he warned, pulling her through the sea of people.

''You don't have to drag me.''

''I know a stubborn mule when I see one,'' he countered, without bothering to lower his voice. Her furious retort was swallowed as Jake presented her to the two men who flanked Lesley.

''Sam, I'd like you to meet George Marshall, Lesley's father.'' Samantha's hand was enveloped in a hearty grip. ''And Jim Bailey,'' he continued, nodding toward the second man.

''Jim only works with cattle on paper. He's a lawyer.''

''My, this is a mighty pretty girl!'' George Marshall boomed. Giving Jake a sly wink, he patted his daughter's shoulder.

''You always manage to rope in the pick of the herd, don't you, Jake?''

Jake slipped his hands easily into his pockets. ''I do my best. But then, roping them's one thing, getting them's another.''

''Well, now, little lady,'' George's genial voice continued, ''Les tells me you're a gym teacher.''

''That's right, Mr. Marshall.''

''Now, you just call me George,'' he instructed, squeezing her shoulder with a genial affection. ''Tell me, why isn't a pretty little thing like you married and settled down instead of running around some gymnasium?''

Jake was grinning with obvious enjoyment. Samantha tossed her hair behind her back, but before she could think of a suitable answer, George's laughter boomed through the room.

''I like this girl,'' George announced to the group. ''Looks like she has spirit. You come over to our ranch any time, little lady, any time at all.''

In spite of herself, Samantha found herself liking his expansive hospitality. ''If you'll excuse me now, I've got...got to get a tray out of the kitchen.'' She gave the group an all-encompassing smile and melted into the crowd.

In the kitchen, she pulled a tray from the refrigerator to give her excuse credibility and was glad she had when Jake followed her in a moment later.

''George is a good man. He has the right ideas when it comes to women.'' Smiling knowingly at her, he leaned against the door watching her every move.

''That's your opinion,'' she returned tartly, bustling around the kitchen in an attempt to ignore him.

''Sit down a minute, Sam.''

She glanced up, immediately wary, then lifted the tray as a defense. ''No, I've got to get back.''

''Please.''

Despite herself, she lowered the tray to the table and herself into a chair.

"I ran into Jack Abbot, the school principal, the other day."

"Oh?"

"He told me the girls' phys ed. instructor isn't coming back next term." Leaning back in his chair, Jake studied her. "He's going to offer you the job."

"Oh," she repeated before she could stop herself.

"He wants you pretty bad. He really needs someone this fall. I told him I'd be seeing you, and that I'd mention it. He's going to call you officially, of course."

How simple, Samantha thought.

How simple it would all be if I didn't love this man. I could stay where I want to stay, work where I want to work. But now, I've got to refuse, I've got to go away.

"I appreciate your telling me, and I appreciate Mr. Abbot wanting me, but…"

"Don't appreciate it, Samantha, think about it."

"You don't know what you're asking me to do."

He rose to pace the room, his hands seeking the depths of his pockets. "I'm just asking you to think about it. You like it here. You've made friends. You like being near your sister. You'd still have the satisfaction of doing what you feel you're suited for. Is it so much to ask that you consider it?"

‘‘Yes, it’s quite a lot. Jake, I don’t want to argue with you. There are things I have to do, the same way there are things you have to do.’’

‘‘All right.’’ He nodded, then repeated slowly, as if coming to a decision. ‘‘All right, there *are* things I have to do.’’ Moving over, he captured her chin between his thumb and fingers.

His arms slipped around her waist to bring her close, his mouth lowering to brush her cheeks and the corners of her lips. ‘‘Come home with me now, Samantha. We can be alone there.’’ His voice had become low and seductive, as his fingers trailed over the bare skin of her back.

‘‘No, please don’t.’’ She turned her face away.

‘‘I want to make love to you. I want to feel your skin under my hands, all of you. I want to hear you sigh when I touch you.’’

‘‘Jake, please.’’ She dropped her head to his chest. ‘‘It’s unfair, here, like this.’’

‘‘Then come home with me.’’

‘‘No, I can’t.’’ She shook her head without raising it. ‘‘I won’t.’’

‘‘All right, Samantha.’’ He framed her face and brought it up to his. ‘‘I said I’d give you until the baby was born. We’ll stick to that. We won’t argue tonight. Let’s call it a truce for your birthday. Agreed?’’

He kissed her once, briefly, and turned to lift the

tray. "Then we'll both do what we have to do when the time comes."

Leaving her confused, Jake moved through the doorway.

Rejoining the festivities, Samantha moved from group to group, but her thoughts were only about Jake. Why was he so interested in her career choices? Why did he want her to take the job in Wyoming? *Maybe he cared for her.* For a brief moment, she allowed hope to shimmer. Her eyes swept the room to find him. Finally she spotted him. He was dancing with Lesley. The shining cap of her raven hair brushing his cheek, the ivory of her hand entwined with the bronze of his. Samantha winced as he threw back his head and laughed at something Lesley had said for his ears alone.

Care for me? her mind repeated in a scathing whisper. Grow up, Samantha, *caring* and *wanting* don't always mean the same thing. In a few weeks, she comforted herself, she would no longer be subjected to this constant pain. When the ache had eased, she could visit Bree again. Jake would probably be too busy with his wife to spare time for visits to the Lazy L. Samantha felt her heart contract with pain.

She turned away and bumped solidly into Jim Bailey.

"Sorry." He took her shoulders to steady her. "I didn't see you."

"It's all right," she returned, offering a smile. "Besides, I think I ran into you."

"Well, no harm done either way." She watched his eyes slide past her and focus on Jake and Lesley. "They look nice together, don't they?"

Embarrassed that he must have seen her staring at them, Samantha nodded, and looked down at her empty glass. "Come on, we better get you a refill."

A few moments later, they joined the group around the piano as Sabrina played.

"So, you're a lawyer." She smiled at Jim. "I don't think I've ever met a lawyer before."

Jim returned her smile. "And you're a gymnast."

"No, actually, I'm a gym teacher now."

He lifted his glass in a toast and drank. "I remember you. I've always been an avid fan of the Olympics. I thought you were fabulous."

"Well, that's nice to hear after a decade."

He tapped his glass to hers. "Well, Olympic star, would you like to dance?"

"I'd love to."

Samantha enjoyed Jim Bailey's easy conversation. She learned during their two dances that he was interested in getting into politics. His dark good looks and ready wit would certainly be assets, she decided.

"Sam." Sabrina motioned to her as they moved back toward the piano. "It's your turn. Union rules."

"Okay," Samantha agreed, sliding onto the bench.

She played with practiced ease, moving from one song to the next. Time slipped through her fingers. As in a dream, she was aware of the voices behind her, the faint, drifting breeze of Wyoming through the opened windows.

Someone sat beside her. Recognizing the lean fingers that lifted to turn the page of her sheet music, she faltered and missed a note.

"You and Jim seem to have hit it off." Samantha heard the click of his lighter over the sounds of the party.

"He's a very nice man. Have you known him long?"

"Oh, only since we were about eight and I gave him a black eye and he loosened a few of my teeth."

"Sounds like a loving friendship."

Jake again turned the page before she could do so herself. "Well, after that we sort of stuck together." He pushed the curtain of hair behind her shoulder, and Samantha struggled not to break the thread of the melody. "The two of you seemed to have a lot to talk about."

"He's very charming, and we have a few mutual interests."

"Hmm." Jake shifted slightly in his seat. His thigh brushed hers, and her fingers responded by hitting three wrong notes.

"You play very well."

Was he being ironic? She turned to look at him, but found no mockery in his jade eyes.

"Pleasantly," she corrected. "I get the general melody, but the details are a bit fuzzy."

"I've noticed that you have a tendency to shrug off your own capabilities. Are you aware of that?"

"That's not true. I just know what I do well and what I don't."

"You're a very tough critic, and you're inclined to underestimate."

"Honesty," she countered, finishing the song with a flourish. "I am a totally honest person."

"Are you, Samantha?" he said softly. "That's what I plan to find out."

Chapter 11

The days grew hot and sultry. The skies were improbably blue, rarely softened by clouds.

Long hours in the sun had deepened the honey of Samantha's skin, teasing out the gold in her hair. As long as she was occupied, she had no time for soul searching. She could enjoy the long summer days without thinking of the fall. As Sabrina wilted like a thirsty rose in the searing heat, Samantha confined her own activities to the early-morning hours. In the long, hot haze of the afternoon, Sabrina moved slowly through the house, her body clumsy. Samantha did not dare leave her. The baby was due in two weeks, and Samantha wanted to remain within calling distance of her sister as much as possible.

One particularly humid afternoon, the two women were sitting idly in the living room. Sabrina got up heavily from her chair to look out the window. ''Sam,'' she said, ''before Dan left for town, he said a storm was brewing. From the looks of the sky, I'd say he was right.''

Before Samantha could answer, there was a sudden flash of lightning. A blast of thunder rolled in on the wind, and the rain began to fall in sheets.

''It's coming down fast,'' Samantha agreed. ''It should cool us off a bit.'' She looked sympathetically at her sister's bulky form.

The storm built in power. Jagged flashes of lightning illuminated the room and an angry wind hurled the rain against the windows. The two women watched in fascination as the storm exhausted itself. Soon rain dripped tentatively from the eaves and the thunder was a mere grumble in the distance.

The sun struggled to reappear, breaking through the gloom with a hazy promise of light.

''That,'' Sabrina commented with an enormous sigh, ''was a mean one.''

Samantha turned from her place by the window and again slumped into a chair. ''Remember when you used to hide in the closet whenever we had a thunderstorm?''

''All too well.'' She gave her sister a pained smile. ''And you used to stand on the porch, loving every minute of it, until Mom dragged you in, soaking wet. On that note from the past,'' Sabrina announced, and struggled to her feet, ''I'm going to take a nap, Sam.'' She turned at the doorway and studied the woman slouched in the chair, bare legs and feet stetched out in unconscious grace. ''I love you.''

With a rather puzzled smile, Samantha watched her walk away.

Wandering out to the porch, Samantha drank in the rain-fresh air. Everything sparkled. Raindrops clung like jewels to blossoms and leaves. Though the flowers had drooped with the weight of the storm, their colors had been washed into brilliant life. A bird, flying by on a shaft of light, trilled above her. She could hear the steady dripping of the rain off the eaves above the whisper of the dying wind. Satisfied, she curled up on a porch rocker and instantly fell asleep.

She had no idea how long she had drifted in the soft twilight world when, with reluctance, she woke at the touch of a hand on her shoulder. She looked up drowsily and yawned. ''Oh, Bree, I must have fallen asleep. It's so wonderfully cool out here.''

''Sam, I think the baby's decided to put in an unscheduled appearance.''

''Huh? Oh!'' Springing to her feet, she was instantly awake. ''Right now? Dan's not here, and it's not time yet. Sit down, sit,'' she ordered, running agitated fingers through her hair.

''I think the first thing to do is to calm down,'' Sabrina suggested.

''You're right. I'm not going to fall apart, it was just a shock. I wasn't expecting this for another week or two.''

''Neither was I.'' Sabrina's smile was half amused, half apologetic.

''All right, how long have you been having contractions, and how far apart are they?''

''Only for an hour or so.''

''That should give us plenty of time.'' Samantha patted Sabrina's hand.

''But they've been getting awfully strong, and...'' Breaking off, she closed her eyes and began to breathe in a deep, methodical rhythm. ''And,'' she continued, after a final long breath, ''awfully close together.''

''How close?'' Samantha asked, feeling new tension at the base of her neck.

''Ten minutes.''

''Ten minutes,'' Samantha repeated. ''I'd better get you to the hospital. I'll bring the car around. Stay put,'' she told her sister, and raced to the garage.

Upon reaching Sabrina's compact and sliding behind the wheel, Samantha was horrified to find the engine unresponsive to the turn of the key. The little car sputtered, emitted an apologetic groan and died.

"You can't," she insisted, and smacked the steering wheel. "We just had you fixed."

There was no use wasting more time trying to figure out what was wrong with the car. It was clearly not going to start, and Samantha hadn't the first idea of where to look for the problem.

Rushing back to the house, she picked up the phone in the kitchen. At least she could call Dr. Gates. A groan of despair was wrenched from her when she heard the dead silence on the line. Oh, no, the storm must have knocked out the phones!

Forcing herself to appear calm, she returned to the living room where Sabrina was waiting for her.

Reaching her sister again, Samantha knelt down so their eyes were level. "Bree, the car won't start. All the trucks and jeeps are out with the men, and the storm must have knocked down the phone lines."

"Looks like we've got a few problems." Sabrina took a deep breath.

"It's going to be all right." Samantha took her hand in reassurance. "I'll help you get into bed, and then I'll take a horse and ride toward the Double T. If I don't see any of the men on the way, I'll get a truck there and bring it back. Most of them have radios, and I can call ahead to the doctor."

''Sam, it's going to take time for you to get there, and to get back. I don't think I'll make it in time to get to the hospital after that. You'll have to have the doctor come here.''

''Here?'' Samantha repeated. Her throat closed on the word. Sabrina nodded. ''All right. Don't worry, I won't be long. I'll be back as soon as I can.'' Samantha raced off to the stables, and without wasting the time for a saddle, she leaped on her mare's back.

The familiar landscape was a blur, as she urged more speed out of the powerful horse. The sound of her own breath was masked by the sound of thudding hooves. Every minute she took was a minute longer that Sabrina was alone. She crouched lower on the horse and dug in bare heels.

When Samantha spotted the men on horseback, she spurred the Arabian over the fence in a fluid leap. As her hooves touched earth, she met the horse's sides again. They streaked across the field, scattering annoyed cattle.

When she reached the group, she reined in sharply. The mare reared, nearly unseating her. Her breath came in gasps as she struggled to keep her seat.

''What are you trying to do, break your neck?'' Furiously Jake snatched the reins from her hands. ''If you're stupid enough not to care about yourself, think of your horse. What do you mean riding like a fool and jumping fences? Where's your saddle? Have you lost your mind?''

''Bree,'' she managed at last between giant gulps of air. ''The baby's coming, and the phone's out. The car wouldn't start, and there's nobody around. Dan's in town. Bree says there's no time to get her into the hospital now, and I have to call the doctor.'' She felt tears of fear burning at her eyes and bit her lip.

''All right, take it easy.'' Twisting in the saddle, Jake called out to one of his men. ''Get back to the ranch and get hold of Dr. Gates on the CB radio. Tell him Sabrina Lomax is in labor and to get to the Lazy L in a hurry.'' Turning back, he handed the reins to Samantha. ''Let's go.''

''Are you coming back with me?'' Flooded with relief, she gripped tight on the leather.

''What do you think?''

Together, they sprang forward in a gallop.

Speed and thundering hooves were all Samantha ever remembered of the ride back. There was no time for conversation, no time for thought. She was sliding to the ground before she came to a full stop and Jake once more secured her reins.

''Keep your head, Samantha,'' he ordered, watching her bound up the steps and through the front door.

The house was silent. Her stomach tightened as

she rushed to the master bedroom. Sabrina sat up in bed, propped by a mound of pillows and greeted her with a cheerful smile.

"That was quick, did you fly?"

"Just about," Samantha returned, faint with relief.

"We've sent for the doctor. Everything's under control." She sat down on the bed, taking her sister's hand. "How are you doing?"

"Not too bad." Her hand closed over Samantha's, as much to reassure as seeking reassurance. "I'm glad you're back. Here comes another one."

Samantha looked on with unfamiliar helplessness. Her fingers grew tighter over her twin's, as if to steal some of her pain.

"We can thank Mom for that book on natural childbirth." Sabrina gave a long, shaky sigh and relaxed against the pillows.

"Don't look so worried, I'm doing fine. Oh, hello, Jake." Glancing at the doorway, Sabrina greeted him with friendly cheerfulness. "I didn't know you were here. Come in. It's not contagious."

He advanced into the room, looking tall, male and out of place. His hands retreated to his pockets. "How're you doing?"

"Oh, well, you've seen a cow in labor before, I don't imagine there's much difference." The small hand tightened on Samantha's. "Here we go again."

Samantha lifted the hand to her cheek. *Where was the doctor?* Sabrina should be in the hospital, surrounded by experts.

"This baby's in a big hurry," Sabrina announced with a small moan. "I'm sorry, Sam, it's not going to wait much longer."

I don't know anything about childbirth, Samantha thought in a moment of terror. *What am I going to do? What do I do first?*

Standing, she turned to Jake. "Go sterilize some towels, lots of them, and some string and scissors."

"All right." His hand rested on her shoulder a moment. "If you need me, give a call."

Nodding, she moved into the adjoining bath and scrubbed her hands and arms until they hurt.

"You're going to be fine," she stated as she reentered the bedroom.

"Yes, I am." Sabrina lay back on the pillows and closed her eyes. "I'm going to have this baby, Sam, and I'm going to do a good job of it. You can't do this for me, I have to be strong."

"You are strong." Brushing away the hair from Sabrina's cheeks, she realized with a sudden jolt that it was true. "You're stronger than I ever knew."

Her calm had returned, and she took over the duties of midwifery with an instinct as old as time. She wiped moisture from her sister's face, working with her, breathing with her, uttering soothing encouragements. Sabrina had not gone through all she had to lose now, and Samantha would not allow anything to go wrong.

"All right." Wiping beads of sweat from her own brow, Samantha straightened. "I think she's going to come this time, it's almost over. You have to help."

Sabrina nodded, her face pale and composed. Her hair had darkened with dampness. She shuddered and moaned with the final pang of childbirth. A thin, shrill cry pierced the stillness of the room. Samantha held new life in her hands.

"Oh, Bree." She stared down at the tiny, wriggling form.

Dan burst into the room two steps ahead of the the doctor.

Suddenly, it was all so simple, Dan standing by Sabrina's side, his large hand clutching hers, the small, fresh form swaddled in the curve of her mother's arms.

"Only one." Sabrina sighed, her eyes luminous. "You'll have to handle the twins, Sam. One at a time is enough for me."

Sometime later, Samantha shut the door behind her and walked toward the kitchen. Jake looked up at her approach.

"A girl." She lowered herself into a chair. "The

doctor says she's perfect, almost seven pounds. Bree's fine.'' She pushed at her tumbled hair and ran a hand across her brow. ''I want to thank you.''

''I didn't do anything.''

''You were here.'' She lifted her eyes, and they were young and vulnerable. ''I needed to know you were here.''

''Samantha.'' He smiled and shook his head. ''You sure find a man's weak points. I'll get you a drink.''

He was back in a moment with a decanter of brandy and two snifters. Sitting across from her, he filled both generously. ''It's not champagne, but it'll do.'' Lifting his glass, he touched it solemnly to hers. ''To mother and child, and to Samantha Evans.'' He paused, his smile fading into seriousness. ''She's one hell of a woman.''

Samantha folded her arms on the table, laid her head on them and burst into tears.

''I was so scared.'' She found her voice muffled against his shoulder as he brought her against him. ''I've never been so scared. I thought I would lose them both.''

He tilted her chin as one hand rubbed the small of her back. ''You're a survivor, Sam, and too stubborn to let anything happen to Sabrina or the baby.''

Her forehead dropped to his chest as she struggled to stem the flow of tears.

"I always seem to fall apart in front of you."

"Don't much care for that, do you?" She felt his lips descend to her hair and allowed herself the joy of being cradled in his arms. "Most people don't look for perfection, Sam, they find it boring. You," he said, framing her face with his hands, "are never boring."

She sniffed and smiled. "I guess that was a compliment." Giving in to impulse, she leaned over and rested her cheek against his. "I don't think you're boring, either."

"Well." He stroked her hair a moment, and his voice was curiously soft. "That's about the nicest thing you've ever said to me.

"Now drink some of that." He pushed her gently away and handed her the brandy.

Obeying, she allowed the warm strength to seep into her veins and relaxed with a sigh. "Bree certainly came through this better than I did." She drank again. Jake straddled a chair, leaning his arms on the back. "When I left her, she was lying there with the baby, looking like she'd just finished having a picnic. Dan looked like he was about to keel over, I was ready for someone to cart me away. Yet Bree lies there, glowing like a rose."

"Your sister's quite a woman."

"I know." Her eyes dropped to the suface of the table. "She said she has someone to depend on her now. I guess the time's come to stop playing big sister. She doesn't need that anymore."

"So, what will you do now?" His voice was casual.

"I'll stay around a couple of weeks, then I'll go on." She struggled, seeing only a void.

"To what?"

Her fingers tightened on her glass. "To my work, to my life." She drank, and the brandy was bitter.

"Still set on leaving?" He lifted his own glass, swirling the liquid. Amber danced under the kitchen light. "You haven't seen Wyoming in the autumn."

"No, I haven't," she answered, evading his prior question. "Maybe I'll come back next year." She stared down at her hands, knowing she never would.

"She's hungry!" Dan charged into the kitchen, his grin threatening to split his face. "Just had a baby, and she says she's hungry. Sam, I love you." Plucking her from her chair, Dan tossed her into the air. Her laughter ended on a shriek as she clutched at him on her journey down. The shriek was strangled as she was smothered by a bear hug. "I swear, if bigamy wasn't against the law, I'd marry you."

"If I was still all in one piece," she managed, turning her face and gulping for air.

"I ask you, Jake." He consulted the other man as his arms threatened to destroy the alignment of

Samantha's rib cage. ''Have you ever known another like this one?''

''Can't say that I have.'' She heard the smile in his voice, though it was impossible in her position to see his face. ''I'd say Samantha is unique. One of a kind.''

Rising, he lifted his brandy and toasted them both.

Chapter 12

"Sam, you're going to spoil her."

"Impossible." Sitting in the front porch rocker with the week-old Jennifer, Samantha smiled at her sister. "She's much too intelligent to be spoiled. Anyway, it's an aunt's privilege."

As she continued to rock, her lips strayed to Jennifer's soft tuft of dark hair. I won't be able to do this much longer. She looked to the massive peaks gleaming silver-blue in the afternoon sun. A light breeze stirred the air, bringing the sweet scent of freshly mowed grass. She breathed it in, and the soft scent of Jennifer's talc mingled with it. A sigh escaped.

She had not realized such a small creature could wrap her way around the heart so completely. Another love to leave behind. In just a week, I'll have to say goodbye to all the things that matter: Bree, Dan, Wyoming, and now Jennifer.

Dents and bruises, she thought again, but not the open wound that comes from leaving the man. Arrogant and gentle, demanding and kind, hot-tempered and easy; the parts that made up Jake Tanner were complicated and many, but to Samantha, it was a simple equation of love.

Blast you, Jake Tanner, if it weren't for you, I could stay. I belong here. I felt it from the first time I saw the mountains. There's nothing for me in Philadelphia. You've left me without anything to go back to.

"Looks like Lesley's coming to pay a visit," Sabrina observed. Samantha jerked back to the present with a snap.

She watched the late-model compact winding down the drive. Ignoring the flare of impossible jealousy, she set her features in casual lines.

"Sabrina, how well you look." Lesley's greeting was obviously tinged by surprise. "It's only been a week, and you look positively..." She hesitated, searching for a word.

"Radiant?" Sabrina suggested, and laughed. "I just had a baby, Lesley, not open-heart surgery."

"But to go through all that here, and without a doctor." She turned to Samantha. "I heard from Jake that you were marvelous and handled everything."

Samantha shrugged, uncomfortable at hearing Jake's praise from Lesley's lips. "It was nice of him to say so, but Sabrina did all the work."

"Well, having a baby is not a prospect I look forward to." Lesley shivered delicately. "I certainly intend to put it off as long as possible." Gliding over, she bent her head over the sleeping infant. "She is quite lovely, Sabrina. Very sweet."

"Would you like to hold her?" Samantha offered.

"Oh, no." Lesley stepped back. "I'm afraid I'm not very good with babies."

As she moved, Samantha caught the glint of the large square-cut diamond on her left hand. Lesley followed her gaze, and held out her hand. "You didn't know I was engaged, did you, Sabrina?"

"No." Sabrina cast a quick glance at her sister. "We hadn't heard."

"Well, you have been rather busy." She moved her fingers, enjoying the changing lights. "And we haven't made any formal announcement yet. We're planning a bit of a party for next week. As a matter of fact, I'm just on my way into town to begin shopping for my trousseau. Of course, I'll have to make a trip into New York for some proper clothes, but

I'll just have to make do locally for the time being. We've set the wedding for the end of September.'' She smoothed her perfectly groomed hair with a well-manicured hand. ''I could have done with a bit more time, but men have no idea how difficult things are to arrange properly.'' She smiled again. ''Well, I must fly. I have so much to do. I do hope you'll be able to make it to the wedding, Samantha.''

Sabrina glanced again at her sister. ''Sam won't be here in September, Lesley.''

''Oh, too bad.'' The regret in Lesley's voice was mild. Her mind had already run ahead to her wardrobe. She opened the door of the compact and slid behind the wheel. Lifting a slim arm in farewell, she drove away.

Rising, Sabrina took the sleeping Jennifer from her sister's arms and went into the house. When she returned, she sat on the arm of the rocker and laid her hand on Samantha's shoulder.

''I knew it was going to happen,'' Samantha murmured. ''I just didn't want to be here when it did. I didn't think it would hurt this much. Oh, Bree.'' She looked up at her twin with helpless, swimming eyes. ''What am I going to do?''

For the first time in their relationship, their situations were reversed, and Samantha was vulnerable, seeking comfort and advice.

"Sam, you can't go on like this. Why don't you talk to him?" Sabrina stroked the thick fall of her sister's hair. "Something is wrong here, and the two of you have to talk things out."

"No. I won't give him the opportunity to feel sorry for me."

"Pride can be a very cold companion," Sabrina murmured.

Samantha stood up. "I'm going back early, Bree. I can have everything arranged by the day after tomorrow, maybe even by tomorrow night."

"Sam, you can't run away from this."

"Just watch me."

"Mom and Dad won't be here for a few more days. They'll be disappointed."

"I'm sorry, I hate to miss them, but I can't handle this." Pausing, she repeated, the admission surprising her, "I *really* can't handle this."

"But, Sam..." Sabrina joined her at the porch rail. "You should at least talk to Jake. Don't you want to know how he feels? You can't just go flying off without speaking to him, without saying good-bye. Something's not right about all this. I've thought about the two of you. I've seen the way he looks at you."

Shaking her head, Samantha moved toward the door. "No, he hasn't shown his face since the baby was born, and Lesley Marshall has his ring on her finger. A diamond. He has what he wants."

Samantha spent the evening packing, while Shylock watched her in silent accusation from his habitual place in the center of her bed.

Once in bed, she spent most of the night staring at a moon-washed ceiling. When the first pale light of dawn crept into the room, she rose. The mauve shadows under her eyes were a sad tribute to the restless hours.

The house slept on, and she deserted it, making her way to the stables. She saddled her mount with quick, deft movements, then galloped over the faint mist of morning.

As the sky lightened, the air came to life with the sweet song of birds. Sadly, she listened to the song of the west, for she knew that the melody would linger forever in her heart. She watched the mountains transformed by the dawn. Ribbons of rose and gold melted into blue until the peaks were no longer silhouettes, but stood proud in the full glory of the sun. She stayed for a last look at the white-faced Herefords grazing on the short, coarse grass. She knew now that her love for this wild, free country was forever bound up with her love for Jake. In saying goodbye to one, she was saying goodbye to the other. Straightening her shoulders, she turned the little mare back to the Lazy L.

When she returned to the house, she greeted her sister with bright chatter, the meaningless words no disguise for sleep-starved eyes. Sabrina made no comment, and shortly disappeared into the bedroom to tend to the baby.

Alone, Samantha wandered aimlessly from window to window. Tonight, she thought, slipping her hands into the pockets of her jeans, I'll be on a plane. And tomorrow morning, all this will just be a dream.

''Morning, ma'am.''

She whirled, nearly upsetting a vase of roses with the movement. Jake leaned against the door frame, legs crossed at the ankles, as if he had been watching for some time.

''What are you doing here?''

He took a few strides into the room. ''Well, now, I came to fetch you.'' This information was imparted in an irritatingly slow drawl.

''Fetch me? What are you talking about? I'm not a dog or a maverick calf to be fetched.''

''Maverick calf sounds pretty close. You're always running off in the wrong direction.'' Reaching out, he took her arm. ''Come on, we're going for a ride.'' His voice was pleasant, but the steel was there. She jerked away, angry with his arrogance, wary of his tone.

"I have no intention of going anywhere with you. Why don't you just go away and leave me alone?"

"Now, I can't do that, Sam," he returned in a reasonable tone. "We have some unfinished business to attend to. Your time's up."

The fire in her eyes flickered and died. "You can't be serious."

"I'm dead serious."

"What…what about Lesley?"

"She's not invited," he returned simply.

"I'm not going with you," she said, somewhere between terror and fury. "You can't make me."

Stopping, he looked down at her from his overpowering height. "Sure I can," he corrected with easy confidence. With a swift movement, he swung her over his shoulder. "See?" He walked effortlessly down the hall. "Nothing to it."

"Let me down!" Furious fists beat against his back. "This is crazy, it's illegal. I'll have you thrown in jail!"

"No kidding? Sam, you're scaring me to death."

He continued easily down the hall, as if he carried an empty sack, rather than an irate woman who was thumping against his back. Pausing, he touched the brim of his hat as Sabrina appeared in the bedroom doorway, the baby in her arms.

''Morning, Sabrina.'' His greeting was genial, and he cocked his head to get a better view of Jennifer. ''She's a real beauty.''

''Thank you, Jake. We certainly think so.'' She shifted the baby and smiled. ''Are you two going out?''

''Thought we'd go for a little ride,'' Jake informed her. ''We may be gone some time.''

''It's a fine day for it, hardly a cloud in the sky.''

''Bree.'' Samantha's voice was desperate. ''Don't just stand there, *do* something.'' She pushed at the hair which hung over her face. ''Don't you see what he's doing? He's kidnapping me. Call the police, call Dan.'' She continued to plead as Jake touched the brim of his hat once more and moved down the hall. ''Bree, say something.''

''Have a good time'' was her sister's surprising response.

Samantha's mouth fell open in dumb astonishment. A stream of imaginative curses was hurled on Jake's unperturbed head as he took the reins of his mount from a grinning cowboy.

''Looks like you got yourself a real handful there, Jake.''

''No more than I can handle,'' he countered, swinging into the saddle with Samantha still held over his shoulder. With a speed that defied his easygoing manner, he had her in front of him in the saddle, spurring the horse into a gallop, before she could think of escape.

"You're going to pay for this," Samantha promised, clutching the saddle horn to keep her balance. "You can't just run off with me this way!"

"I didn't see anybody try to stop me," Jake pointed out.

He followed the road for some time without decreasing his pace, then cut across an open field. At a small grove of trees, he reined in, gripping Samantha around the waist when she attempted to wiggle down.

"Now, don't do that, Sam," he warned in a friendly voice. "I'd just have to catch you, and I throw a mean lasso."

He slid from the chestnut, and before her feet could touch the ground, she was back over his shoulder. Without ceremony, she was dumped under the fragile, bending leaves of a willow while he towered over her, grinning with obvious enjoyment.

"You're going to be sorry," she predicted, smoldering with fury. "I'm going to..." The rest of her words slipped back down her throat as he dropped down next to her. "You—you can't do this, Jake. You're not the kind of man who forces himself on a woman."

"Who says?" Pushing her back on the soft grass, he covered her body with his.

Her body betrayed her with instant response. Her skin tingled as his mouth brushed over it. ''You're not really going to do this.''

''I told you once—'' his mouth moved to her ear, and his words were warm and soft against it ''—not to forget your own words. There are some things you just have to do.''

His kiss was long and lingering.

When her mouth was free, she drew in a deep breath and spit out with all her strength, ''What kind of man are you, to make love to one woman and plan to marry another?''

His eyes lazily narrowed. He propped himself on one elbow, his other arm pinning her down. Lifting his head from his elbow, he undid the top button of her blouse. ''Suppose,'' he continued, moving down to the next button, ''you tell me whom I'm supposed to marry.''

His fingers trailed a slow line from her throat, down the smooth skin her open blouse revealed, and rested on the next button. The blood began to pound in her ears. His eyes alone held her still as he spread her blouse apart. Slowly, his fingers roamed up the warmth of her skin, moving with casual possession over her. Her eyes clouded with growing need as he explored.

''Tell me who I'm going to marry, Samantha.''

His body shifted again, molding to hers. His shirt was warm against her naked flesh.

"L-Lesley," she stammered.

"No." His mouth lowered to the curve of her throat, his tongue teasing the vulnerable skin.

She felt the waist of her jeans loosen under his hand. His finger pushed away the material and moved along her hip. With her last claim to lucidity, she pushed against his chest.

"Please stop."

"Now I just can't do that, Sam." His hands teased the curve of her hip, trailing back up to the side of her breast. "I've waited a good long time to get you where I want you."

"I'm not staying… Did you say you weren't marrying Lesley?"

He frowned down in consideration, winding her hair around his finger. "Seems to me I did mention that. I don't know why you're always piling your hair on top of your head when it looks so good spread all over."

"But she was wearing your ring."

"Not mine," Jake corrected, still concentrating on the hair around his fingers. "Your hair's gotten lighter these past few weeks, you haven't been wearing a hat. Les has a diamond, doesn't she? I told you once diamonds don't suit you. They're cold, and they don't have much imagination. But that's Les."

He shrugged and began to move his mouth over her face again. ‘‘It doesn’t seem to matter to Jim.’’

Valiantly, Samantha attempted to follow his words. Her head shook with the effort.

‘‘Les is engaged to Jim Bailey. I’m sure you remember Jim Bailey, you spent enough time with him at the party.’’

‘‘Yes, but…’’

‘‘No buts,’’ he interrupted. ‘‘Les likes to have a couple of fish on the line, and when she got it through her head I wasn’t in season, she netted Jim without a struggle.’’

‘‘But I thought…’’

‘‘I know what you thought.’’ He cut her off again and smiled. ‘‘Running away a few days early, weren’t you?’’

‘‘I wasn’t running. How did you know I was leaving?’’

‘‘Sabrina told me.’’

‘‘Bree?’’ Samantha whispered. Bree did that?

‘‘Yeah, yesterday. She came to see me while you were packing. I like this spot right here,’’ he stated, planting his lips against the hollow of her throat. ‘‘I’ve had a devil of a time putting things in order since then, so I could take time for a honeymoon. Busy time of year for a cattleman.’’

‘‘Honeymoon?’’ Her skin was trembling where his lips continued to taste.

"I've got a good foreman," he continued, as if thinking aloud. "I reckon he can manage things for a while. I could use another day or two. I had a nice long honeymoon in mind, someplace quiet." He brought his attention back to her stunned face. "You've never been to Bora Bora, have you?"

"Are you talking about getting your ranch in order so you can take time off to marry me?" She attempted to speak slowly and clearly while her emotions whirled like a summer tornado.

"Just being practical," he explained with a bland smile.

"Why you conceited, overbearing… Just what makes you think I'll marry you? You sit back and make all these plans and expect me to run off to Bora Bora with you like a passive little puppy. Of all the chauvinist—"

"How about Antarctica?" he suggested, willing to be reasonable. "Not too many people there, either."

"You're crazy. I never said I'd marry you. What makes you think…" Her tirade was cut off effectively as his mouth coaxed her silence. When he let her breathe, her voice had lost its strength. "That's not going to help you. I'm not in love with you."

"Seems to me I recall someone telling me she was a totally honest person." His gaze was disconcertingly direct. He held her chin, preventing her face from turning away. ''You want to look at me and tell me that again? You've been fighting me all along, and I think I've just about used up my patience.'' His lips were teasing hers again, and his hands moved over her with more urgency. ''Mmm, but you have a nice body. I can't take much more of this waiting around. Six months is a long time, Sam. I've wanted you from the minute you stood there ordering Dan to have his man tend to the horses.''

''Yes, you let me know very early what you wanted.'' She no longer struggled, but lay passive in his arms.

''Gave you something to think about. Of course, you didn't know I wanted you to be my wife, too. It was easy to tell you I wanted you, but a bit difficult to tell you I loved you. Sam, look at me.'' She shook her head, but the fingers on her chin tightened in authority. ''Look at me.'' She obeyed, her lids opening to reveal eyes veiled with tears. ''You stubborn little idiot. Listen carefully, I've never said this to another woman, and I've had to wait too long to say it to you. If you don't marry me soon, I'm going to lose my mind.'' His mouth took hers, spinning the world into nothing. Her arms flew around him as pain evaporated into unspeakable joy. ''Samantha.'' He buried his face in the lushness of her hair. ''It's been quite a race.''

"I don't understand." She brought his face back to hers, needing to see the truth in his eyes. "Why didn't you tell me before?"

"I didn't think you'd believe that a man had nearly been knocked off his feet by a picture of a girl less than half his age, then had completely lost his balance when he saw the woman she'd become. If you hadn't been so wrapped up in Sabrina those first few minutes, you'd have seen how a man looks when he gets hit by lightning."

"Just like that?" Stunned, she traced the angles of his face to assure herself she was not dreaming.

"Just like that," he agreed, bringing her palm to his lips. "Then, after I'd recovered a bit, I knew I had to work around your dedication to Sabrina until you'd figured out there was room in your life for someone else. Then you stood there telling me you were going back home as soon as the baby was born. I nearly strangled you." His fingers tightened on her hand as he brought his eyes back to hers. "How was I supposed to tell you that I loved you, that I wanted to marry you, wanted you to stay in Wyoming? The night of the party, in the kitchen, I made up my mind I wasn't letting you go, no matter what I had to do to keep you."

"But I never wanted to leave." She shook her head in brisk denial, as if he should have realized it all along. ''It was just that I couldn't bear to see you married to Lesley.''

''You know, things might have gotten even more complicated if Sabrina hadn't come by and laid things out for me. She's got a bit more of you in her than I had thought.'' Laughing, he lifted his face from hers. ''She told me to sit down and listen. She'd never seen two people run around in circles so long and get nowhere.''

''It's not like Bree to interfere.''

''She interfered beautifully. First thing she did was ask me what business I had getting engaged to Lesley. I must have stared at her like she'd lost her mind. After I managed to tell her I was definitely not engaged to Lesley, she let me have it with both barrels. Mixed with the buckshot was the information that you were miserable about going home, and that I was a fool for not seeing it myself. Then she folded her arms, stuck out her chin exactly like someone else has a habit of doing and asked me what the devil I intended to do about it.''

Samantha stared up at him and shook her head in astonishment. ''I wish I could have seen that.''

He smiled and lowered his mouth. ''Just look in the mirror sometime.'' Flesh met flesh with no barriers, and with a small sound of desperation he savaged her mouth. The hard lines of his chest pressed into her breasts. ''Let me hear you say it, Samantha,'' he murmured, unable to resist the curve of her neck. ''I need to hear you say it.''

''I love you.'' Her mouth searched for his, her arms urging him closer. ''I love you. I love you.'' Her lips found their objective, and her silence told him again.

''I need you, Samantha.'' His mouth and hands continued to seek, growing wilder, possessive, demanding. ''I never knew I could need anyone the way I need you. I want you for myself for a while, no distractions, no complications, just you. We've got six months of loving to make up for. I'm going to keep you fully occupied for a very long time.'' Lifting his face, he smiled down at her, running his hand through the hair spread over the grass. ''A very long time.''

She smiled back, running her hands up his chest to circle his neck. ''I intend to keep you occupied, as well. Your cows are going to get very lonely.'' Removing his hat, she tossed it carelessly aside, then turned back to him with raised brows. ''Okay, cowboy.'' Her arms lifted to lock around his neck, fingers tangling possessively in his hair. ''Start occupying.''

''Yes, ma'am.'' With a polite nod, he lowered his mouth and followed orders.

* * * * *

HER MOTHER'S KEEPER

Chapter 1

The taxi zipped through the airport traffic. Gwen let out a long sigh as the Louisiana heat throbbed around her. She shifted as the thin material of her ivory lawn blouse dampened against her back. The relief was brief. Squinting out of the window, she decided the July sun hadn't changed in the two years she had been away. The cab veered away from downtown New Orleans and cruised south. Gwen reflected that very little else here had changed in the past two years but herself. Spanish moss still draped the roadside trees, giving even the sun-drenched afternoon a dreamlike effect. The warm, thick scent of flowers still wafted through the air. The atmosphere was touched with an easygoing indolence she nearly had forgotten during the two years she'd spent in Manhattan. Yes, she mused, craning her neck to catch a glimpse of a sheltered bayou, I'm the one who's changed. I've grown up.

When she had left Louisiana, she'd been twenty-one and a starry-eyed innocent. Now, at twenty-three, she felt mature and experienced. As an assistant to the fashion editor of *Style* magazine, Gwen had learned how to cope with deadlines, soothe ruffled models, and squeeze in a personal life around her professional one. More, she had learned how to cope alone, without the comfort of familiar people and places. The gnawing ache of homesickness she had experienced during her first months in New York was forgotten, the torture of insecurity and outright fear of being alone were banished from her memory. Gwen Lacrosse had not merely survived the transplant from magnolias to concrete, she felt she had triumphed. This is one small-town southern girl who can take care of herself, she reflected with a flash of defiance. Gwen had come home not merely for a visit, a summer sabbatical. She had come on a mission. She folded her arms across her chest in an unconscious gesture of determination.

In the rearview mirror, the taxi driver caught a glimpse of a long, oval face surrounded by a shoulder-length mass of caramel curls. The bone structure of his passenger's face was elegant, but the rather sharp features were set in grim lines. Her huge brown eyes were focused on some middle distance, and her full, wide mouth was unsmiling. In spite of her severe expression, the cabbie decided, the face was a winner. Unaware of the scrutiny, Gwen continued to frown, absorbed by her thoughts. The landscape blurred, then disappeared from her vision.

How, she wondered, could a forty-seven-year-old woman be so utterly naive? What a fool she must be making of herself. Mama's always been dreamy and impractical, but this! It's all *his* fault, she thought resentfully. Her eyes narrowed as she felt a fresh surge of temper, and color rose to warm the ivory tone of her skin. *Luke Powers*—Gwen gritted her teeth on the name—successful novelist and screenwriter, sought-after bachelor and globe-trotter. *And rat,* Gwen added, unconsciously twisting her leather clutch bag in a movement suspiciously akin to that of wringing a neck. A thirty-five-year-old rat. Well, Mr. Powers, Gwen's thoughts continued, your little romance with my mother is through. I've come all these miles to send you packing. And by hook or crook, fair means or foul, that's what I'm going to do.

Gwen sat back, blew the fringe of curls from her eyes and contemplated the pleasure of ousting Luke Powers from her mother's life. Researching a new book, she sniffed. He'll have to research his book without researching my mother. She frowned, remembering the correspondence from her mother over the past three months. Luke Powers had been mentioned on almost every page of the violet-scented paper; helping her mother garden, taking her to the theater, hammering nails, making himself generally indispensable.

At first Gwen had paid little attention to the constant references to Luke. She was accustomed to her mother's enthusiasm for people, her flowery, sentimental outlook. And, to be honest, Gwen reflected with a sigh, I've been preoccupied with my own life, my own problems. Her thoughts flitted back to Michael Palmer—practical, brilliant, selfish, dependable Michael. A small cloud of depression threatened to descend on her as she remembered how miserably she had failed in their relationship. He deserved more than I could give him, she reflected sadly. Her eyes became troubled as she thought of her inability to share herself as Michael had wanted. Body and mind, she had held back both, unwilling or unable to make the commitment. Quickly shaking off the encroaching mood, Gwen reminded herself that while she had failed with Michael, she was succeeding in her career.

In the eyes of most people, the fashion world was glamorous, elegant, full of beautiful people moving gaily from one party to the next. Gwen almost laughed out loud at the absurdity of the illusion. What it really was, as she had since learned, was crazy, frantic, grueling work filled with temperamental artists, high-strung models and impossible deadlines. And I'm good at handling all of them, she mused, automatically straightening her shoulders. Gwen Lacrosse was not afraid of hard work any more than she was afraid of a challenge.

Her thoughts made a quick U-turn back to Luke Powers. There was too much affection in her mother's words when she wrote of him, and his name cropped up too often for comfort. Over the past three months, Gwen's concern had deepened to worry, until she felt she had to do something about the situation and had arranged for a leave of absence. It was, she had decided, up to her to protect her mother from a womanizer like Luke Powers.

She was not intimidated by his reputation with words or his reputation with women. He might be said to be an expert with both, she mused, but I know how to take care of myself and my mother. Mama's trouble is that she's too trusting. She sees only what she wants to see. She doesn't like to see faults. Gwen's mouth softened into a smile, and her face was suddenly, unexpectedly breathtaking. I'll take care of her, she thought confidently, I always have.

The lane leading to Gwen's childhood home was lined with fragile magnolia trees. As the taxi turned in and drove through patches of fragrant shade, Gwen felt the first stirrings of genuine pleasure. The scent of wisteria reached her before her first glimpse of the house. It had three graceful stories and was made of white-washed brick with high French windows and iron balconies like lacework. A veranda flowed across the entire front of the house, where the wisteria was free to climb on trellises at each end. It was not as old or as elaborate as many other antebellum houses in Louisiana, but it had the charm and grace so typical of that period. Gwen felt that the house suited her mother to perfection. They were both fragile, impractical and appealing.

She glanced up at the third story as the taxi neared the end of the drive. The top floor contained four small suites that had been remodeled for "visitors," as her mother called them, or as Gwen more accurately termed them, boarders. The visitors, with their monetary contributions, made it possible to keep the house in the family and in repair. Gwen had grown up with these visitors, accepting them as one accepts a small itch. Now, however, she scowled up at the third-floor windows. One of the suites housed Luke Powers. Not for long, she vowed, as she slipped out of the cab with her chin thrust forward.

As she paid her fare, Gwen glanced absently toward the sound of a low, monotonous thudding. In the side yard, just past a flourishing camellia, a man was in the process of chopping down a long-dead oak. He was stripped to the waist, and his jeans were snug over narrow hips and worn low enough to show a hint of tan line. His back and arms were bronzed and muscled and gleaming with sweat. His hair was a rich brown, touched with lighter streaks that showed a preference for sun. It curled damply at his neck and over his brow.

There was something confident and efficient in his stance. His legs were planted firmly, his swing effortless. Though she could not see his face, she knew he was enjoying his task: the heat, the sweat, the challenge. She stood in the drive as the cab drove off and admired his raw, basic masculinity, the arrogant efficiency of his movements. The ax swung into the heart of the tree with a violent grace. It occurred to her suddenly that for months she had not seen a man do anything more physical than jog in Central Park. Her lips curved in approval and admiration as she watched the rise and fall of the ax, the tensing and flow of muscle. The ax, tree and man were a perfect whole, elemental and beautiful. Gwen had forgotten how beautiful simplicity could be.

The tree shuddered and moaned, then hesitated briefly before it swayed and toppled to the ground.

There was a quick whoosh and thump. Gwen felt a ridiculous urge to applaud.

"You didn't say timber," she called out.

He had lifted a forearm to wipe the sweat from his brow, and at her call, he turned. The sun streamed behind his back. Squinting against it, Gwen could not see his face clearly. There was an aura of light around him, etching the tall, lean body and thickly curling hair. He looks like a god, she thought, like some primitive god of virility. As she watched, he leaned the ax against the stump of the tree and walked toward her. He moved like a man more used to walking on sand or grass than on concrete. Ridiculously, Gwen felt as though she were being stalked. She attributed the strange thrill she felt to the fact that she could not yet make out his features. He was a faceless man, therefore somehow the embodiment of man, exciting and strong. In defense against the glare of the sun, she shaded her eyes with her hand.

"You did that very well." Gwen smiled, attracted by his uncomplicated masculinity. She had not realized how bored she had become with three-piece suits and smooth hands. "I hope you don't mind an audience."

"No. Not everyone appreciates a well-cut tree." His voice was not indolent with vowels. There was nothing of Louisiana in his tone. As his face at last came into focus, Gwen was struck with its power. It was narrow and chiseled, long-boned and with the faintest of clefts in the chin. He had not shaved, but the shadow of beard intensified the masculinity of the face. His eyes were a clear blue-gray. They were calm, almost startlingly intelligent under rough brows. It was a calm that suggested power, a calm that captivated the onlooker. Immediately, Gwen knew he was a man who understood himself. Though intrigued, she felt discomfort under the directness of his gaze. She was almost sure he could see beyond her words and into her thoughts.

"I'd say you have definite talent," she told him. There was an aloofness about him, she decided, but it was not the cold aloofness of disinterest. He has warmth, she thought, but he's careful about who receives it. "I'm sure I've never seen a tree toppled with such finesse." She gave him a generous smile. "It's a hot day for ax swinging."

"You've got too many clothes on," he returned simply. His eyes swept down her blouse and skirt and trim, stockinged legs, then up again to her face. It was neither an insolent assessment nor an admiring one; it was simply a statement. Gwen kept her eyes level with his and prayed she would not do anything as foolish as blushing.

"More suitable for plane travelling than tree chopping I suppose," she replied. The annoyance in her voice brought a smile to the corners of his mouth. Gwen reached for her bags, but her hand met his on the handle. She jerked away and stepped back as a new source of heat shot through her. It seemed to dart up her fingers, then explode. Stunned by her own reaction, she stared into his calm eyes. Confusion flitted across her face and creased her brow before she smoothed it away. Silly, she told herself as she struggled to steady her pulse. Absolutely silly. He watched the shock, confusion and annoyance move across her face. Like a mirror, her eyes reflected each emotion.

"Thank you," Gwen said, regaining her poise. "I don't want to take you away from your work."

"No hurry." He hoisted her heavy bags easily. As he moved up the flagstone walk, she fell into step beside him. Even in heels, she barely reached his shoulder. Gwen glanced up to see the sun play on the blond highlights in his hair.

"Have you been here long?" she asked as they mounted the steps to the veranda.

"Few months." He set down her bags and placed his hand on the knob. Pausing, he studied her face with exacting care. Gwen felt her lips curve for no reason at all. "You're much lovelier than your picture, Gwenivere," he said unexpectedly. "Much warmer, much more vulnerable." With a quick twist, he opened the door, then again picked up her bags.

Breaking out of her trance, Gwen followed him inside, reaching for his arm. ''How do you know my name?'' she demanded. His words left her puzzled and defenseless. He saw too much too quickly.

''Your mother talks of you constantly,'' he explained as he set her bags down in the cool, white-walled hallway. ''She's very proud of you.'' When he lifted her chin with his fingers, Gwen was too surprised to protest. ''Your beauty is very different from hers. Hers is softer, less demanding, more comfortable. I doubt very much that you inspire comfort in a man.'' His eyes were on her face again, and fascinated, Gwen stood still. She could nearly feel the heat flowing from his body into hers. ''She worries about you being alone in New York.''

''One can't be alone in New York, it's a contradiction in terms.'' A frown shadowed her eyes and touched her mouth with a pout. ''She's never told me she worried.''

''Of course not, then you'd worry about her worrying.'' He grinned.

Resolutely Gwen ignored the tingle of pleasure his touch gave her. ''You seem to know my mother quite well.'' Her frown deepened and spread. The grin reminded her of someone. It was charming and almost irresistible. Recognition struck like a thunderbolt. *"You're Luke Powers,"* she accused.

"Yes." His brows lifted at the tone of her voice, and his head tilted slightly, as if to gain a new perspective. "Didn't you like my last book?"

"It's your current one I object to," Gwen snapped. She jerked her chin from his hold.

"Oh?" There was both amusement and curiosity in the word.

"To the fact that you're writing it here, in this house," Gwen elaborated.

"Have you a moral objection to my book, Gwenivere?"

"I doubt you know anything about morals," Gwen tossed back as her eyes grew stormy. "And don't call me that, no one but my mother calls me that."

"Pity, such a romantic name," he said casually. "Or do you object to romance, as well?"

"When it's between my mother and a Hollywood Casanova a dozen years younger than she, I have a different name for it." Gwen's face flushed with the passion of her words. She stood rigid. The humor faded from Luke's face. Slowly, he tucked his hands in his pockets.

"I see. Would you care to tell me what you'd call it?"

"I won't glorify your conduct with a title," Gwen

retorted. ''It should be sufficient that you understand I won't tolerate it any longer.'' She turned, intending to walk away from him.

''Won't you?'' There was something dangerously cold in his tone. ''And your mother has no voice in the matter?''

''My mother,'' Gwen countered furiously, ''is too gentle, too trusting and too naive.'' Whirling, she faced him again. ''I won't let you make a fool of her.''

''My dear Gwenivere,'' he said smoothly. ''You do so well making one of yourself.''

Before Gwen could retort, there was the sharp click of heels on wood. Struggling to steady her breathing, Gwen moved down the hall to greet her mother.

''Mama.'' She embraced a soft bundle of curves smelling of lilac.

''Gwenivere!'' Her mother's voice was low and as sweet as the scent she habitually wore. ''Why, darling, what are you doing here?''

''Mama,'' Gwen repeated and pulled away far enough to study the rosy loveliness of her mother's face. Her mother's skin was creamy and almost perfectly smooth, her eyes round and china blue, her nose tilted, her mouth pink and soft. There were two tiny dimples in her cheeks. Looking at her sweet prettiness, Gwen felt their roles should have been reversed. "Didn't you get my letter?" She tucked a stray wisp of pale blond hair behind her mother's ear.

"Of course, you said you'd be here Friday."

Gwen smiled and kissed a dimpled cheek. "This is Friday, Mama."

"Well, yes, it's *this* Friday, but I assumed you meant *next* Friday, and… Oh, dear, what does it matter?" Anabelle brushed away confusion with the back of her hand. "Let me look at you," she requested and, stepping back, subjected Gwen to a critical study. She saw a tall, striking beauty who brought misty memories of her young husband. Widowed for more than two decades, Anabelle rarely thought of her late husband unless reminded by her daughter. "So thin," she clucked, and sighed. "Don't you eat up there?"

"Now and again." Pausing, Gwen made her own survey of her mother's soft, round curves. How could this woman be approaching fifty? she wondered with a surge of pride and awe. "You look wonderful," Gwen murmured, "but then, you always look wonderful."

Anabelle laughed her young, gay laugh. "It's the climate," she claimed as she patted Gwen's cheek. "None of that dreadful smog or awful snow you have up there." New York, Gwen noted, would always be "up there." "Oh, Luke!" Anabelle caught sight of him as he stood watching the reunion. A smile lit up her face. "Have you met my Gwenivere?"

Luke shifted his gaze until his eyes met Gwen's. His brow tilted slightly in acknowledgement. "Yes." Gwen thought his smile was as much a challenge as a glove slapped across her cheek. "Gwen and I are practically old friends."

"That's right." Gwen let her smile answer his. "Already we know each other quite well."

"Marvelous." Anabelle beamed. "I do want you two to get along." She gave Gwen's hand a happy squeeze. "Would you like to freshen up, darling, or would you like a cup of coffee first?"

Gwen struggled to keep her voice from trembling with rage as Luke continued to smile at her. "Coffee sounds perfect," she answered.

"I'll take your bags up," Luke offered as he lifted them again.

"Thank you, dear." Anabelle spoke before Gwen could refuse. "Try to avoid Miss Wilkins until you have a shirt on. The sight of all those muscles will certainly give her the vapors. Miss Wilkins is one of my visitors," Anabelle explained as she led Gwen down the hall. "A sweet, timid little soul who paints in watercolors."

"Hmm," Gwen answered noncommittally as she glanced back over her shoulder. Luke stood watching them with sunlight tumbling over his hair and bronzed skin. "Hmm," Gwen said again, and turned away.

The kitchen was exactly as Gwen remembered: big, sunny and spotlessly clean. Tillie, the tall, waspishly thin cook stood by the stove. "Hello, Miss Gwen," she said without turning around. "Coffee's on."

"Hello, Tillie." Gwen walked over to the stove and sniffed at the fragrant steam. "Smells good."

"Cajun jambalaya."

"My favorite," Gwen murmured, glancing up at the appealingly ugly face. "I thought I wasn't expected until next Friday."

"You weren't," Tillie agreed, with a sniff. Lowering her thick brows, she continued to stir the roux.

Gwen smiled and leaned over to peck Tillie's tough cheek. "How are things, Tillie?"

"Comme ci, comme ça," she muttered, but pleasure touched her cheeks with color. Turning, she gave Gwen a quick study. "Skinny" was her quick, uncomplimentary conclusion.

"So I'm told." Gwen shrugged. Tillie never flattered anyone. "You have a month to fatten me up."

"Isn't that marvellous, Tillie?" Anabelle carefully put a blue delft sugar and creamer set on the kitchen table. "Gwen is staying for an entire month.

Perhaps we should have a party! We have three visitors at the moment. Luke, of course, and Miss Wilkins and Mr. Stapleton. He's an artist, too, but he works in oils. Quite a talented young man.''

Gwen seized the small opening. ''Luke Powers is considered a gifted young man, too.'' She sat across from her mother as Anabelle poured the coffee.

''Luke *is* frightfully talented,'' Anabelle agreed with a proud sigh. ''Surely you've read some of his books, seen some of his movies? Overwhelming. His characters are so real, so vital. His romantic scenes have a beauty and intensity that just leave me weak.''

''He had a naked woman in one of his movies,'' Tillie stated in an indignant mutter. ''Stark naked.''

Anabelle laughed. Her eyes smiled at Gwen's over the rim of her cup. ''Tillie feels Luke is singlehandedly responsible for the moral decline in the theater,'' Anabelle continued.

''Not a stitch on,'' Tillie added, setting her chin.

Though Gwen was certain Luke Powers had no morals whatsoever, she made no reference to them. Her voice remained casual as instead she commented, ''He certainly has accomplished quite a bit for a man of his age. A string of best-sellers, a clutch of popular movies...and he's only thirty-five.''

''I suppose that shows how unimportant age really is,'' Anabelle said serenely. Gwen barely suppressed a wince. "And success hasn't spoiled him one little bit," she went on. "He's the kindest, sweetest man I've ever known. He's so generous with his time, with himself." Her eyes shone with emotion. "I can't tell you how good he's been for me. I feel like a new woman." Gwen choked on her coffee. Anabelle clucked in sympathy as Tillie gave Gwen a sturdy thump on the back. "Are you all right, honey?"

"Yes, yes, I'm fine." Gwen took three deep breaths to steady her voice. Looking into her mother's guileless blue eyes, she opted for a temporary retreat. "I think I'll go upstairs and unpack."

"I'll help you," Anabelle volunteered, and started to rise.

"No, no, don't bother." Gwen placed a gentle hand on her shoulder. "It won't take long. I'll shower and change and be down in an hour." In an hour, Gwen hoped to have her thoughts more in order. She looked down at her mother's smooth, lovely face and felt a hundred years old. "I love you, Mama," she sighed, and kissed Anabelle's brow before she left her.

As Gwen moved down the hall, she realigned her strategy. Obviously, there was little she could say to her mother that would discourage her relationship with Luke Powers. It was going to be necessary, she decided, to go straight to the source. While climbing the stairs, she searched her imagination for an appropriate name for him. She could find nothing vile enough.

Chapter 2

A shaft of sunlight poured over the floor in Gwen's room. The walls were covered in delicate floral paper. Eggshell-tinted sheer curtains were draped at the windows, matching the coverlet on the four-poster bed. As she always did when she entered the room, Gwen crossed to the French windows and threw them open. Scents from Anabelle's flower garden swam up to meet her. Across the lawn was a spreading cypress, older than the house it guarded, festooned with gray-green moss. The sun filtered through it, making spiderweb patterns on the ground. Birdsong melded with the drone of bees. She could barely glimpse the mystery of the bayou through a thick curtain of oaks. New York's busy streets seemed nonexistent. Gwen had chosen that world for its challenges, but she discovered that coming home was like a sweet dessert after a full meal. She had missed its taste. Feeling unaccountably more lighthearted, she turned back into her room. She plucked up her white terry-cloth robe and headed for the shower.

Mama's romanticizing again, Gwen mused as the water washed away her travel weariness. She simply doesn't understand men at all. *And you do?* her conscience asked as she thought uncomfortably of Michael. Yes, I do understand them, she answered defiantly as she held her face up to the spray. I understand them perfectly. I won't let Luke hurt my mother, she vowed. I won't let him make a fool of her. I suppose he's used to getting his own way because he's successful and attractive. Well, I deal with successful, attractive people every day, and I know precisely how to handle them. Refreshed and ready for battle, Gwen stepped from the shower. With her confidence restored, she hummed lightly as she towel-dried her hair. Curls sprang to life on her forehead. Slipping on her robe, she tied the belt at her waist and strolled back into the bedroom.

"You!" Gwen jerked the knot tight as she spied Luke Powers standing beside her dresser. "What are you doing in my room?"

Calmly, his eyes traveled over her. The frayed robe was short, revealing slender legs well above the knee. Its simplicity outlined her nearly boyish slenderness. Without makeup, her eyes were huge and dark and curiously sweet. Luke watched her damp curls bounce with the outraged toss of her head.

"Anabelle thought you'd like these," he said as he indicated a vase of fresh yellow roses on the dresser. His hand made the gesture, but his eyes remained on Gwen. Gwen frowned.

"You should have knocked," she said ungraciously.

"I did," he said easily. "You didn't answer." To her amazement, he crossed the distance between them and lifted a hand to her cheek. "You have incredibly beautiful skin. Like rose petals washed in rainwater."

"Don't!" Knocking his hand away, Gwen stepped back. "Don't touch me." She pushed her hair away from her face.

Luke's eyes narrowed fractionally at her tone, but his voice was calm. "I always touch what I admire."

"I don't want you to admire me."

Humor lit his face and added to its appeal. "I didn't say I admired you, Gwen, I said I admired your skin."

"Just keep your hands off my skin," she snapped,

wishing the warmth of his fingers would evaporate and leave her cheek as it had been before his touch. "And keep your hands off my mother."

"What gives you the notion I've had my hands on your mother?" Luke inquired, lifting a bottle of Gwen's scent and examining it.

"Her letters were clear enough." Gwen snatched the bottle from him and slammed it back on the dresser. "They've been full of nothing but you for months. How you went to the theater or shopping, how you fixed her car or sprayed the peach trees. Especially how you've given her life fresh meaning." Agitated, Gwen picked up her comb, then put it down again. His direct, unruffled stare tripped her nerves.

"And from that," Luke said into the silence, "you've concluded that Anabelle and I are having an affair."

"Well, of course." His tone confused her for a moment. Was he amused? she wondered. His mouth was beautiful, a smile lurking on it. Furious with herself, Gwen tilted her chin. "Do you deny it?"

Luke slipped his hands into his pockets and wandered about the room. Pausing, he studied the view from the open French windows. "No, I don't believe I will. I believe I'll simply tell you it's none of your business."

"None of my..." Gwen sputtered, then swallowed in a torrent of fury. "None of my business? She's my mother!"

"She's also a person," Luke cut in. When he turned back to face her, there was curiosity on his face. "Or don't you ever see her that way?"

"I don't feel it's—"

"No, you probably don't," he interrupted. "It's certainly time you did, though. I doubt you feel Anabelle should approve of every man you have a relationship with."

Color flared in Gwen's cheeks. "That's entirely different," she fumed, then stalked over to stand in front of him. "I don't need you to tell me about my mother. You can flaunt your affairs with actresses and socialites all you want, but—"

"Thank you," Luke replied evenly. "It's nice to have your approval."

"I won't have you flaunting your affair with my mother," Gwen finished between her teeth. "You should be ashamed," she added with a toss of her head, "seducing a woman a dozen years older than you."

"Of course, it would be perfectly acceptable if I were a dozen years older than she," he countered smoothly.

"I didn't *say* that," Gwen began. Her brow creased with annoyance.

"You look too intelligent to hold such views,

Gwen. You surprise me.'' His mild voice was infuriating.

''I don't!'' she denied hotly. Because the thought made her uncomfortable, her mouth moved into a pout. Luke's eyes dropped to her lips and lingered.

''A very provocative expression,'' he said softly. ''I thought so the first time I saw it, and it continues to intrigue me.'' In one swift motion, he gathered her into his arms. At her gasp of surprised protest, he merely smiled. ''I told you I always touch what I admire.'' Gwen squirmed, but she was pinned tight against him, helpless as his face lowered toward her.

His lips feathered lightly along her jawline. Gwen was caught off guard by the gentleness. Though his chest was solid and strong against her yielding breasts, his mouth was soft and sweet. Disarmed, she stood still in the circle of his arms as his mouth roamed her face. Through the slight barrier of the robe, she could feel every line of his body. They merged together as if destined to do so. Heat began to rise in her, a sudden, unexpected heat as irresistible as his mouth. Her lips throbbed for the touch of his. She moaned softly as he continued to trace light, teasing kisses over her skin. Her hands slipped up from his chest to find their way into his hair, urging him to fulfill a silent promise. At last his lips brushed hers. They touched, then clung, then devoured.

Lost in pleasure, riding on sensations delirious and new, Gwen answered his demands with fervor. She rose on her toes to meet them. The kiss grew deeper. The roughness of his beard scratched her skin and tripled her heartbeat. A tenuous breeze fanned the curtains at the open windows, but Gwen felt no lessening of heat. Luke moved his hands down her spine, firmly caressing her curves before he took her hips and drew her away.

Gwen stared up at him with dark, cloudy eyes. Never had a kiss moved her more, never had she been so filled with fire and need. Her soft mouth trembled with desire for his. The knowledge of what could be hers lay just beyond her comprehension. Luke lifted his hand to her damp curls, tilting back her head for one last, brief kiss. "You taste every bit as good as you look."

Abruptly Gwen remembered who and where she was. The fires of passion were extinguished by fury. "Oh!" She gave Luke's chest a fierce push and succeeded in putting an entire inch between them. "How could you?"

"It wasn't hard," he assured her.

Gwen shook her head. Tiny droplets of water danced in the sunlight. "You're despicable!"

"Why?" Luke's smile broadened. "Because I made you forget yourself for a moment? You made me forget myself for a moment too." He seemed to enjoy the confession. ''Does that make you despicable?''

''I didn't... It was you...I just...'' Her words stumbled to a halt, and she made ineffectual noises in her throat.

''At least try to be coherent,'' Luke said.

''Just let me go,'' Gwen demanded. She began a violent and fruitless struggle. ''Just let me go!''

''Certainly,'' Luke said obligingly. He brushed back her disheveled hair with a friendly hand. ''You know, one day you might just be the woman your mother is.''

''Oh!'' Gwen paled in fury. ''You're disgusting.''

Luke laughed with pure masculine enjoyment. ''Gwenivere, I wasn't speaking of your rather exceptional physical virtues.'' He sobered, then shook his head. ''Anabelle is the only person I know who looks for the good in everyone and finds it. It's her most attractive asset.'' His eyes were calm again and thoughtful. ''Perhaps you should take time to get to know your mother while you're here. You might be surprised.''

Gwen retreated behind a film of ice. ''I told you, I don't need you to tell me about my mother.''

''No?'' Luke smiled, shrugged, and moved to the door. ''Perhaps I'll spend my time teaching you about yourself, then. See you at dinner.'' He closed the door on her furious retort.

* * *

The front parlor had both the color and the scent of roses. It was furnished in Anabelle's delicate and feminine style. The chairs were small and elegant, with dusky pink cushions; the lamps, china and terrifyingly fragile; the rugs, faded and French. Even when she was not there, Anabelle's presence could be felt.

Gwen pushed aside a pale pink curtain and watched the sun go down while Anabelle chattered happily. The sky gradually took on the hues of sunset, until it glowed with defiant gold and fiery reds. Its passion suited Gwen much more than the soft comfort of the room at her back. She lifted her palm to the glass of the window, as if to touch that explosion of nature. She still felt the aftershocks of the explosion that had burst inside her only a few hours before in the arms of a stranger.

It meant nothing, she assured herself for the hundredth time. I was off guard, tired, confused. I'm sure most of what I felt was pure imagination. I'm on edge, that's all, everything's exaggerated. She ran the tip of her tongue experimentally along her lips, but found no remnants of the heady flavor she remembered. Exaggerated, she told herself again.

"A month's quite a long time for you to be away from your job," Anabelle said conversationally as she sorted through a basket of embroidery thread.

Gwen shrugged and made a small sound of agreement. "I haven't taken more than a long weekend in nearly two years."

"Yes, darling, I know. You work too hard."

The cerulean blue dress suited Gwen well, but as Anabelle glanced up at her, she again thought how thin her daughter looked. She was slim and straight as a wand. Gwen's hair caught some of the last flames of the sun, and the mass of curls became a flood of rose-gold light. *How did she get to be twenty-three?* Anabelle wondered. She went back to sorting her thread. "You always were an overachiever. You must get that from your father's side. His mother had two sets of twins, you know. That's overachievement."

With a laugh, Gwen rested her forehead against the glass of the window. It was as refreshing as her mother. "Oh, Mama, I do love you."

"I love you, too, dear," she answered absently as she scrutinized two tones of green. "You haven't mentioned that young man you were seeing, the attorney. Michael, wasn't it?"

"It was," Gwen returned dryly. Dusk began to fall as she watched. With the mellowing of light came an odd, almost reverent hush. She sighed. Dusk, she thought, was the most precious time, and the most fleeting. The sound of the first cricket brought her out of her reverie. "I'm not seeing Michael anymore."

"Oh, dear." Anabelle looked up, distressed. "Did you have a disagreement?"

"A series of them. I'm afraid I don't make the ideal companion for a corporate attorney." Gwen made a face in the glass and watched it reflect. "I have too many deep-rooted plebeian values. Mostly, I like to see the little guy get a break."

"Well, I hope you parted friends."

Gwen closed her eyes and stifled a sardonic laugh as she recalled the volatile parting scene. "I'm sure we'll exchange Christmas cards for years to come."

"That's nice," Anabelle murmured comfortably as she threaded her needle. "Old friends are the most precious."

With a brilliant smile, Gwen turned toward her mother. The smile faded instantly as she spotted Luke in the doorway. As her eyes locked with his, she felt herself trembling. He had changed into tan slacks and a rust-colored shirt. The effect was casual and expensive. But somehow there seemed little difference between the clean-shaven, conventionally clad man Gwen now saw and the rugged woodsman she had met that morning. Clothes and a razor could not alter the essence of his virility.

"It's a fortunate man who has two exquisite women to himself."

"Luke!" Anabelle's head lifted. Instantly, her

face was touched with pleasure. "How lovely it is to be flattered! Don't you agree, Gwen?"

"Lovely," Gwen assented, as she sent him her most frigid smile.

With easy assurance, Luke crossed the room. From Gwen's grandmother's Hepplewhite server, he lifted a crystal decanter. "Sherry?"

"Thank you, darling." Anabelle turned her smile from him to Gwen. "Luke bought the most delightful sherry. I'm afraid he's been spoiling me."

I'll just bet he has, Gwen muttered silently. Temper flared in her eyes. Had she seen it, Anabelle would have recognized the look. Luke both saw it and recognized it. To Gwen's further fury, he grinned.

"We shouldn't dawdle long," Anabelle said, unconscious of the war being waged over her head. "Tillie has a special supper planned for Gwen. She dotes on her, you know, though she wouldn't admit it for the world. I believe she's missed Gwen every bit as much as I have these past two years."

"She's missed having someone to scold," Gwen smiled ruefully. "I still carry the stigma of being skinny and unladylike that I acquired when I was ten."

"You'll always be ten to Tillie, darling." Anabelle sighed and shook her head. "I have a difficult time realizing you're more than twice that myself."

Gwen turned toward Luke as he offered her a glass of sherry. "Thank you," she said in her most graciously insulting voice. She sipped, faintly disappointed to find that it was excellent. "And will you be spoiling me, as well, Mr. Powers?"

"Oh, I doubt that, Gwenivere." He took her hand, although she stiffened and tried to pull it away. His eyes laughed over their joined fingers. "I doubt that very much."

Chapter 3

Over dinner Gwen met Anabelle's two other visitors. Though both were artists, they could not have been more different from each other. Monica Wilkins was a small, pale woman with indifferent brown hair. She spoke in a quiet, breathy voice and avoided eye contact at all costs. She had a supply of large, shapeless smocks, which she wore invariably and without flair. Her art was, for the most part, confined to illustrating textbooks on botany. With a touch of pity, Gwen noticed that her tiny, birdlike eyes often darted glances at Luke, then shifted away quickly and self-consciously.

Bradley Stapleton was tall and lanky, casually

dressed in an ill-fitting sweater, baggy slacks and battered sneakers. He had a cheerful, easily forgettable face and a surprisingly beautiful voice. He studied his fellow humans with unquenchable curiosity and painted for the love of it. He yearned to be famous but had settled for regular meals.

Gwen thoroughly enjoyed dinner, not only because of Tillie's excellent jambalaya but for the oddly interesting company of the two artists. Separately, she thought each might be a bore, but somehow together, the faults of one enhanced the virtues of the other.

"So, you work for *Style,*" Bradley stated as he scooped up a second, generous helping of Tillie's jambalaya. "Why don't you model?"

Gwen thought of the frantic, nervous models, with their fabulous faces. She shook her head. "No, I'm not at all suitable. I'm much better at stroking."

"Stroking?" Bradley repeated, intrigued.

"That's what I do, basically." Gwen smiled at him. It was better, she decided, that her mother had seated her next to Luke rather than across from him. She would have found it uncomfortable to face him throughout an entire meal. "Soothe, stroke, bully. Someone has to keep the models from using their elegant nails on each other and remind them of the practical side of life."

"Gwen's so good at being practical," Anabelle

interjected. ''I'm sure I don't understand why. I've never been. Strange,'' she said, and smiled at her daughter. ''She grew up long before I did.''

''Practicality wouldn't suit you, Anabelle,'' Luke told her with an affectionate smile.

Anabelle dimpled with pleasure. ''I told you he was spoiling me,'' she said to Gwen.

''So you did.'' Gwen lifted her water glass and sipped carefully.

''You must sit for me, Gwen,'' Bradley said, as he buttered a biscuit.

''Must I?'' Knowing the only way she could get through a civilized meal was to ignore Luke, Gwen gave Bradley all her attention.

''Absolutely.'' Bradley held both the biscuit and knife suspended while he narrowed his eyes and stared at her. ''Fabulous, don't you agree, Monica? A marvelous subject,'' he went on without waiting for her answer. ''In some lights the hair would be the color Titian immortalized, in others, it would be quieter, more subtle. But it's the eyes, isn't it, Monica? It's definitely the eyes. So large, so meltingly brown. Of course, the bone structure's perfect, and the skin's wonderful, but I'm taken with the eyes. The lashes are real, too, aren't they, Monica?''

''Yes, quite real,'' she answered as her gaze flew swiftly to Gwen's face and then back to her plate. ''Quite real.''

"She gets them from her father," Anabelle explained as she added a sprinkle of salt to her jambalaya. "Such a handsome boy. Gwen favors him remarkably. His eyes were exactly the same. I believe they're why I first fell in love with him."

"They're very alluring," Bradley commented with a nod to Anabelle. "The size, the color, the shape. Very alluring." He faced Gwen again. "You will sit for me, won't you, Gwen?"

Gwen gave Bradley a guileless smile. "Perhaps."

The meal drifted to a close, and the evening waned. The artists retreated to their rooms, and Luke wandered off to his. At Gwen's casual question, Anabelle told her that Luke "worked all the time." It was odd, Gwen mused to herself, that a woman as romantic as her mother wasn't concerned that the man in her life was not spending his evening with her.

Anabelle chattered absently while working tiny decorative stitches into a pillowcase. Watching her, Gwen was struck with a sudden thought. Did Anabelle seem happier? Did she seem more vital? If Luke Powers was responsible, should she, Gwen, curse him or thank him? She watched Anabelle delicately stifle a yawn and was swept by a fierce protective surge. She needs me to look out for her, she decided, and that's what I plan to do.

* * *

Once in her bedroom, however, Gwen could not get to sleep. The book she had brought with her to pass the time did not hold her attention. It grew late, but her mind would not allow her body to rest. A breeze blew softly in through the windows, lifting the curtains. It beckoned. Rising, Gwen threw on a thin robe and went outside to meet it.

The night was warm and lit by a large summer moon. The air was filled with the scent of wisteria and roses. She could hear the continual hum of the crickets. Now and then, there was the lonely, eerie call of an owl. Leaves rustled with the movements of night birds and small animals. Fireflies blinked and soared.

As Gwen breathed in the moist, fragrant air, an unexpected peace settled over her. Tranquility was something just remembered, like a childhood friend. Tentatively Gwen reached out for it. For two years, her career had been her highest priority. Independence and success were the goals she had sought. She had worked hard for them. And I've got them, she thought as she plucked a baby coral rose from its bush. Why aren't I happy? I am happy, she corrected as she lifted the bloom and inhaled its fragile scent, but I'm not as happy as I should be. Frowning, she twisted the stem between her fingers. *Complete.* The word came from nowhere. I don't feel complete. With a sigh, she tilted her head and studied the star-studded sky. Laughter bubbled up in her throat suddenly and sounded sweet in the silence.

"Catch!" she cried as she tossed the bloom in the air. She gasped in surprise as a hand plucked the rose on its downward journey. Luke had appeared as if from nowhere and was standing a few feet away from her twirling the flower under his nose. "Thanks," he said softly. "No one has ever tossed me a rose."

"I wasn't tossing it to you." Automatically, Gwen clutched her robe together where it crossed her breasts.

"No?" Luke smiled at her and at the gesture. "Who then?"

Feeling foolish, Gwen shrugged and turned away. "I thought you were working."

"I was. The muse took a break so I called it a night. Gardens are at their best in the moonlight." He paused, and there was an intimacy in his voice. Stepping closer, he added, "I've always thought the same held true for women."

Gwen felt her skin grow warm. She struggled to keep her tone casual as she turned to face him.

Luke tucked the small flower into her curls and lifted her chin. "They are fabulous eyes, you know. Bradley's quite right."

Her skin began to tingle where his fingers touched it. Defensively, she stepped back. "I wish you wouldn't keep doing that.'' Her voice trembled, and she despised herself for it.

Luke gave her an odd, amused smile. ''You're a strange one, Gwenivere. I haven't got you labeled quite yet. I'm intrigued by the innocence.''

Gwen stiffened and tossed back her hair. ''I don't know what you're talking about.''

Luke's smile broadened. The moonlight seemed trapped in his eyes. ''Your New York veneer doesn't cover it. It's in the eyes. Bradley doesn't know why they're appealing, and I won't tell him. It's the innocence and the promise.'' Gwen frowned, but her shoulders relaxed. Luke went on, ''There's an unspoiled innocence in that marvelous face, and a warmth that promises passion. It's a tenuous balance.''

His words made Gwen uncomfortable. A warmth was spreading through her that she seemed powerless to control. Tranquility had vanished. An excitement, volatile and hot, throbbed through the air. Suddenly she was afraid. ''I don't want you to say these things to me,'' she whispered, and took another step in retreat.

''No?'' The amusement in his voice told her that a full retreat would be impossible. ''Didn't Michael ever use words to seduce you? Perhaps that's why he failed.''

''Michael? What do you know about...?'' Abruptly she recalled the conversation with her mother before dinner. ''You were listening!'' she began, outraged. ''You had no right to listen to a private conversation! No gentleman listens to a private conversation!''

''Nonsense,'' Luke said calmly. ''Everyone does, if he has the chance.''

''Do you enjoy intruding on other people's privacy?''

''People interest me, emotions interest me. I don't apologize for my interests.''

Gwen was torn between fury at his arrogance and admiration for his confidence. ''What *do* you apologize for, Luke Powers?''

''Very little.''

Unable to do otherwise, Gwen smiled. Really, she thought, he's outrageous.

''Now that was worth waiting for,'' Luke murmured, as his eyes roamed her face. ''I wonder if Bradley can do it justice? Be careful,'' he warned, ''you'll have him falling in love with you.''

''Is that how you won Monica?''

''She's terrified of me,'' Luke corrected as he reached up to better secure the rose in her hair.

''Some terrific observer of humanity you are.'' Gwen sniffed, fiddling with the rose herself and managing to dislodge it. As it tumbled to the ground, both she and Luke stooped to retrieve it. Her hair brushed his cheek before she lifted her eyes to his. As if singed, she jolted back, but before she could escape, he took her arm. Slowly, he rose, bringing her with him. Involuntarily, she shivered as he brought her closer until their bodies touched. Just a look from him, just the touch of him, incited her to a passion that she had not known she possessed. His hands slid up her arms and under the full sleeves of her robe to caress her shoulders. She felt her mantle of control slip away as she swayed forward and touched her lips to his.

His mouth was avid so quickly, her breath caught in her throat. Then all was lost in pleasure. Lights fractured and exploded behind her closed lids as her lips sought to give and to take with an instinct as old as time. Beneath her palms she felt the hard, taut muscles of his back. She shuddered with the knowledge of his strength and the sudden realization of her own frailty. But even her weakness had a power she had never tapped, never experienced.

His hands roamed over her, lighting fires, learning secrets, teaching and taking. Gwen was pliant and willing. He was like a drug flowing into her system, clouding her brain. Only the smallest grain of denial struggled for survival, fighting against the growing need to surrender. Reason surfaced slowly, almost reluctantly. Suddenly, appalled by her own behavior, she began to struggle. But when she broke away, she felt a quick stab of loneliness.

''No.'' Gwen lifted her hands to her burning cheeks. ''No,'' she faltered.

Luke watched in silence as she turned and fled to the house.

Chapter 4

The morning was hazy and heavy. So were Gwen's thoughts. As dawn broke with a gray, uncertain light, she stood by her window.

How could I? she demanded of herself yet again. Closing her eyes and groaning, Gwen sank down onto the window seat. I kissed him. *I* kissed *him.* Inherent honesty kept her from shifting what she considered blame. I can't say I was caught off guard this time. I knew what was going to happen, and worse yet, I *enjoyed* it. She brought her knees up to her chin. I enjoyed the first time he kissed me too. The silent admission caused her to shut her eyes again. *How could I?* As she wrestled with this question, she rose and paced the room. I came thousands of miles to get Luke Powers out of Mama's life, and I end up kissing him in the garden in the middle of the night. And liking it, she added wretchedly. What kind of a person am I? What kind of a daughter am I? I never thought of Mama once in that garden last night. Well, I'll think of her today, she asserted, and pulled a pair of olive-drab shorts from her drawer. I've got a month to move Luke Powers out, and that's just what I'm going to do.

As she buttoned up a short-sleeved khaki blouse, Gwen nodded confidently at herself in the mirror. No more moonlit gardens. I won't take the chance of having midsummer madness creep over me again. That's what it was, wasn't it? she asked the slender woman in the glass. She ran a nervous hand through her hair. Another answer seemed just beyond her reach. Refusing any attempt to pursue it, Gwen finished dressing and left the room.

Not even Tillie was in the kitchen at such an early hour. There was a certain enjoyment in being up alone in the softly lit room. She made the first pot of coffee in the gray dawn. She sipped at a cupful while watching dark clouds gather. Rain, she thought, not displeased. The sky promised it, the air smelled of it. It gave an excitement to the quiet, yawning morning. There would be thunder and lightning and cooling wind. The thought inexplicably lifted Gwen's spirits. Humming a cheerful tune, she began searching the cupboards. The restless night was forgotten.

"What are you up to?" Tillie demanded, sweeping into the room. Hands on her bony hips, she watched Gwen.

"Good morning, Tillie." Used to the cook's abrasiveness, Gwen answered good-naturedly.

"What do you want in my kitchen?" she asked suspiciously. "You made coffee."

"Yes, it's not too bad." Gwen's tone was apologetic, but her eyes danced with mischief.

"I make the coffee," Tillie reminded her. "I always make the coffee."

"I've certainly missed it over the past couple of years. No matter how I try, mine never tastes quite like yours." Gwen poured a fresh cup. "Have some," she offered. "Maybe you can tell me what I do wrong."

Tillie accepted the cup and scowled. "You let it brew too long," she complained. Lifting her hand, she brushed curls back from Gwen's forehead. "Will you never keep your hair out of your eyes? Do you want to wear glasses?"

"No, Tillie," Gwen answered humbly. It was an old gesture and an old question. She recognized the tenderness behind the brisk words and quick fingers. Her lips curved into a smile. "I made Mama's breakfast.'' Turning, Gwen began to arrange cups and plates on a tray. ''I'm going to take it up to her, she always liked it when I surprised her that way.''

''You shouldn't bother your *maman* so early in the morning,'' Tillie began.

''Oh, it's not so early,'' Gwen said airily as she lifted the tray. ''I didn't leave much of a mess,'' she added with the carelessness of youth. ''I'll clean it up when I come back.'' She whisked through the door before Tillie could comment.

Gwen moved quickly up the stairs and down the corridor. Balancing the tray in one hand, she twisted the knob on her mother's door with the other. She was totally stunned to find it locked. Automatically, she jiggled the knob in disbelief. Never, as far back as her childhood memories stretched, did Gwen remember the door of Anabelle's room being locked.

''Mama?'' There was a question in her voice as she knocked. ''Mama, are you up?''

''What?'' Anabelle's voice was clear but distracted. ''Oh, Gwen, just a minute, darling.''

Gwen stood outside the door listening to small, shuffling sounds she could not identify. ''Mama,'' she said again, ''are you all right?''

''Yes, yes, dear, one moment.'' The creaks and shuffles stopped just before the door opened. ''Good morning, Gwen.'' Anabelle smiled. Though she wore a gown and robe and her hair was mussed by sleep, her eyes were awake and alert. ''What have you got there?''

Blankly, Gwen looked down at the tray she carried. ''Oh, chocolate and *beignets.* I know how you like them. Mama, what were you…?''

''Darling, how sweet!'' Anabelle interrupted, and drew Gwen into the room. ''Did you really make them yourself? What a treat. Come, let's sit on the balcony. I hope you slept well.''

Gwen evaded a lie. ''I woke early and decided to test my memory with the *beignet* recipe. Mama, I don't remember you ever locking your door.''

''No?'' Anabelle smiled as she settled herself in a white, wrought-iron chair. ''It must be a new habit, then. Oh, dear, it looks like rain. Well, my roses will be thankful.''

The locked door left Gwen feeling slighted. It reminded her forcibly that Anabelle Lacrosse was a person, as well as her mother. Perhaps she would do well to remember it, Gwen silently resolved. She set the tray on a round, glass-topped table and bent to kiss Anabelle's cheek. ''I've really missed you. I don't think I've told you that yet.''

''Gwenivere.'' Anabelle smiled and patted her daughter's fine-boned hand. ''It's so good to have you home. You've always been such a pleasure to me.''

''Even when I'd track mud on the carpet or lose

frogs in the parlor?'' Grinning, Gwen sat and poured the chocolate.

''Darling.'' Anabelle sighed and shook her head. ''Some things are best forgotten. I never understood how I could have raised such a hooligan. But even as I despaired of you ever being a lady, I couldn't help admiring your freedom of spirit. Hot-tempered you might have been,'' Anabelle added as she tasted her chocolate, ''but never malicious and never dishonest. No matter what dreadful thing you did, you never did it out of spite, and you always confessed.''

Gwen laughed. Her curls danced as she tossed back her head. ''Poor Mama, I must have done so many dreadful things.''

''Well, perhaps a bit more than your share,'' Anabelle suggested kindly. ''But now you're all grown up, so difficult for a mother to accept. Your job, Gwen, you do enjoy it?''

Gwen's automatic agreement faltered on her lips. Enjoy, she thought. I wonder if I do. ''Strange,'' she said aloud, ''I'm not at all certain.'' She gave her mother a puzzled smile. ''But I need it, not just for the money, I need the responsibility it imposes, I need to be involved.''

''Yes, you always did... My, the *beignets* look marvelous.''

''They are,'' Gwen assured her mother as she rested her elbows on the table and her chin on her open palms. ''I felt obligated to try one before I offered them to you.''

''See, I've always told you you were sensible,'' Anabelle said with a smile before she tasted one of the oddly shaped doughnuts. ''Delicious,'' she proclaimed. ''Tillie doesn't make them any better, though that had best be our secret.''

Gwen allowed time to pass with easy conversation until she poured the second cup of chocolate. ''Mama,'' she began cautiously, ''how long does Luke Powers plan to stay here?''

The lifting of Anabelle's delicate brows indicated her surprise. ''Stay?'' she repeated as she dusted powdered sugar from her fingers. ''Why, I don't know precisely, Gwen. It depends, I should say, on the stage of his book. I know he plans to finish the first draft before he goes back to California.''

''I suppose,'' Gwen said casually as she stirred her chocolate, ''he'll have no reason to come back here after that.''

''Oh, I imagine he'll be back.'' Anabelle smiled into her daughter's eyes. ''Luke is very fond of this part of the country. I wish I could tell you what his coming here has meant to me.'' Dreamily, she stared out into the hazy sky. Gwen felt a stab of alarm. ''He's given me so much. I'd like you to spend some time with him, dear, and get to know him.''

Gwen's teeth dug into the tender inside of her lip.

For the moment, she felt completely at a loss. She raged in silence while Anabelle smiled secretly at rain clouds. Despicable man. How can he do this to her? Gwen glanced down into the dregs of her cup and felt a weight descend on her heart. And what is he doing to me? No matter how she tried to ignore it, Gwen could still feel the warmth of his lips on hers. The feeling clung, taunting and enticing. She was teased by a feeling totally foreign to her, a longing she could neither identify nor understand. Briskly, she shook her head to clear her thoughts. Luke Powers was only a problem while he was in Louisiana. The aim was to get him back to the West Coast and to discourage him from coming back.

"Gwen?"

"Hmm? Oh, yes, Mama." Blinking away the confused images and thoughts of Luke, Gwen met Anabelle's curious look.

"I said blueberry pie would be nice with supper. Luke's very fond of it. I thought perhaps you'd like to pick some berries for Tillie."

Gwen pondered briefly on the attractive prospect of sprinkling arsenic over Luke's portion, then rejected the idea. "I'd love to," she murmured.

The air was thick with moisture when, armed with a large bucket, Gwen went in search of blueberries. With a quick glance and shrug at the cloudy sky, she opted to risk the chance of rain. She would use her berry picking time to devise a plan to send Luke Powers westward. Swinging the bucket, she moved across the trim lawn and into the dim, sheltering trees that formed a border between her home and the bayou. Here was a different world from her mother's gentle, tidy, well-kept home. This was a primitive world with ageless secrets and endless demands. It had been Gwen's refuge as a child, her personal island. Although she remembered each detail perfectly, she stood and drank in its beauty anew.

There was a mist over the sluggish stream. Dull and brown, cattails peeked through the surface in search of the hidden sun. Here and there, cypress stumps rose above the surface. The stream itself moved in a narrow path, then curved out of sight. Gwen remembered how it twisted and snaked and widened. Over the straight, slender path, trees arched tunnellike, garnished with moss. The water was silent, but Gwen could hear the birds and an occasional plop of a frog. She knew the serenity was a surface thing. Beneath the calm was a passion and violence and wild, surging life. It called to her as it always had.

With confidence, she moved along the riverbank and searched out the plump wild berries. Silence and the simplicity of her task were soothing. Years slipped away, and she was a teenager again, a girl whose most precious fantasy was to be a part of a big city. She had dreamed in the sheltered bayou of the excitement, the mysteries of city life, the challenges of carving out her own path. Hard work, determination and a quick mind had hurried her along that path. She had earned a responsible job, established an interesting circle of friends and acquired just lately a nagging sense of dissatisfaction.

Overwork, Gwen self-diagnosed, and popped a berry into her mouth. Its juice was sweet and full of memories. *And, of course, there's Michael.* With a frown, Gwen dropped a handful of berries into the bucket. *Even though it was my idea to end things between us, I could be suffering from the backlash of a terminated romance. And those things he said...* Her frown deepened, and unconsciously she began to nibble on berries. *That I was cold and unresponsive and immature...I must not have loved him.* Sighing, Gwen picked more berries and ate them, one by one. *If I had loved him, I'd have wanted him to make love to me.*

I'm not cold, she thought. *I'm not unresponsive. Look at the way I responded to Luke!* She froze with a berry halfway to her mouth. Her cheeks filled with color. *That was different*, she assured herself quickly. *Entirely different.* She popped the berry into her mouth. *That was simply physical, it had* nothing to do with emotion. Chemistry, that's all. Why, it's practically scientific.

She speculated on the possibility of seducing Luke. She could flirt and tease and drive him to the point of distraction, make him fall in love with her and then cast him off when all danger to Anabelle was past. It can't be too difficult, she decided. I've seen lots of the models twist men around their fingers. She looked down at her own and noted they were stained with berry juice.

"Looks as though you've just been booked by the FBI."

Whirling, Gwen stared at Luke as he leaned back comfortably against a thick cypress. Again he wore jeans and a T-shirt, both faded and well worn. His eyes seemed to take their color from the sky and were more gray now than blue. Gwen's heart hammered at the base of her throat.

"Must you continually sneak up on me?" she snapped. Annoyed with the immediate response of her body to his presence, she spoke heatedly. "You have the most annoying habit of being where you're not wanted."

"Did you know you become more the Southern belle when you're in a temper?" Luke asked with an easy, unperturbed smile. "Your vowels flow quite beautifully."

Gwen's breath came out in a frustrated huff. "What do you want?" she demanded.

"To help you pick berries. Though it seems you're doing more eating than picking."

It trembled on her tongue to tell him that she didn't need or want his help. Abruptly, she remembered her resolve to wind him around her berry-stained finger. Carefully she smoothed the frown from between her brows and coaxed her mouth into a charming smile. "How sweet of you."

Luke raised a quizzical eyebrow at her change of tone. "I'm notoriously sweet," he said dryly. "Didn't you know?"

"We don't know each other well, do we?" Gwen smiled and held out the bucket. "At least, not yet."

Slowly, Luke straightened from his stance and moved to join her. He accepted the bucket while keeping his eyes fastened on hers. Determinedly, Gwen kept her own level and unconcerned. She found it difficult to breathe with him so close. "How is your book going?" she asked, hoping to divert him while she regained control of her respiratory system.

"Well enough." He watched as she began to tug berries off the bush again.

"I'm sure it must be fascinating." Gwen slid her eyes up to his in a manner she hoped was provocative and exciting. "I hope you won't think me a bore if I confess I'm quite a fan of yours. I have all your books.'' This part was easier because it was true.

''It's never a bore to know one's work is appreciated.''

Emboldened, Gwen laid her hand on his on the handle of the bucket. Something flashed in his eyes, and her courage fled. Quickly slipping the bucket from his hold, she began to pick berries with renewed interest while cursing her lack of bravery.

''How do you like living in New York?'' Luke asked as he began to add to the gradually filling bucket.

''New York?'' Gwen cleared her head with a quick mental shake. Resolutely, she picked up the strings of her plan again. ''It's very exciting—such a sensual city, don't you think?'' Gwen lifted a berry to Luke's lips. She hoped her smile was invitingly alluring, and wished she had thought to practice in a mirror.

Luke opened his mouth to accept her offering. His tongue whispered along the tips of her fingers. Gwen felt them tremble. It took every ounce of willpower not to snatch her hand away. ''Do you—do you like New York?'' Her voice was curiously husky as she began to pull berries again. The tone was uncontrived and by far the most enticing of her tactics.

''Sometimes,'' Luke answered, then brushed the hair away from her neck.

Moistening her lips, Gwen inched away. ''I suppose you live in Louisiana.''

''No, I have a place near Carmel, at the beach. What marvellously soft hair you have,'' he murmured, running his hand through it.

''The beach,'' Gwen repeated, swallowing. ''It must be wonderful. I've—I've never seen the Pacific.''

''It can be very wild, very dangerous,'' Luke said softly before his lips brushed the curve of Gwen's neck.

There was a small, strangled sound from Gwen's throat. She moved farther away and fought to keep up a casual front. ''I've seen pictures, of course, and movies, but I expect it's quite different to actually see it. I'm sure it's a wonderful place to write.''

''Among other things.'' From behind, Luke dropped his hands to her hips as he caught the lobe of her ear between his teeth. For a moment, Gwen could only lean back against him. Abruptly she stiffened, straightened, and put a few precious inches between them.

''You know,'' she began, completely abandoning her plans to seduce him, ''I believe we have enough.'' As she turned around, her breasts brushed against his chest. She began to back up, stammering.

"Tillie won't want to make more than two—two pies, and there's plenty here for that." Her eyes were wide and terrified.

Luke moved forward. "Then we won't have to waste any more time picking berries, will we?" The insinuation was clear.

"No, well..." Her eyes clung helplessly to his as she continued to back up. "Well, I'll just take these in to Tillie. She'll be waiting."

He was still advancing, slowly. Just as Gwen decided to abandon her dignity and run, she stepped backward into empty space. With a sharp cry, she made a desperate grab for Luke's hand. He plucked the bucket from her as she tumbled into the stream.

"Wouldn't want to lose the berries," he explained as Gwen surfaced, coughing and sputtering. "How's the water?"

"Oh!" After beating the surface of the water violently with her fists, Gwen struggled to her feet. "You did that on purpose!" Her hair was plastered to her face, and impatiently she pushed it out of her eyes.

"Did what?" Luke grinned, appreciating the way her clothes clung to her curves.

"Pushed me in." She took two sloshing steps toward the bank.

"My dear Gwenivere," Luke said in a reasonable tone. "I never laid a hand on you."

"Exactly." She kicked at the water in fury. "It's precisely the same thing."

"I suppose it might be from your point of view," he agreed. "But then, you were getting in over your head in any case. Consider the dunking the lesser of two evils. By the way, you have a lily pad on your..." His pause for the sake of delicacy was belied by the gleam in his eyes.

Flushing with embarrassment and fury, Gwen swiped a hand across her bottom. "As I said before, you are no gentleman."

Luke roared with laughter. "Why, Miss Gwenivere, ma'am, your opinion devastates me." His drawl was mocking, his bow low.

"At least," she began with a regal sniff, "you could help me out of this mess."

"Of course." With a show of gallantry, Luke set down the bucket and reached for Gwen's hand. Her wet shoes slid on the slippery bank. To help balance her, he offered his other hand. Just as she reached the top edge, Gwen threw all her weight backward, tumbling them both into the water. This time, Gwen surfaced convulsed with laughter.

As she stood, she watched him rise from the water and free his eyes of wet hair with a jerk of his head. Laughter blocked her speech. In silence, Luke watched as the sounds of her uninhibited mirth filled the air.

"How's the water?" she managed to get out before dissolving into fresh peals of laughter. Though she covered her mouth with both hands, it continued to escape and dance on the air. A quick hoot of laughter emerged as she saw his eyes narrow. He took a step toward her, and she began a strategic retreat. She moved with more speed than grace through the water, kicking it high. Giggles caused her to stumble twice. She scrambled up the slope but before she could rise to her feet, Luke caught her ankle. Pulling himself up onto the grass, he pinned Gwen beneath him.

Breathless, Gwen could still not stop laughing. Water dripped from Luke's hair onto her face, and she shook her head as it tickled her skin. A smile lurked in Luke's eyes as he looked down on her.

"I should have known better, I suppose," he commented. "But you have such an innocent face."

"You don't." Gwen took deep gulps of air in a fruitless effort to control her giggles. "Yours isn't innocent at all."

"Thank you."

Abruptly, the heavens opened and rain fell, warm and wild. "Oh!" Gwen began to push against him. "It's raining."

"So it is," Luke agreed, ignoring her squirms. "We might get wet."

The absurdity of his statement struck her suddenly. After staring up at him a moment, Gwen began to laugh again. It was a young sound, appealing and free. Gradually, Luke's expression sobered. In his eyes appeared a desire so clear, so unmistakable, that Gwen's breath caught in her throat. She opened her mouth to speak, but no words came.

"My God," he murmured. "You are exquisite."

His mouth took hers with a raw, desperate hunger. Her mouth was as avid as his, her blood as urgent. Their wet clothing proved no barrier as their bodies fused together in ageless intimacy. His caress was rough, and she reveled in the exquisite pain. The soft moan might have come from either of them. He savaged the vulnerable curve of her neck, tasting, arousing, demanding. His quick, desperate loving took her beyond the edge of reason and into ecstasy.

She felt no fear, only excitement. Here was a passion that sought and found her hidden fires and set them leaping. Rain poured over them unfelt, thunder bellowed unheard. His hands were possessive as they moved over her. Through the clinging dampness of her blouse, his mouth found the tip of her breast. She trembled, murmuring his name as he explored the slender smoothness of her thigh. She wanted him as she had never wanted anyone before.

"Luke?" His name was half question, half invitation.

Lightning flashed and illuminated the bayou. Just as swiftly they were plunged again into gloom.

"We'd better get back," Luke said abruptly, rising. "Your mother will be worried."

Gwen shut her eyes on a sudden stab of hurt. Hurriedly, she scrambled to her feet, avoiding Luke's outstretched hand. She swayed under a dizzying onslaught of emotions. "Gwen," Luke said, and took a step toward her.

"No." Her voice shook with the remnants of passion and the beginning of tears. Her eyes as they clung to his were young and devastated. "I must be losing my mind. You had no right," she told him shakily, "you had no right."

"To what?" he demanded roughly and grasped her shoulders. "To begin to make love with you or to stop?" Anger crackled in his voice.

"I wish I'd never seen you! I wish you'd never touched me."

"Oh, yes." Temper whipped through Luke's voice as he pulled her close to him again. "I can only say I wish precisely the same, but it's too late now, isn't it?" She had never seen his eyes so lit with fury. "Neither of us seems pleased with what's been started, but perhaps we should finish it." Rain swept around them, slicing through the trees and battering the ground. For a moment, Gwen knew terror. He could take her, she knew, even if she fought him. But worse, she knew he would need no force, no superior strength, after the first touch. Abruptly, he released her and stepped away. ''Unless that's what you want,'' he said softly, ''you'd best get out of here.''

This time Gwen took his advice. Sobbing convulsively, she darted away among the moss-draped trees. Her one thought...to reach the safety of home.

Chapter 5

The rain had awakened the garden. Twenty-four hours later it was still vibrant. Rose petals dried lazily in the sun while dew clung tenaciously to the undersides of leaves. Without enthusiasm, Gwen moved from bush to bush, selecting firm young blooms. Since the day before, she had avoided Luke Powers. With a determination born of desperation, she had clung to her mother's company, using Anabelle as both a defense and an offense. If, she had decided, *she* was always with Anabelle, Luke could not be. Nor could he take another opportunity to confuse and humiliate Gwen herself.

The basket on her arm was half filled with flowers, but she felt no pleasure in their colors and scents. Something was happening to her—she knew it, felt it, but could not define it. More and more often, she caught her thoughts drifting away from whatever task she was performing. It is, she reflected as she snipped a slender, thorny rose stem with Anabelle's garden shears, as if even my thoughts aren't wholly mine any longer.

When she considered her behavior over the past two days, Gwen was astounded. She had come to warn her mother about her relationship with Luke Powers and instead had found herself responding to him as she had never responded to Michael or any other man. But then, she admitted ruefully, she had never come into contact with a man like Luke Powers. There was a basically sensual aura about him despite his outward calm. She felt that he, like the bayou, hid much below the surface. Gwen was forced to admit that she had no guidelines for dealing with such a man. Worse, he had kindled in her a hitherto-buried part of her nature.

She had always thought her life and her needs simple. But suddenly, the quiet dreams inside her had risen to the surface. She was no longer the uncomplicated, controlled woman she had thought herself to be. The somewhat volatile temper she possessed had always been manageable, but in just two days the reins of restraint had slipped through her fingers.

His fault, Gwen grumbled to herself as she glared at a pale pink peony. He shouldn't be here—he should be in his beach house in California. If he were in California, perhaps battling an earthquake or hurricane, I'd be having a nice, uncomplicated visit with Mama. Instead he's here, insinuating himself into my life and making me feel… Gwen paused a moment and bit her lip. How does he make me feel? she thought. With a sigh, she let her gaze wander over the variety of colors and hues in the garden. I'm not sure how he makes me feel. He frightens me. The knowledge came to her swiftly, and her eyes reflected her surprise. Yes, he frightens me, though I'm not altogether sure why. It's not as if I thought he'd hurt me physically, he's not that sort of man, but still… Shaking her head, Gwen moved slowly down the walkway, digesting the new thought. He's a man who controls people and situations so naturally you're hardly aware you've been controlled.

Unconsciously, Gwen lifted her finger and ran it along her bottom lip. Vividly she remembered the feel of his mouth on hers. Its touch had ranged from gentle and coaxing to urgent and demanding, but the power over her had been the same. It was true—there was something exhilarating about fencing with him, like standing on the bow of a ship in a storm. But no matter how adventurous she might be, Gwen was forced to concede that there was one level on which she could not win. When she was in his arms, it was not surrender she felt, but passion for passion, need for need. Discovering this new facet of herself was perhaps the most disturbing knowledge of all.

I won't give up. Gwen lifted her chin and straightened her shoulders. I won't let him intimidate me or dominate my thoughts any longer. Her eyes glittered with challenge. Luke Powers won't control me. He'll find out that Gwen Lacrosse is perfectly capable of taking care of herself *and* her mother.

"Just a minute longer." Bradley Stapleton held up a pencil briefly, then continued to scrawl with it on an artist's pad. He sat crosslegged in the middle of the walkway, his feet sandaled, wearing paint-spattered carpenter's pants, a checked sport shirt unbuttoned over his thin chest and a beige fisherman's cap on his head. Surprised and intrigued, Gwen stopped in her tracks.

"Wonderful!" With surprising agility, Bradley unfolded himself and rose. His eyes smiled with genuine pleasure as he strolled over to Gwen. "I knew you'd be a good subject, but I didn't dare hope you'd be spectacular. Just look at this range of emotions!" he commanded as he flipped back several pages in his pad.

Gwen's initial amusement altered to astonishment. That the pencil sketches were exceptionally good was obvious, but it was not his talent as much as the content of the sketches that surprised her. She saw a woman with loose, curling hair and a coltish slenderness. There was a vulnerability she had never perceived in herself. As Gwen turned the pages, she saw herself dreaming, pouting, thinking and glaring. There was something disturbing about seeing her feelings of the past half hour so clearly defined. She lifted her eyes to the artist.

"They're fabulous," she told him. Bradley's face crinkled into a grin. "Bradley," she searched for the right words. "Am I really…so, well…artless as it seems here?" She looked back down at the sketches with a mixture of conflicting emotions. "What I mean is, are my thoughts, my feelings, so blatantly obvious? Am I so transparent?"

"That's precisely what makes you such a good model," Bradley said. "Your face is so expressive."

"But—" With a gesture of frustration, Gwen ran a hand through her hair. "Do they always show? Are they always there for people to examine? I feel defenseless and, well, naked somehow."

Bradley gave her a sympathetic smile and patted her cheek with his long, bony fingers. "You have an honest face, Gwen, but if it worries you, remember that most people don't see past the shape of a nose or the color of eyes. People are usually too busy with their own thoughts to notice someone else's."

"Yet you certainly did," Gwen replied, but she felt more comfortable.

"It's my business."

"Yes." With a smile, Gwen began flipping through the pages again. "You're very good..." She stopped, speechless as the pad fell open to a sketch of Luke.

It was a simple sketch of him sitting on the rail of the veranda. He was dressed casually, and his hair was tousled, as though he had been working. Bradley had captured the strength and intelligence in his face, as well as the sensual quality she had not expected another man to notice. But it was Luke's eyes, which seemed to lock on to hers, that impressed her. The artist had caught the strange melding of serenity and power that she had felt in them. Gwen was conscious of an odd quickening of her breath. Irresistibly, she was drawn to the picture just as she was drawn to the man.

"I'm rather pleased with it." Gwen heard Bradley's voice and realized with a jolt that he had been speaking for several seconds.

"It's very good," she murmured. "You understand him.'' She was unaware of the wistfulness and touch of envy in her voice.

After a brief, speculative glance at her lowered head, Bradley nodded. ''To an extent, I suppose. I understand he's a complicated man. In some ways, he's much like you.''

''Me?'' Genuinely shocked, Gwen lifted her eyes.

''You're both capable of a wide range of emotions. Not everyone is, you know. The main difference is, he channels his, while yours are fully expressed. Will you sit for me?''

''What?'' Gwen tried to focus on him again. The question was out of context with the rest of his statement. She shook her head to clear it of the disturbing thoughts his words had aroused in her.

''Will you sit for me?'' Bradley repeated patiently. ''I very much want to do you in oils.''

''Yes, of course.'' She shrugged and conjured up a smile to dispel her own mood. ''It sounds like fun.''

''You won't think so after a couple of hours of holding a pose,'' Bradley promised good-naturedly. ''Come on, we'll get started now, before you change your mind.'' Taking her hand, he pulled her up the walkway.

Several hours later, Gwen clearly understood the truth of Bradley's statement. Posing for a temperamental artist, she discovered, was both exhausting and demanding. Her face had been sketched from a dozen angles while she stood or sat or twisted in accordance with his commands. She began to feel more sympathy for the models at *Style.*

She had been amused at first when Bradley rooted through her wardrobe in search of attire suitable to sitting for the portrait. When he selected a thin white silk robe, she had taken what she considered a firm stand against his choice. He ignored her objections and, to her amazement, Gwen found herself doing exactly as he instructed.

Now, tired and alone, Gwen stretched out on her bed and relaxed her muscles. A smile lurked at the corners of her mouth as she recalled how Bradley had gently steamrolled her. Any embarrassment she had felt about wearing only the robe while he studied her or moved her this way and that had been swiftly eradicated. She might as easily have been an interesting tree or a fruit bowl. He had not been interested in the body beneath the robe but in the way the material draped.

I don't have to worry about fending off a passionate attack, Gwen reflected as she shut her eyes, only about stiffening joints. With a deep sigh, she snuggled into the pillow.

Her dreams were confused. She dreamed she was roaming through the bayou picking roses and blueberries. As she passed through a clearing, she saw

Luke chopping down a thick, heavy tree. The sound of the ax was like thunder. The tree fell soundlessly at her feet. As Luke watched, she walked to him and melted into his arms. For an instant she felt violent joy, then, just as suddenly, she found herself hurled into the cool stream.

From behind a curtain of water, Gwen saw Anabelle, a gentle smile on her lips as she offered her hand to Luke. Gwen struggled for the surface but found it just beyond her reach. Abruptly she was standing on the bank with Bradley sitting at her feet sketching. Ax in hand, Luke approached her, but Gwen found her arms and legs had turned to stone. As he walked, he began to change, his features dissolving, his clothing altering.

It was Michael who came to her now, a practical briefcase taking the place of the ax. He shook his head at her stone limbs and reminded her in his precise voice that he had told her she was cold. Gwen tried to shake her head in denial, but her neck had turned to stone, as well. When Michael took her by the shoulders and prepared to carry her away, she could only make a small sound of protest. From a distance, she heard Luke call her name. Michael dropped her, and as her stone limbs shattered, she awoke. Dazed, Gwen stared into blue-gray eyes. "Luke," she murmured, "I'm not cold."

"No." He brushed the hair from her cheek, then let his palm linger. "You're certainly not."

"Kiss me again, I don't want to turn to stone." She made the request petulantly. Amusement touched Luke's mouth as he lowered it to hers.

"Of course not, who could blame you?"

Sighing, Gwen locked her arms around his neck and enjoyed the warm gentleness of the kiss. Her limbs grew warm and fluid, her lips parted and begged for more. The kiss deepened until dream and reality mixed. A sharp stab of desire brought Gwen crashing through the barriers of lingering sleep. She managed a muffled protest against his mouth as she struggled for release. Luke did not immediately set her free but allowed his lips to linger on hers until he had had his fill. Even then, his face remained dangerously close. His mouth was only a sigh away.

"That must've been some dream," he murmured. With easy intimacy, he rubbed his nose against hers. "Women are so irresistibly soft and warm when they've been sleeping."

Cheeks flaming, Gwen managed to struggle up to a sitting position. "You have a nerve," she flared. "What do you mean by coming into my bedroom and molesting me?"

"Take a guess," he invited with a wolfish grin. Her color grew yet deeper as she gripped the V of her robe. "Relax," Luke continued. "I didn't come to steal your virtue, I came to wake you for dinner." He ran a fingertip along her jawline. "The rest was your idea."

Indignation stiffened Gwen's spine but muddled her speech. "You—you…I was asleep, and you took advantage…"

"I certainly did," Luke agreed, then pulled her close for a hard, brief kiss. "And we both enjoyed every second of it." He rose gracefully. "White suits you," he commented, his gaze wandering over the soft folds of the robe, "but you might want to change into something a bit less informal for dinner, unless your object is to drive Bradley into a frenzy of desire."

Gwen rose, wrapping the robe more tightly about her. "Don't worry about Bradley," she said icily. "He spent all afternoon sketching me in this robe."

The humor disappeared so swiftly from Luke's face, Gwen wondered if she had imagined its existence. His mouth was grim as he stepped toward her. "What?" The one word vibrated in the room.

"You heard me. I've agreed to let Bradley paint me."

"In that?" Luke's eyes dropped the length of the robe, then returned to her face.

"Yes, what of it?" Gwen tossed her head and turned to walk away from him. The silk of her robe floated around her legs and clung to her hips as she moved. When she reached the window, she turned and leaned back against the sill. Her stance was at once insolent and sensual. "What business is it of yours?"

"Don't play games unless you're prepared to lose," Luke warned softly.

"You're insufferable." The brown of her eyes grew molten.

"And you're a spoiled child."

"I'm not a child," Gwen retorted. "I make my own decisions. If I want to pose for Bradley in this robe or in a suit of armor or in a pair of diamond earrings and nothing else, that's nothing to do with you."

"I'd consider the diamond earrings carefully, Gwen." The soft tone of Luke's voice betrayed his rising temper. "If you try it, I'd have to break all of Bradley's fingers."

His calm promise of violence added fuel to Gwen's fire. "If that isn't typical male stupidity! If something doesn't work, kick it or swear at it! I thought you were more intelligent."

"Did you?" A glimmer of amusement returned to Luke's eyes. Reaching out, he gave her hair a sharp tug. "Too bad you were wrong."

"Men!" she expostulated, lifting her palms and eyes to the ceiling. "You're all the same."

"You speak, of course, from vast personal experience."

The sarcasm in his voice did not escape Gwen. "You're all arrogant, superior, selfish—"

"Beasts?" Luke suggested amiably.

"That'll do," she agreed with a nod.

"Glad to help." Luke sat back on the edge of the bed and watched her. The flickering lights of the setting sun accentuated the hollows and shadows of her face.

"You always think you know best and that women are too muddleheaded to decide things for themselves. All you do is give orders, orders, orders, and when you don't get your own way, you shout or sulk or, worse, patronize. I hate, loathe and despise being patronized!" Balling her hands into fists, Gwen thrust them into the pockets of her robe. "I don't like being told I'm cute in a tone of voice that means I'm stupid. I don't like being patted on the head like a puppy who can't learn to fetch. Then, after you've finished insulting my intelligence, you want to breathe all over me. Of course, I should be grateful for the attention because I'm such a sweet little simpleton." Unable to prevent herself any longer, Gwen gave the bedpost a hard slap. "I am not," she began, and her voice was low with fury, "I am *not* cold and unresponsive and sexually immature."

"Good Lord, child." Gwen, jolted by Luke's voice, blinked as she refocused on him. "What idiot ever told you that you were?"

Gwen stared at Luke in frozen silence.

"Your opinion of men obviously comes from the same source," he continued. "Your Michael must have been really convincing." Embarrassed, Gwen shrugged and turned back to the window. "Were you in love with him?"

The question caught her so off balance that she answered automatically. "No, but I thought I was, so it amounts to the same thing, I imagine."

"Bounced around a bit, were you?" His tone was surprisingly gentle as were the hands that descended to her shoulders.

"Oh, please." Quickly, Gwen moved away as she felt a strange, sweet ache. "Don't be kind to me. I can't fight you if you're kind."

"Is that what you want to do?" Luke took her shoulders firmly now and turned her around to face him. "Do you want to fight?" His eyes dropped to her lips. Gwen began to tremble.

"I think it's better if we do." Her voice was suddenly breathless. "I think fighting with you is safer."

"Safer than what?" he inquired. He smiled, a quick, flashing movement that was both charming and seductive. The room grew dim in the dusk, silhouetting them in the magic light of a dying day. "You are beautiful," he murmured, sliding his hand along the slope of her shoulders until his fingers traced her throat.

Mesmerized, Gwen stared up at him. "No, I—I'm not. My mouth's too wide, and my chin's pointed."

"Of course," Luke agreed as he drew her closer. "I see it now, you're quite an ugly little thing. It's a pity to waste velvet eyes and silken skin on such an unfortunate-looking creature."

"Please." Gwen turned her head, and his mouth brushed her cheek rather than her lips. "Don't kiss me. It confuses me—I don't know what to do."

"On the contrary, you seem to know precisely what to do."

"Luke, please." She caught her breath. "Please, when you kiss me, I forget everything, and I only want you to kiss me again."

"I'll be happy to do so."

"No, don't." Gwen pushed away and looked at him with huge, pleading eyes. "I'm frightened."

He studied her with quiet intensity. He watched her lip tremble, her teeth digging into it to halt the movement. The pulse in her neck throbbed under his palm. Letting out a long breath, he stepped back and slipped his hands into his pockets. His look was thoughtful. "I wonder, if I make love to you, would you lose that appealing air of innocence?"

"I'm not going to let you make love to me." Even to herself, Gwen's voice sounded shaky and unsure.

"Gwen, you're much too honest to make a statement like that, let alone believe it yourself." Luke turned and walked to the door. "I'll tell Anabelle you'll be down in a few minutes."

He closed the door behind him, and Gwen was left alone with her thoughts in the darkening room.

Chapter 6

Gwen endured Bradley's sketching for nearly an hour. His eyes were much sharper in his plain, harmless face than she had originally thought. And, she had discovered, he was a quiet tyrant. Once she had agreed to pose for him, he had taken over with mild but inescapable efficiency. He placed her on a white wrought-iron chair in the heart of the garden.

The morning was heavy and warm, with a hint of rain hovering despite the sunshine. A dragonfly darted past, zooming over a rosebush to her right. Gwen turned her head to watch its flight.

"Don't do that!" Bradley's beautifully modulated voice made Gwen guiltily jerk her head back. "I'm only sketching your face today,'' he reminded her. She murmured something unintelligible that had him smiling. ''Now I understand why you work behind the scenes at *Style* and not in front of the camera.'' His pencil paused in midair. ''You've never learned how to sit still!''

''I always feel as though I should be doing something,'' Gwen admitted. ''How does anyone ever just sit like this? I had no idea how difficult it was.''

''Where's your Southern languor?'' Bradley asked, sketching in a stray wisp of hair. She would sit more quietly if he kept up a conversation, he decided, even though he did not particularly care for splitting his concentration between sketching and talking.

''Oh, I don't think I ever had it,'' Gwen told him. She brought up her foot to rest on the chair and laced her hands around her knee. Enjoying the heady perfumes of the garden, she took a deep breath. ''And living in New York has made it worse. Although...'' She paused, looking around her again, though this time remembering to move only her eyes. ''There is something peaceful here, isn't there? I'm discovering how much I've missed that.''

''Is your work very demanding?'' Bradley asked, perfecting the line of her chin with a dash of his pencil.

''Hmm.'' Gwen shrugged and longed to take a

good stretch. ‘‘There’s always some deadline that no one could possibly meet that, of course, we meet. Then there are the models and photographers who need their artistic egos soothed—’’

‘‘Are you good at soothing artistic egos?’’ Bradley narrowed his eyes to find the perspective.

‘‘Surprisingly, yes.’’ She smiled at him. ‘‘And I like the challenge of meeting deadlines.’’

‘‘I’ve never been good with deadlines,’’ he murmured. ‘‘Move your chin, so.’’ He gestured with a fingertip, and Gwen obeyed.

‘‘No, some people aren’t, but I have to be. When you’re a monthly publication, you have no choice.’’

For a moment, Gwen fell silent, listening to the hum of bees around the azalea bushes in back of her. Somewhere near the house, a bird sent up a sudden, jubilant song. ‘‘Where are you from, Bradley?’’ she asked at length, turning her eyes back to him. He was a strange man, she thought, with his gangly body and wise eyes.

‘‘Boston.’’ His eyes went briefly to her, then back to his sketch pad. ‘‘Turn your head to the right a bit… There, good.’’

‘‘Boston. I should have guessed. Your voice is very…elegant.’’ Bradley chuckled. ‘‘How did you decide to become an artist?’’

‘‘It’s my favorite mode of communication. I’ve always loved sketching. In school my teachers had to confiscate my sketchbooks. And some people are very impressed when they hear you're an artist.''

Gwen laughed. ''The last's not a real reason.''

''Don't be too sure,'' Bradley murmured, involved with the curve of her cheek. ''I enjoy flattery. Not everyone is as self-sufficient as you.''

Forgetting his instructions, Gwen turned to him again. ''Is that the way you see me?''

''Sometimes.'' He lifted a brow and motioned for her to turn away again. For a moment he studied her profile before beginning to draw again. ''To be an artist, a good one, without the driving passion to be a great one, suits me perfectly.'' He smiled at her thoughtful expression. ''It wouldn't suit you at all. You haven't the patience for it.''

Gwen thought of the brisk, no-nonsense Gwen Lacrosse of *Style* magazine—a practical, efficient woman who knew her job and did it well, a woman who knew how to handle details and people, who was good at facts and figures. And yet…there was another Gwen Lacrosse who loved old, scented gardens and watched weepy movies on television, who hopped into hansom cabs in the rain. Michael had been attracted to the first Gwen but despaired of the second. She sighed. Perhaps she had never understood the mixture herself. She had not even questioned it. At least not until she had met Luke Powers.

Luke Powers. She didn't want to think about him. Things were not working out quite the way she had planned in that department. Worse yet, she wasn't at all sure they ever would.

Gwen tilted her head up to the sky. Bradley opened his mouth to remonstrate, then finding a new angle to his liking, continued sketching. The sun lit reddish sparks in her hair. She noticed that the clouds were rolling in from the west. A storm was probably brewing, she thought. It was still far off, hovering, taking its time. She had a feeling that it would strike when least expected. Though the day appeared to be sunny and pleasant, she felt the passion there, just below the surface. The air throbbed with it. In spite of the heat, Gwen shivered involuntarily. Irresistibly, her eyes were drawn to the house and up.

Luke was watching her from the window of his room. She wondered how long he had been there, looking down with that quiet, direct expression that she had come to expect from him. His eyes never wavered as hers met them.

He stared without apology, without embarrassment. For the moment, Gwen found herself compelled to stare back. Even with the distance between them, she could feel the intrusion of his gaze. She stiffened against it.

As if sensing her response, Luke smiled…slowly,

arrogantly, never shifting his eyes from hers. Gwen read the challenge in them. She tossed her head before turning away.

Bradley cocked a brow at Gwen's scowling face. "It appears," he said mildly, "that we're done for the day." He rose from his perch on a stone, unexpectedly graceful. "Tomorrow morning, I want you in the robe. I've a pretty good idea on the pose I want. I'm going in to see if I can charm Tillie out of a piece of that chocolate cake. Want some?"

Gwen smiled and shook her head. "No, it's a bit close to lunch for me. I think I'll give Mama a hand and do some weeding." She glanced down at the petunia bed. "She seems to be neglecting it a bit."

"Busy lady," Bradley said and, sticking the pencil behind his ear, sauntered down the path.

Busy lady? Gwen frowned after him. Her mother did not seem preoccupied...but *what* precisely was she doing? Perhaps it was just her way of intimating to Gwen that she, too, had a life, just as important as Gwen's big-city profession. Moving over to the petunia bed, Gwen knelt down and began to tug at stray weeds.

Anabelle had developed a habit of disappearing from time to time—that was something new. Unable to do otherwise, she glanced up at Luke's window again. He was gone. With a scowl, she went back to her weeding.

If only he would leave, she thought, everything would be fine. Her mother was a soft, gentle creature who trusted everyone. She simply had no defenses against a man like Luke Powers. And you do? she mocked herself. Swearing, Gwen tugged and unearthed a hapless petunia.

"Oh!" She stared down at the colorful blossom, foolishly guilty. A shadow fell across her, and she stiffened.

"Something upsetting you?" Luke asked. He crouched down beside her; taking the blossom from her hand, he tucked it behind her ear. Gwen remembered the rose and blushed before she could turn her face away.

"Go away. I'm busy," she said.

"I'm not." His voice was carelessly friendly. "I'll help."

"Don't you have work to do?" She shot him a scornful glance before ripping savagely at another weed.

"Not at the moment." Luke's tone was mild as he felt his way among the flowers. His fingers were surprisingly deft. "The advantage of being self-employed is that you make your own hours—at least most of the time."

"Most of the time?" Gwen queried, curiously overcoming her dislike for this annoying man.

"When it works, you're chained to the typewriter, and that's that."

"Strange," Gwen mused aloud, forgetting to ignore him. "I can't picture you chained to anything. You seem so free. But it must be difficult putting all those words on paper, making the people inside your head walk and talk and think. Why did you decide to become a writer?"

"Because I have an affection for words," he said. "And because those people in my head are always scrambling to get out. Now I've answered your question frankly." Luke turned to her as he twirled a blade of grass between his fingers. "It's my turn to ask one. What were you thinking of when you were watching the sky?"

Gwen frowned. She wasn't at all sure she wanted to share her private thoughts with Luke Powers. "That we're in for some rain," she compromised. "Must you watch me that way?"

"Yes."

"You're impossible," she told him crossly.

"You're beautiful." His look was suddenly intense, shooting a quiver up her spine. He cupped her chin before she could turn away. "With the sunlight on your hair and your eyes misty, you were all I have ever dreamed of. I wanted you." His mouth drew closer to hers. His breath fluttered over her skin.

"Don't!" Gwen started to back away, but his fingers on her chin held her steady.

"Not so fast," Luke said softly.

His kiss was surprisingly gentle, brushing her mouth like a butterfly's wing. Instinctively, she parted her lips to receive his probing tongue. With a sigh, she succumbed to the mood of the waiting garden. Her passion had lain sleeping, like the threatened storm behind the layer of soft clouds. She trembled with desire as his fingers carefully traced the planes of her face. They caressed her cheekbones, the line of her jaw, the thick tousle of her hair at her temples, before he kissed her again. His tongue teased and tasted with only the slightest pressure. She gripped his shirt front tightly and moaned his name. Her skin was alive with him. Wanting, needing, she twined her arms around his neck and pulled him against her. Her mouth was avid, seeking.

For one blazing moment, the flame rose and consumed them both, as they embraced in the fragrant morning heat. Then he had drawn her away, and Gwen was staring up at him, trying to catch her breath.

"No." She shook her head, pressing her hands to her temples as she waited for her thoughts to steady. "No." Before she could turn and flee, Luke had sprung up, grabbing her wrist.

"No what?" His voice was deeper, but still calm.

"This isn't right." The words tumbled out of her as she tried to find reason. "Let me go."

"In a minute." Luke kept his hand on her wrist and stepped toward her. A sweeping gaze took in her frantic color and widened eyes. "You want it, and so do I."

"No, no, I don't!" She shot out the fierce denial and jerked her arm. Her wrist stayed in his grip.

"I don't remember your protesting too much!" he said mildly. She was annoyed to recognize amusement in his eyes. "Yes, I distinctly recall it was you who took matters to the boiling point."

"All right, all right. You win." She took a breath. "I did. I forgot, that's all."

He smiled. "Forgot what?"

Gwen narrowed her eyes at his amusement. It fanned her temper more than his anger would have. "Forgot that I don't like you," she tossed out. "Now let me go, my memory's back."

Luke laughed a joyous masculine laugh before he pulled Gwen back into his arms. "You tempt me to make you forget again, Gwenivere." He kissed her again, a hard and possessive kiss. It was over almost before it had begun, but her senses were already reeling from it. "Shall we go back to weeding?" he asked pleasantly, as he released her.

She drew herself straight, indignant, furious. "You can go..."

"Gwen!" Anabelle's soft voice cut off Gwen's suggestion. Her mother had drifted into the garden. "Oh, here you are, both of you. How nice."

"Hello Anabelle." Luke gave her an easy smile. "We thought we'd give you a hand with the garden!"

"Oh?" She looked vaguely at her flowers, then her face brightened with a smile. "That's sweet, I'm sure I haven't been as diligent as I should be, but..." She trailed off, watching a bee swoop down on a rosebud. "Perhaps we can all get back to this later. Tillie's got lunch ready and insists on serving right away. It's her afternoon off, you know." She turned her smile on Gwen. "You'd better wash your hands, dear," she looked anxiously at Gwen, "and perhaps you should stay out of the sun for a while, you're a bit flushed."

Gwen could feel Luke grin without looking at him. "You're probably right," she mumbled. Detestable man! Why did he always succeed in confusing her?

Unaware of the fires raging in her daughter, Anabelle smilingly laid a hand on Gwen's cheek, but whatever she planned to say was distracted by the drone of a furry bee. "My, my," she said, watching it swoop greedily down on an azalea blossom.

"He's certainly a big one." Having forgotten Tillie's instructions, she glanced back up at Gwen. "You were sitting for Bradley this morning, weren't you, dear?"

"Yes." Gwen made a face. "For almost two hours."

"Isn't that exciting?" Anabelle glanced up at Luke for his confirmation, then continued before he could comment. "A portrait painted by a real artist! I can hardly wait to see it when it's all finished! Why, I'll have to buy it, I suppose." Her blue eyes brightened. "Perhaps I'll hang it right over the mantel in the parlor. That is..." Another thought intruded, and she stopped her planning and rearranging to look at her daughter. "Unless you want it for you and your Michael."

"He isn't *my* Michael, Mama, I told you." Gwen stuck her hands in her pockets, wishing Luke would say something instead of simply watching her with those cool blue-gray eyes. Why was it never possible to tell what he was thinking? "And in any case, he'd never buy a painting from an unknown. He wouldn't be assured of the investment value," she added. She was sorry that a note of rancor slipped into her voice.

Luke's eyes remained cool, but Gwen saw his brow lift fractionally. He doesn't miss anything, she thought with a stab of resentment. Turning, she began to pull loose petals from an overbloomed rose.

"Oh, but surely, if it were a portrait of you..." Anabelle began. Observing her daughter's expression, she hastily changed her course. "I'm sure it's going to be just beautiful," she said brightly. She turned to Luke. "Don't you think so, Luke?"

"Undoubtedly," he agreed as Gwen gave the rose her fiercest attention. "Bradley has the raw material to work with. That is..." He paused and, unable to resist, Gwen looked over her shoulder to meet his eyes again. "If Gwenivere manages to hold still until it's finished."

Gwen's spine stiffened at the amusement in his voice, but before she could retort, Anabelle laughed gaily. "Oh, yes, Gwen's a ball of fire, I declare," she emoted. "Even as a youngster, flitting here and there, quicker than a minute. Why, I'd have to nearly chain her to a chair to braid her hair." She smiled in maternal memory, absently fluffing her own hair. "Then, at the end of the day, or most times long before, it looked as though I had never touched it! And her clothes!" She clucked her tongue and rolled her eyes. "Oh, what a time I used to have with torn knees and ripped seams."

"Mama." Gwen interrupted before Anabelle could launch into another speech on her girlhood.

"I'm sure Luke's not interested in the state of my clothes."

He grinned at that, widely, irreverently. Gwen blushed to the roots of her hair. "On the contrary," he said as she groped around for something scathing and dignified to say. "I'm extremely interested." His eyes softened as he smiled at Anabelle. "It's all grist for my mill—just the sort of background material a writer needs."

"Why, yes, I suppose so." Gwen saw that her mother found this extremely profound. Anabelle lapsed into silence again, dreaming off into the middle distance. Luke grinned at Gwen over her head.

"And I've always had a fondness for little girls," he told her. "Particularly ones whose braids won't stay tied, and who regularly scrape their knees." He glanced down, letting his eyes run over Gwen's French-cut T-shirt and cinnamon-colored shorts. "I imagine over the years Anabelle was pretty busy administering first aid." His eyes traveled up on the same slow, casual journey before meeting hers.

"I didn't make a habit of falling down," Gwen began, feeling ridiculous.

Anabelle came out of her trance for a moment. "Oh, yes." She picked up on Luke's comment. "I don't think a day went by when I wasn't patching up some hurt. A fishhook in your hand one day..." She shuddered at the memory. "And a lump the size of a goose egg on your forehead the next. It was always one thing or another.''

''Mama.'' Gwen crushed what was left of the rose between her fingers. ''You make it sound as if I had been a walking disaster.''

''You were just spirited, darling.'' Anabelle frowned a bit at the damaged rose, but made no comment. ''Though there were times, I admit, I wasn't certain you'd live to grow up. But, of course, you have, so I probably shouldn't have worried so much.''

''Mama.'' Gwen was suddenly touched. How difficult it must have been, she reflected, for such a young, dreamy woman to raise a lively youngster all on her own! How many sacrifices Anabelle must have made that Gwen had never even considered. Stepping over, Gwen put her hands on Anabelle's soft rounded shoulders. ''I love you, and I'm terribly glad you're my mother.''

With a sound of surprised pleasure, Anabelle framed Gwen's face and kissed both her cheeks. ''What a sweet thing to hear, and from a grown daughter, too.'' She gave Gwen a quick, fragrant hug.

Over her mother's shoulder, Gwen saw that Luke was still watching them. His direct intensity made her feel self-conscious.

How do I really feel about him? she asked herself.

And how can I feel anything, anything at all, when the woman I love most in the world stands between us? She felt trapped, and something of her panic showed in her eyes.

Luke tilted his head. "You're very fortunate, Anabelle." He spoke to the mother, though his eyes remained on the daughter. "Love is very precious."

"Yes." She kissed Gwen's cheek again, then linked her arm through her daughter's. "I'm in a festive mood," she told them both, glowing. "I think we should be daring and have some wine with lunch." Her eyes widened. "*Lunch!* Oh, dear, Tillie will be furious! I completely forgot." She rested a hand against her heart as if to calm it. "I'll go smooth things along. Give me a minute." She assumed a businesslike air. "Then come right in. And see that you make a fuss over whatever she's fixed. We don't want to hurt her feelings any more than we have." She gave the final instructions as she swept back up the path and disappeared.

Gwen started to follow. Luke neatly cut off her retreat by taking her hand. "You'd better let her play diplomat first," he told her.

Gwen swung around to face him. "I don't want to be here with you."

Luke lifted a brow, letting his eyes play over her face. "Why not? I can't imagine more attractive circumstances. This lovely garden… A beautiful day…

Tell me something,'' he continued, interrupting whatever retort she might have made. Casually, he tangled the fingers of his other hand in her hair. ''What were you thinking of when you hugged your mother and looked at me?''

''That's none of your business.'' Gwen jerked her head, trying to free her hair from his curious fingers.

''Really?'' He lifted and stroked a straying lock of her hair. Somewhere in the distant west, she heard the first rumbles of thunder. ''I had the impression whatever was going through your mind at that moment was very much my business.'' He brought his eyes back down to hers and held them steady. ''Why do you suppose I did?''

''I haven't the faintest idea,'' Gwen returned coolly. ''Probably an author's overheated imagination.''

Luke's smile moved slowly, touching his eyes seconds before it touched his lips. ''I don't think so, Gwen. I prefer thinking of it as a writer's intuition.''

''Or a man's overinflated ego,'' she shot back, lifting her hand to her hair in an attempt to remove his exploring fingers. ''Would you stop that!'' she demanded, trying to ignore the dancing of nerves at the back of her neck.

''Or a man's sensitivity to a woman,'' he countered, bringing her hand to his lips. He kissed her fingers one at a time until she regained the presence of mind to try to jerk free. Instead of releasing her, Luke simply laced fingers with hers. They stood, joined as carelessly as schoolchildren, while she frowned at him. The thunder came again, closer. "Sensitive enough to know when a woman who is attracted to me," he went on lazily, "is not willing to admit it."

Her eyes narrowed. "You're impossibly conceited."

"Hopelessly honest," he corrected. "Shall I prove it to you?"

Gwen lifted her chin. "There's nothing to prove." She knew the hopelessness of attempting to pull her hand from his. Casually, she looked past him to the sky. "The clouds are coming in. I don't want to get caught in the rain."

"We've got a minute," he said, without even glancing at the sky. He smiled. "I believe I make you nervous."

"Don't flatter yourself," she tossed back, and kept her hands calm in his.

"The pulse in your throat is hammering." His eyes dropped and lingered on it, further increasing its pace. "It's strangely attractive—"

"It always does when I'm annoyed," she said, fighting for poise as the sweep of his eyes from her throat to her face threatened to destroy her composure.

"I like you when you're annoyed. I like to watch the different expressions on your face and to see your eyes darken…but…" He trailed off, slipping his hands to her wrists. "At the moment, I believe it's nerves."

"Believe what you like." It was impossible to prevent her pulse from pounding against his fingers. She tried to calm her rebel blood. "You don't make me the least bit nervous."

"No?" His grin turned wolfish. Gwen braced for a struggle. "A difference of opinion," he observed. "And one I'm tempted to resolve." He drew her closer, letting his eyes rest on her mouth. Gwen knew he was baiting her and held her ground. She said nothing, waiting for him to make his move.

"At the moment, however, I'm starved." Luke grinned, then gave her a quick, unexpected kiss on the nose. "And I'm too much of a coward to risk Tillie's bad temper." He dropped one of her hands, but kept the other companionably linked with his. "Let's eat," he suggested, ignoring Gwen's frown.

Chapter 7

Gwen noticed several small changes in Anabelle. There was an air of secrecy about her that Gwen found out of character. She disappears so often, Gwen thought as she seated herself in front of the vintage Steinway in the parlor. She's here one minute and gone the next. And she spends too much time with Luke Powers. There are too many discussions that stop abruptly when I walk in on them. They make me feel like an intruder. With little interest, she began to pick out a melody. The breeze came softly through the window, barely stirring the curtain. The scent of jasmine was elusive, teasing the senses.

I'm jealous, Gwen realized with a jolt of surprise. I expected Mama's undivided attention, and I'm not getting it. With a rueful laugh, Gwen began to play Chopin. Now when have I ever had Mama's undivided attention? She's always had her "visitors," her antiques, her flowers.

Thinking back over childhood memories, Gwen played with absentminded skill. She had forgotten how soothing the piano was to her. I haven't given myself enough time for this, she reflected. I should take a step back and look at where my life is going. I need to find out what's missing. Her fingers stilled on the last note, which floated quietly through the air and then vanished.

"Lovely," Luke said. "Really lovely."

Gwen suppressed the desire to jump at the sound of his voice. She forced herself to raise her eyes and meet his, struggling to keep the color from tinting her cheeks. It was difficult, after what she had said the evening before, to face him. She felt her defenses were shaky, her privacy invaded. He knew more of her now than she wanted him to.

"Thank you," she said politely. "I am, as Mama always said I would be, grateful for the music lessons she forced me to take."

"Forced?" To Gwen's consternation, Luke sat down on the stool beside her.

"As only she can." Gwen relieved a portion of

her tension by giving her attention to another melody. "With quiet, unarguable insistence."

"Ah." Luke nodded in agreement. "And you didn't want to study piano?"

"No, I wanted to study crawfishing." She was stunned when he began to play along with her, picking out the melody on the treble keys. "I didn't know you played." The utter disbelief in her voice brought on his laugh.

"Believe it or not, I, too, had a mother." He gave Gwen his swift, conspiratorial grin. "I wanted to study rock skipping."

Totally disarmed, Gwen smiled back at him. Something passed between them. It was as strong and as real as the passion that had flared with their kiss, as gentle and soothing as the music drifting from the keys.

"Isn't that sweet." Anabelle stood in the doorway and beamed at both of them. "Duets are so charming."

"Mama." Gwen was relieved her voice did not tremble. "I looked for you earlier."

"Did you?" Anabelle smiled. "I'm sorry, dear, I've been busy with…this and that," she finished vaguely. "Aren't you sitting for Bradley today?"

"I've already given him his two hours this morning," Gwen answered. "It's lucky for me he wants the early light, or I'd be sitting all day. I thought perhaps you had something you'd like me to do or someplace you'd like me to take you. It's such a lovely day.''

''Yes, it is, isn't it?'' Anabelle agreed. Her eyes drifted momentarily to Luke's. Abruptly, her cheeks dimpled and her lips curved. ''Why, as a matter of fact, darling, there *is* something you could do for me. Oh—'' She paused and shook her head. ''But it's so much trouble.''

''I don't mind,'' Gwen interrupted, falling into a childhood trap.

''Well, if it really isn't a bother,'' Anabelle continued, beaming again. ''I especially wanted some embroidery thread, very unusual shades, difficult to find, I'm afraid. There's a little shop in the French Market that carries them.''

''In New Orleans?'' Gwen's eyes widened.

''Oh, it is a bother, isn't it?'' Anabelle sighed. ''It's not important, dear. Not important at all,'' she added.

''It's not a bother, Mama,'' Gwen corrected, smiling at the old ruse. ''Besides, I'd like to get into New Orleans while I'm home. I can be a tourist now.''

''What a marvelous idea!'' Anabelle enthused. ''Wouldn't it be fun? Roaming through the Vieux Carré, wandering through the shops, listening to the music in Bourbon Street. Oh, and dinner at some lovely gallery restaurant. Yes.'' She clapped her hands together and glowed. ''It's just the thing.''

''It sounds perfect.'' Anabelle's childlike enthusiasm caused Gwen to smile. Shopping, she remembered, had always been Anabelle's favorite pastime. ''I can't think of a better way to spend the day.''

''Good. It's settled, then.'' She turned to Luke with a pleased smile. ''You'll go with Gwen, won't you, dear? It wouldn't do for her to go all alone.''

''Alone?'' Gwen cut in, confused. ''But, Mama, aren't you—?''

''It's such a long drive, too,'' Anabelle bubbled on. ''I'm sure Gwen would love the company.''

''No, Mama, I—''

''I'd love to.'' Luke easily overruled Gwen's objections. He gave Gwen an ironic smile. ''I can't think of a better way to spend the day.''

''Gwen, dear, I'm so glad you thought of it.'' The praise was given with a sigh as Anabelle moved over to pat Gwen's cheek.

Looking up into the ingenuous eyes, Gwen felt the familiar sensations of affection and frustration. ''I'm very clever,'' she murmured, moving her lips into a semblance of a smile.

''Yes, of course you are,'' Anabelle agreed, and gave her a quick, loving hug. ''I would change, though, darling. It wouldn't do to go into the city in those faded old jeans. Didn't I throw those out when you were fifteen? Yes, I'm sure I did. Well, run along and have fun,'' she ordered as she began to drift from the room. ''I've just so much to do, I can't think of it all.''

''Mama.'' Gwen called after her. Anabelle turned at the door, lifting her brows in acknowledgement. ''The thread?''

''Thread?'' Anabelle repeated blankly. ''Oh, yes, of course. I'll write down the colors and the name of the shop.'' She shook her head with a self-deprecating smile. ''My, my, I'm quite the scatter-brain. I'll go in right now and tell Tillie you won't be here for dinner. She gets so annoyed with me when I forget things. Do change those pants, Gwen,'' she added as she started down the hall.

''I'd hide them,'' Luke suggested confidentially. ''She's liable to throw them out again.''

Rising with what she hoped was dignity, Gwen answered, ''If you'll excuse me?''

''Sure.'' Before she could move away, Luke took her hand in a light but possessive grip. ''I'll meet you out front in twenty minutes. We'll take my car.''

A dozen retorts trembled on Gwen's tongue and were dismissed. ''Certainly. I'll try not to keep you waiting.'' She walked regally from the room.

* * *

The weather was perfect for a drive—sunny and cloudless, with a light breeze. Gwen had replaced her jeans with a snowy crepe de chine dress. It had a high, lacy neck and pleated bodice, its skirt flowing from a trim, tucked waist. She wore no jewelry. Her hair lay free on her shoulders. Hands primly folded in her lap, she answered Luke's easy conversation with polite, distant monosyllables. I'll get Mama's thread, she determined, have a token tour of the city and drive back as quickly as possible. I will be perfectly polite the entire time.

An hour later, Gwen found that maintaining her aloof sophistication was a difficult task. She had forgotten how much she loved the Vieux Carré. It was not just the exquisite iron grillwork balconies, the profusion of flowering plants, the charm of long wooden shutters and buildings that had stood for centuries. It was the subtle magic of the place. The air was soft and seemed freshly washed, its many scents ranging from flowery to spicy to the rich smell of the river.

"Fabulous, isn't it?" Luke asked as they stood on the curb of a street too narrow for anything but pedestrian traffic. "It's the most stable city I know."

"Stable?" Gwen repeated, intrigued enough to turn and face him directly.

"It doesn't change," he explained with a gesture of his hand. "It just continues on." Before she realized his intent, he laced his fingers with hers and began to walk. She tugged and was ignored.

"There's no reason to hold my hand," Gwen told him primly.

"Sure there is," he corrected, giving her a friendly smile. "I like to."

Gwen subsided into silence. Luke's palm was hard, the palm of a man used to doing manual labor. She remembered suddenly the feel of it caressing her throat. He sighed, turned and pulled her hard against him, covering her mouth in an unexpected and dizzying kiss. Gwen had no time to protest or respond before she was drawn away again. Along the crowded street, several people applauded.

Gwen and Luke walked past the many street artists in Jackson Square. They paused briefly to admire the chalk portraits of tourists, the oils of city scenes and the mysterious studies of the bayous. Gwen was torn between her desire to share her pleasure at returning to the city of her childhood and the feeling that she should ignore the dominating man by her side. She was not here to have a good time, she reminded herself sternly. She was here to do an errand. It was on the tip of her tongue to remind Luke of the purpose of their trip when she saw the magician. He was dressed in black, with spangles and a rakish beret and a flowing moustache.

"Oh, look!" Gwen pointed. "Isn't he wonderful?" She moved closer, unconsciously pulling Luke along by tightening her grip on his hand.

They watched brilliantly colored scarves appear from nowhere, huge bouquets of paper flowers grow from the magician's palm and coins sprout from the ears of onlookers. Two young clowns in whiteface entertained the stragglers by twisting balloons into giraffe and poodle shapes. Some distance away, guitarists sold their songs to passing tourists. Gwen could just hear their close-knit harmony.

Forgetting all her stern resolutions, she turned to grin at Luke. He dropped a bill into the cardboard box that served as the portable cash register for the magician. Reaching out, he pinched her chin between his thumb and forefinger. "I knew it wouldn't last too long."

"What wouldn't?" She brushed the hair from her eyes in a habitual gesture.

"You enjoy things too much to remain cool for long," he told her. "No, now don't do that," he ordered, running a finger down her nose as she frowned. He smiled, then brushed his lips over her fingertips. "Shall we be friends?"

Her hand, already warm from his, grew warmer at the kiss. She knew his charm was practiced, his smile a finely tuned weapon. She forced herself to be cautious.

"I don't know that I'd go as far as that," she replied, studying him with eyes that were warily amused.

"Fellow tourists?" he suggested. His thumb moved gently across her knuckles. "I'll buy you an ice cream cone."

Gwen knew she was losing to the smile and the persuasive voice. "Well..." It would do no harm to enjoy the day. No harm in enjoying the city, the magic...in enjoying him. "Two scoops," she demanded, answering his smile with her own.

They moved at an easy pace through the park, enjoying both shade and sun. All around was the soft, continuous cooing from hundreds of pigeons. They flocked along the ground, scattered when chased by children, sunned atop the statue of Andrew Jackson on a rearing horse. Here and there people sat or slept on curved black benches. A young girl sat in a patch of shade and played softly on a recorder.

They walked along the levee and looked at the brown waters of the Mississippi. Lazy music from calliopes provided a pleasant background as they talked of everything and of nothing. The bells of Saint Louis Cathedral chimed the hour. They laughed at the toddler who escaped from his mother and splashed in the cool waters of a fountain.

They walked along Bourbon Street, listening to

the tangled, continuous music that poured from open doors. Jazz and country and rock merged into one jumbled, compelling sound. They applauded the old man who danced in the street to the demanding strains of "Tiger Rag." They listened to the corner saxophone player whose lonely song brought Gwen to tears.

On a gallery overlooking a narrow street surging with people, they ate shrimp gumbo and drank cold, dry wine. They lingered over the leisurely meal, watching the sun slowly disappear. Pleasantly weary, Gwen toyed with the remains of her cheese-cake and watched the first stars come out. Laughter rose from the street below. When she turned, she found Luke studying her over the rim of his glass.

"Why do you look at me like that?" Her smile was completely relaxed as she rested her chin on her palm.

"A remarkably foolish question," Luke answered as he set down his glass. "Why do you think?"

"I don't know." She took a deep breath. The scent of the city assailed her senses. "No one's ever looked at me quite the way you do. You can tell too much about people. It's not fair. You study them and steal their thoughts. It's not a very comfortable feeling."

Luke smiled, and his fingers were light on the back of her hand.

Gwen lifted an eyebrow, then strategically moved her hand out of reach. ''You also have a way of making people say things. Yesterday I...'' Gwen hesitated and twisted the stem of her glass between her fingers. ''I said things to you I shouldn't have. It's disturbing to know you've revealed your emotions to someone else.'' She sipped her wine. ''Michael always says I'm too open.''

''Your emotions are beautiful.'' Gwen looked up, surprised at the tenderness in his voice. ''Michael is a fool.''

Quickly she shook her head. ''Oh, no, he's really quite brilliant, and he never does anything foolish. He has an image to maintain. It's just that I was beginning to feel as if I were being molded into his conception of a proper attorney's wife.''

''He asked you to marry him?'' Luke asked, as he poured wine into both glasses.

''He was sure that I would. He was furious when I didn't jump at the offer.'' Gwen sighed and made a restless movement with her shoulders. ''I kept seeing a long, narrow tunnel, very straight, no curves, no detours, no surprises. I guess I developed claustrophobia.'' She made a frustrated sound, wrinkling her nose. ''There, you've done it again.''

''I have?'' He smiled as he leaned back in his seat. Moonlight spilled over her hair.

''I'm telling you things...things I've barely told

myself. You always manage to find out what's in a person's mind, but you keep your own thoughts all tidy and tucked away."

"I put them in print," he corrected. "For anyone who cares to read them."

"Yes," she said slowly. "But how does one know if they're your real thoughts? Your books are interesting, but how do I know who you really are?"

"Do you want to?" There was a soft challenge in his voice.

Gwen hesitated, but the answer was already moving to her lips. "Yes, I do."

"But you're not quite sure." He rose, then held out his hand to her. "The wine's made you sleepy," he said, looking down into her heavy eyes. "Shall I take you home?"

"No." Gwen shook her head. "No, not yet." She slipped her hand back into his.

Luke drove down the magnolia-lined lane. The scent of the night was delicate, mixing with the fragrance of the woman who slept on his shoulder. After stopping the car, he turned his head and looked down at her. Gwen's mouth was soft and vulnerable in sleep. There was a moment's hesitation before he lifted her chin and drew away from her.

"Gwen." He moved his thumb gently over her lips. She gave a soft, pleased sigh. "Gwen," he said again with more firmness. Her lashes fluttered and opened. ''We're home.'' He massaged her shoulders lightly, and she stretched under his hands.

''Did I fall asleep?'' Her eyes were huge and dark as she smiled at him. ''I didn't mean to.''

''It's late.''

''I know.'' She smiled sleepily. ''I had fun. Thank you.'' On impulse, she bent forward and brushed her lips over his. His fingers tightened on her shoulders as he pulled away from her sharply. Gwen blinked in confusion. ''Luke?''

''I have my limits,'' he said tersely. He made a quick, impatient sound as her face registered consternation. ''I told you once, women are very soft and warm when they've been sleeping. I have a weakness for soft, warm women.''

''I didn't mean to fall asleep,'' she murmured as his hand slipped around to cradle the back of her neck. Her head felt light, her limbs heavy.

A cloud drifted over the moon. The light shifted, dimmed and glowed again. He was watching her, studying each feature with absorption. She could feel his fingers on the base of her neck. They were hard and long, their strength obvious even in the gentle touch. She whispered, ''What do you want?''

In answer, he bent slowly toward her. His mouth was easy, teasing the corners of hers, drifting to her closed lids, exploring the hollows of her cheeks.

Passion lay simmering beneath the surface as he began to caress her body with slow, patient hands. He traced her parted lips with the tip of his tongue. "Beautiful," he murmured, moving his mouth to her ear. She shivered with pleasure as his thumb lingered on the point of her breast. "When I touch you, I feel your body melt under my hands." He met her mouth with a long, tender kiss. "What do I want?" he answered as he tasted the heated skin of her throat. "What I want more than anything at this moment is to make love with you. I want to take you slowly, until I know all of you."

She felt her body growing fluid, and her will flowed with it. "Will you make love with me?" She heard herself ask, heard the tone that was request rather than question. Luke's mouth paused on her skin. Slowly he tightened his grip on her hair, then drew her head back until their eyes met. For a moment, they hung suspended in silence with only the echo of her voice between them.

"No." His answer was cool and quick as a slap. Gwen jerked away from it and him and fumbled with the handle of the door. She stumbled out of the car, but before she could escape into the house, Luke captured her arms in a firm grip. "Wait a minute."

Shaking her head, Gwen pushed against him. "No, I want to go in. I didn't know what I was saying. It was crazy."

''You knew exactly what you were saying,'' Luke corrected, tightening his grasp.

Gwen wanted to deny it, but found it impossible. She had wanted him, she knew she still wanted him. ''All right, I knew what I was saying. Now will you let me go?''

''I won't apologize for touching you,'' he said.

''I'm not asking for apologies, Luke,'' she told him evenly. ''I'm simply asking for my freedom.'' She realized uncomfortably that it was not freedom from his arms that she meant, but freedom from the power he held over her. The struggle inside her was reflected briefly in her face. Luke's frown deepened before he released her arms. ''Thank you,'' she said.

She walked quickly inside the house before he could say another word.

Chapter 8

A yellow butterfly fluttered delicately over a pot of white impatiens. From the veranda, Gwen watched its dance until it skimmed away, light as the air. Sitting in the white porch rocker, dressed in a yellow sundress, Anabelle looked as fragile as the butterfly. Gwen studied her mother's soft pink cheeks and gentle blue eyes. Anabelle's small hands were busy with the domestic task of shelling peas, but her eyes were, as always, dreamy. Watching her, Gwen was swamped with waves of love and helplessness.

Who am I? she demanded of herself. Who am I to advise anyone on men? For a moment, Gwen wished desperately that she could seek from Anabelle advice for herself. Her own emotions were chaotic. She was terrified that her own feelings for Luke were approaching a dangerous level. Falling in love with a man like Luke was courting disaster. And yet, Gwen wondered unhappily, is it really possible for the mind to control the heart? In this case it must…there's no choice. I have to forget about last night. The sigh escaped before she could stop it. Priorities, she reminded herself. Gwen watched a bumblebee dive into a cluster of wisteria, then took a deep breath and turned to Anabelle. ''Mama.'' Anabelle went on shelling peas, a misty smile on her lips. ''Mama,'' Gwen repeated more sharply, placing a hand over her mother's.

''Oh, yes, dear?'' Anabelle looked up with the open, expectant look of a child. ''Did you say something?''

For an instant, Gwen teetered on the brink, then plunged. ''Mama, don't you think twelve years is a terribly big gap?''

Gravely, Anabelle considered. ''Why, I suppose it could be, Gwenivere, but then, as you grow older, twelve years is hardly any time at all.'' Her momentary seriousness vanished with a fresh smile. ''Why, it seems like yesterday that you were twelve years old. I remember quite clearly when you fell out of that old cypress in the backyard and broke your arm. Such a brave child…'' She began shelling peas again. ''Never shed a tear. I cried enough for both of us, though.''

''But, Mama.'' Valiantly Gwen tried to keep Anabelle's thoughts from straying. ''Twelve years, when you're speaking of a man and a woman....'' Anabelle failed to respond to the prompting, only nodding to indicate she was listening. ''The age difference, Mama,'' Gwen blurted out. ''Isn't twelve years a terribly wide age gap?''

''Sally Deumont's girls are nearly twelve years apart,'' Anabelle stated with another series of nods. ''I suppose having children that far apart has its drawbacks.''

''No, Mama.'' Gwen ran both hands through her hair.

''And its advantages, certainly,'' Anabelle said soothingly, not wanting to be critical of an old friend.

''No, Mama, I don't mean that at all. I'm speaking of men and women...of relationships. Romantic relationships.''

''Oh!'' Anabelle blinked in surprise and smiled. ''That's a different matter altogether, isn't it?'' Gwen resisted grinding her teeth as her mother continued to shell peas for a moment in silence. ''I'm surprised,'' Anabelle said at length, giving Gwen a look of gentle curiosity. ''I'm surprised you would think that age and love had anything to do with each other. I've always thought of the heart as ageless."

The words caused Gwen to falter a moment. Slowly she leaned forward and took both her mother's hands in hers. "Mama, don't you think, sometimes, that love can blind people to what's right for them? Don't people often put themselves into a position where getting hurt is the only possible outcome?"

"Yes, of course." Anabelle shook her head, as if startled by the question. "That's part of life. If you never open yourself for pain, you never open yourself for joy. How empty life would be then. This Michael of yours," Anabelle continued with a light of concern in her eyes, "did he hurt you terribly?"

"No." Gwen released her mother's hands and rose to walk the length of the veranda. "No, basically only my pride."

"That can happen by a fall off a horse," Anabelle stated. Abandoning her peas, she moved to join Gwen. "Darling, how young you are." She turned to face her, studying her with rare total concentration. "I sometimes forget that, because you're so much more practical and organized than I am. I suppose I always let you take care of me, much more than I took care of you."

"Oh, no, Mama," Gwen protested, but Anabelle placed a finger on her lips.

''It's true. I never like to look at the unpleasant side of things. I'm afraid I've always let you do that for me. In some ways you matured so quickly, but in others...'' Anabelle sighed and slipped an arm around Gwen's waist. ''Perhaps at last we've found something I can help you with.''

''But, Mama, it's not me...'' Gwen began, only to be ignored.

''Did you know I was only eighteen when I first saw your father? I fell instantly, wildly in love.'' The soft look in Anabelle's eyes halted Gwen's interruption. ''Who would have thought his life would be so short? He never even got to see you. I always thought that the greatest tragedy. He would have been so proud to see himself in you.'' She sighed, then smiled at Gwen. ''Ours was a first love, a desperate love, and often I've wondered if it would have withstood all the tests of time. I'll never know.'' Gwen remained silent, fascinated by a side of her mother she was seeing for the first time. ''I learned so many things from that short, crowded marriage. I learned you must always accept love when it's offered, always give it when it's needed. There might not be a second chance. And I know, too, that until your heart's been broken, you never know the full beauty of love.''

Gwen watched a squirrel dart across the lawn and scurry up a tree. It was an odd feeling, hearing her mother speak of being in love. She wondered if their relationship had blinded her from seeing Anabelle as a woman with needs and desires. Looking down, Gwen saw the smooth, untroubled skin of a woman at the peak of her beauty. There was still a youthful sweetness in the shape of the mouth, an impossible air of innocence in the eyes. Impulsively, Gwen asked the question that had lurked in her mind for years.

"Mama, why haven't you ever gotten married again?"

"I haven't wanted to," Anabelle answered instantly. She moved away with a swish of her skirts. "At first, I was too much in love with your father's memory, and later I was having too much fun raising you." She plucked a withered fuchsia bloom from a hanging basket and dropped it over the railing of the veranda. "I'm quite good with babies, you know. Later you became more and more independent, so I moved on to the next stage. I've had some admirers." She smiled, pleased with the thought. "I've simply never had the urge to settle down with any of them." In silence, Gwen watched Anabelle move from flower to flower. It occurred to her for the first time that her mother had probably enjoyed love affairs over the past twenty years. She had not been exclusively Gwen's dreamy, gentle mother but Anabelle Lacrosse, a lovely, desirable woman. For one brief moment, Gwen felt ridiculously like an orphan.

I'm being a fool, Gwen told herself, resting her head against the rail post. She's still the same person—I'm the one who's changing. I grew up, but I've kept her locked in a childhood image. It's time I let her out. But I can't bear to see her hurt, and I'm so afraid Luke will leave her wounded. He can't love her, not when he can kiss me the way he does. No… She closed her eyes. He wants me, but it has nothing to do with his heart. He wants me, but he turned away from me. Why else would he have done that, if not for her? A bright flash of jealousy both stunned and shamed her. With a shuddering sigh, she turned to find Anabelle studying her.

"You're not happy," her mother said simply.

"No." Gwen shook her head with the word.

"Confused?"

"Yes." Quickly she swallowed the tears that threatened to come.

"Men do that to us so easily." Anabelle smiled as if the prospect was not altogether unappealing. "Try a rare piece of advice from your mother, darling. Do nothing." With a little laugh, she tossed back a stray wisp of golden hair. "I know how difficult that is for you, but do try. Just let the pieces fall into place around you for a time. Sometimes doing nothing is doing everything."

"Mama." Gwen was forced to smile. "How can something so silly make so much sense?"

"Luke says I've an intuitive understanding," Anabelle replied with a glow of pride.

"He has a way with words," Gwen muttered.

"Tools of the trade." Luke spoke as the screen door swung shut behind him. His eyes met Gwen's. There was something intimate in the glance, something possessive. Even as the stirring began inside her, she lifted her chin in defense. A smile teased his mouth. "Guns primed, Gwenivere?"

"I'm a dead shot," she returned evenly.

"Oh dear." Anabelle moved lightly across the veranda and began to gather her peas. "You didn't tell me you were going hunting. I hope Tillie packed you a lunch."

Luke grinned over her head with such easy boyish charm, Gwen was helpless to resist. Her eyes warmed and her mouth softened as they shared the intimacy of a joke.

"Actually, I had fishing in mind," Luke countered, keeping his eyes on Gwen's. "I thought I'd walk down to Malon's cabin."

"That's nice." Anabelle straightened and smiled. "Malon still brings up fresh fish," she told Gwen. "You run along, too, darling. You know he would be hurt if you didn't visit."

"Oh, well, I..." Seeing the amusement on Luke's

face, Gwen continued smoothly, ''I'll visit him, Mama, another time. I told Tillie I'd help her do some canning.''

''Nonsense.'' Anabelle flitted to the screen door, beaming at Luke as he held it open for her. ''Thank you, darling,'' she said before giving Gwen a look over her shoulder. ''You're on vacation. That's no time to be standing in a hot kitchen over boiling tomatoes. Run along and have fun. She's always loved to fish,'' she added to Luke before she stepped inside. ''Tell Malon I'd adore some fresh shrimp.'' The door closed behind her. Gwen had the odd feeling that she had just been pushed gently out of the way. Luke gave her slim blue jeans and plain white T-shirt a cursory glance.

''Looks like you're dressed for fishing,'' he said with a nod. ''Let's go.''

''I have no intention of going anywhere with you.'' Gwen dusted her hands on her hips and started to move by him. She was brought up short by his hand on her arm. They stood side by side. Gwen let her eyes rest on his imprisoning hand and then slid them slowly to meet his. It was her most disdainful stare. ''I beg your pardon?'' she said icily. To her dismay, Luke burst out laughing. The warm, deep tones of it caused a bird to dart from the lawn to the shelter of a tree. ''Let me go, you...you...''

"Wasn't it 'beast' before?" he asked as he began to assist her down the stairs.

"You are the most outrageous man." She continued to struggle as she trotted to keep pace.

"Thanks."

Gwen dug in her heels and managed to persuade Luke to stop. Staring up at him, she took a long, deep breath. "You are the most arrogant, officious, egotistical, thick-skinned man I have ever met."

"You forgot unreasonable, tyrannical and incredibly attractive. Really, Gwen, you surprise me. I thought you had more imagination. Are those your best insults?"

"Off the cuff, yes." She sniffed and tried not to respond to the humor in his eyes. "If you'll give me a little time, I can be more articulate."

"Don't trouble, I got the idea." He released her arm, held up one hand in the air, and the other out to her. "Truce?"

Gwen's guard relaxed before she realized it. Her hand moved to meet his.

"Truce," she agreed, with only a token trace of reluctance.

"Until…?" he asked as he rubbed his thumb lightly across the back of her hand.

"Until I decide to be annoyed with you again." Gwen smiled, tossing back her curls as she enjoyed his laugh. It was, she decided, the most pleasing, infectious laugh she had ever heard.

"Well, will you fish with me?" he asked.

"Perhaps I will." For a moment she pursed her lips in thought. When she smiled again, it was the smile of challenge. "Ten bucks says I catch a bigger fish than you."

"Done." Casually, Luke laced his fingers through hers. This time Gwen made no objection.

Gwen knew every twist of the river and every turn of the paths in the bayou. Automatically, she moved north toward Malon's cabin. They walked under cascading moss and filtered sunlight.

"Do you really know how to can tomatoes, Gwenivere?" Luke asked as he bent under a low-hanging branch.

"Certainly, and anything else that comes out of a garden. When you're poor, a garden can mean the difference between eating or not."

"I've never known poor people who eat with Georgian silver," Luke commented dryly.

"Heirlooms." Gwen gave a sigh and a shrug. "Mama always considered heirlooms a sacred trust. One can't sell a sacred trust. Nor," she added with a wry smile, "can one comfortably wear or eat a sacred trust. Mama loves that house, it's her Camelot. She's a woman who needs a Camelot."

"And Gwenivere doesn't?" A great egret, startled by their intrusion, unfolded himself from the water and rose into the sky. Gwen felt an old, familiar stir of pleasure as she watched.

"I suppose I've always wanted to find my own. Heirlooms belong to someone else first. I'd nearly forgotten the scent of wild jasmine," she murmured as the fragrance drifted to her.

There was a dreamlike stillness around them. Beside them, the stream moved on its lackadaisical journey to the Gulf. Its water mirrored the moss-dripping trees. Gwen tossed a pebble and watched the ripples spread and vanish. "I spent most of my leisure time out here when I was younger," she said. "I felt more at home here than inside my own house. There was never any real privacy there, with strangers always coming and going. I never wanted to share my kingdom with anyone before...."

She could feel Luke's big hand tighten his grasp on hers. He met her eyes with perfect understanding.

Chapter 9

Malon's cabin hung over the water. It was built of split logs with a low, wide A roof and a porch that doubled as a dock for his pirogue. On a small, spare patch of grass beside the cabin, half a dozen chickens clucked and waddled. Somewhere deep in the marsh, a woodpecker drummed. A scratchy recording of music by Saint-Saëns came from the cabin to compete with the drumming and clucking. Stretched lengthwise on a narrow railing above the water, a tabby cat slept.

"It's just the same," Gwen murmured. She was unaware of the relief in her voice or the pleasure that lit her face. She smiled up at Luke and pulled him quickly across the lawn and up the three wooden steps. ''Raphael,'' she said to the snoozing cat. Lazily he opened one eye, made a disinterested noise and shut it again. ''Affectionate as ever,'' Gwen remarked. ''I was afraid he'd forget me.''

''Raphael is too old to forget anything.''

Gwen turned quickly at the sound of the voice. Malon stood in the cabin doorway, a mortar and pestle in his hand. He was a small man, barely taller than Gwen herself, but with powerful arms and shoulders. His middle had not gone to flesh with age, but remained as flat as a boxer's, as he had indeed once been. His hair was white, thick and curly, his face brown and lined, his eyes were a faded blue under dark brows. His age was a mystery. The bayou had been his home for an unspecified number of years. He took from the stream what he needed and was content. He had both a passionate love and a deep respect for the bayou. These he had passed on to the young girl who had found his cabin more than fifteen years before. Gwen checked the impulse to run into his arms.

''Hello, Malon. How are you?''

''Comme ci, comme ça.'' He gave a tiny shrug, then set down his mortar and pestle. He nodded a greeting to Luke before concentrating on Gwen. For a full minute she stood silent under his scrutiny. At length he said, ''Let me see your hands.'' Obedi-

ently, Gwen held them out. ''Soft,'' Malon said with a snort. ''Lady's hands now, *hein?* Why didn't you get a lady's figure in New York, too?''

''I could only afford the hands. I'm still saving up for the rest. And Tillie's still pressing your shirts, I see,'' Gwen ran an experimental finger over the faded but crisp material of his cotton shirt. ''When are you going to marry her?''

''I'm too young to get married,'' he said. ''I have not finished sowing wild oats.''

Gwen laughed and laid her cheek against his. ''Oh, I've missed you, Malon.'' He answered her laugh and gave her one quick, bruising and unexpected hug. From the outset, they had spoken in Cajun French, a dialect that Gwen used again without the slightest thought. She closed her eyes a moment, enjoying the strength in his burly arms, the feel of his leathery cheek against hers, the scent of woodsmoke and herbs that was his personal cologne. She realized suddenly why she had not come to see him earlier. He had been the one constant male figure in her life. She had been afraid she would find him changed.

''Everything's the same,'' she murmured.

''But you.'' There was a smile in his voice, and she heard it.

''I should have come sooner.'' For the first time

since she had known him, Gwen dared kiss his cheek.

"You are forgiven," he said.

Gwen was suddenly conscious of Luke beside her. She flushed. "I'm sorry," she said to him, "I—I didn't realize that we were rambling on in French."

Luke smiled while absently scratching Raphael's ears. "You don't have to apologize—I enjoyed it."

Gwen forced her thoughts into order. She would not fall under the charm of that smile again. "Do you speak French?" she asked with casual interest.

"No. But I still enjoyed it." She had the uncomfortable feeling he knew precisely how deeply his smile affected her. He turned his clear, calm eyes to Malon. "Anabelle says she'd like some shrimp."

"I go shrimping tomorrow," Malon answered with an agreeable nod. "Your book goes well?"

"Well enough."

"So, you take the day off, *hein?* You take this one fishing?" A jerk of his thumb in Gwen's direction accompanied the question.

"Thought I might," Luke replied without glancing at her.

Malon shrugged and sniffed. "Use t'be she knew which end of the pole to hold and which to put in the water, but that was before she went up there." A snap of his head indicated "up there." Even a town twenty miles from Lafitte was regarded with suspicion.

"Perhaps she remembers," Luke suggested. "She seems reasonably intelligent."

"She was raised good," Malon added, softening a bit. "Her papa was a good boy. She has his face. She don't favor her mama."

Gwen straightened her shoulders and raised her brows ever so slightly. "*She* remembers *everything.* My mother can outfish both of you in her sleep."

"Poo-yie!" Malon shook his hand and wrist as if he had touched something hot. "This city girl, she scare me out of my shoe. You take her. Me, I'm too old to fight with mean women."

"A minute ago you were too young to get married," Gwen reminded him.

"Yes, it's a good age I have." He smiled contentedly. "*Allez,* I have medicine to make. Take the poles and the pirogue and bring me a fish for my dinner." Without another word, he walked into the cabin, letting the screen door slam shut behind him.

"He hasn't changed," Gwen stated, trying to sound indignant.

"No," Luke agreed, taking two fishing poles and putting them across his shoulder. "He's still crazy about you." After stepping into the pirogue, he held out a hand to her. With the ease of experience, Gwen settled into the canoe. Soundlessly, Raphael leaped from rail to boat and fell instantly back to sleep.

"He doesn't want to miss the fun," Gwen explained.

Luke poled away from the dock. "Tell me, Gwenivere," he asked, "how do you come to speak the dialect so fluently? Anabelle can barely read a French menu." Sunshine dappled their heads as they passed under a canopy of trees.

"Tillie taught me." Gwen leaned her head back and let the warm sunlight play on her face. She remembered Malon saying long ago that his pirogue could ride on a film of dew. "I've spoken the coastal dialect for as long as I can remember. For the most part, the people here treat outsiders as beneath their notice; it's a very closed society. But I speak Cajun—therefore, I *am* Cajun. I'm curious, though, why Malon accepts you. It's obvious that you're on easy terms."

"I don't speak Cajun." Luke stood in the pirogue and poled down the river as if born to it. "But we speak the same language nonetheless."

They cleared the trees and drifted into a ghost forest shadowed by stumps of cypress. The boat moved through floating mats of hyacinths. Tiny baby crawfish clung to the clumped roots, while a fat cottonmouth disappeared into the lavender blooms. The winding river was teeming with life.

Gwen watched a marsh raccoon fishing from the sloping bank.

"How is it," Gwen mused aloud, "that a Pulitzer Prize winner speaks the same language as a Louisiana *traiteur?*"

"Traiteur?" Luke repeated, meeting the frank curiosity in her eyes.

"Folk doctor. Malon fishes and trades and lumbers sometimes, but primarily he's the local *traiteur.* He cures snakebites, illness and spells. Spells are his specialty."

"Hmm. Did you ever wonder why he lives here, alone with his cat, his music and his books?" Gwen did not answer, content to watch Luke pole through the scattered stumps. "He's been to Rome and London and Budapest, but he lives here. He's driven tanks, broken horses, boxed and flown planes. Now he fishes and cures spells. He knows how to fix a carburetor, how to play classical guitar and how to cure snakebites. He does as he pleases and no more. He's the most successful man I know."

"How did you find out so much about him in such a short time?"

"I asked," Luke told her simply.

"No. No, it's not as easy as that." Gwen made a frustrated gesture with her hand. "People tell you things, I don't know why. I've told you things I have no business telling you, and I tell you before I realize it.'' She examined his face. ''And worse, you don't always need to be told, you know. You see people much too clearly.''

He smiled down at her. ''Does it make you uncomfortable that I know who you are?''

The river widened. Gwen's pout became a frown. ''Yes, I think it does. It makes me feel defenseless, the same way I felt when I first saw Bradley's sketches.''

''An invasion of privacy?''

''Privacy's important to me,'' Gwen admitted.

''I understand,'' Luke leaned on the pole. ''You grew up having to share your home with strangers, having to share Anabelle. The result is a desire for privacy and independence. I apologize for invading your privacy, but, after all, it's partly my profession.''

''Are we all characters to you?'' Gwen asked as she baited her hook and cast her line.

''Some more than others,'' he returned dryly, casting his line on the opposite side of the boat from hers.

Gwen shook her head. ''You know,'' she began, then settled back, stretching her legs and crossing them, ''I'm finding it very hard not to like you.''

At the other end of the canoe, Luke mirrored her position. ''I'm a very charming person.''

''Unfortunately, that's true.'' With a contented

sigh, Gwen closed her eyes. "You're not at all how I pictured you."

"Oh?"

"You look more like a woodchopper than a world-renowned writer."

Luke grinned. "And how should a world-renowned writer look?"

"Several different ways, I suppose. Intellectual, with small glasses and narrow shoulders. Or prominent..."

"Heaven forbid."

"Or prominent," Gwen continued, ignoring him. "Wearing a well-cut suit and with just a hint of a paunch. Dashing, maybe, with a faint scar along the jawline. Or Byronic..."

"Oh, good Lord."

"With a romantic pallor and tragic eyes."

"It's difficult to maintain a pallor in California."

"The trouble is, you're too physical." Gwen was enjoying the gentle drift of the boat and the warm fingers of sun. "What's your new book about?"

"A man and a woman."

"It's been done before," Gwen commented as she opened her eyes.

Luke smiled. His legs made a friendly tangle with hers. "It's *all* been done before, child. It's simply that each person believes his is a fresh experience."

Gwen tilted her head, waiting for his explanation.

Luke obliged. "Endless numbers of symphonies are composed on the same eighty-eight keys." He closed his eyes, and Gwen took the opportunity to study him.

"Will you let me read it?" she asked suddenly. "Or are you temperamental and sensitive?"

"I'm only temperamental when it's to my advantage," Luke told her lazily, opening one eye. "How's your spelling?"

"Comme ci, comme ça," Gwen grinned across at him.

"You can proof my rough draft, my spelling's only half that good."

"That's generous of you." Abruptly she let out a cry. "Oh, I've got one!" Instantly she was sitting up, giving all her attention to the fish on the end of her line. Her face was animated as she tossed her hair back with an impatient jerk of her head. There was competence in her hands and a gleam of challenge in her eyes. "Eight pounds easy," she announced as she plopped the defeated fish on deck. "And that was just for practice." Raphael roused himself to inspect the first catch, then curled up beside Gwen's hip and went back to sleep.

The silence lay comfortably between them. There was no need for conversation or small talk. Dragonflies streaked by now and then with a flash of color and a quick buzz. Occasionally birds called to each other. It seemed natural to Gwen to loll drowsily across from Luke under the hazy sun. Her legs crossed over his with absent camaraderie. The shadows lengthened. Still they lingered, drifting among the stumps of once-towering cypress.

"The sun'll be gone in a couple of hours," Luke commented. Gwen made an unintelligible sound of agreement. "We should be heading back." The boat rocked gently as Luke got to his feet.

Under the cover of gold-tipped lashes, Gwen watched him. He stretched, and muscles rippled. His eyes were clear and light, an arresting contrast to the burnished tone of his skin. They flicked over her as she lay still, too comfortable to stir herself. She knew that he was aware of her scrutiny.

"You owe me ten dollars," she reminded him smiling.

"A small price to pay for the afternoon." The water sighed as the boat glided over it. "Did you know you have five pale gold freckles on your nose?"

Gwen laughed as she stretched her arms luxuriously over her head. "I believe you're quite mad."

He watched her as the lashes shadowed her cheeks and her mouth sweetened with a smile. "I begin to be sure of it," he murmured.

It wasn't until the pirogue bumped noiselessly against its home dock that Gwen stirred again. The thin wisps of clouds were pink now with the setting sun, and there was a coolness in the air.

''Mmm.'' Her sigh was filled with the simple pleasure of the moment. ''What a lovely ride.''

''Next time, you pole,'' Luke stated. He watched Raphael stand, stretch and leap nimbly onto the dock and then joined him. After securing the boat, he offered a hand to Gwen.

''I suppose that's only fair.'' Gwen stood in one fluid movement. As nimbly as Raphael, she leaped onto the dock. She tilted back her head to give Luke a flippant grin, but found her lips captured by his.

One hand tangled in her hair while his other pressed into the small of her back, demanding she come closer. His mouth was desperate in its need for possession. There was a tension in him, a whisper of power held tightly in check. Gwen's pulses hammered at the thought of it unleashed. There was no gentleness in the mouth that claimed hers nor in the arms that held her, and she asked for none. There was a wild, restless thing in her that cried for release. She explored the strength of his arms, then the softness of his hair, as she plunged deeper into sensations she could no longer measure. Touching him, she felt there were no limits to the power flooding her. What filled her was more than the quick heat of passion, more than a transient surge of desire. It was an all-consuming need to be his. She wanted to travel where only he could take her and to learn what only he could teach her. Then Luke's hands were on her shoulders, pushing her away.

"Gwen," he began in a voice roughened with desire.

"No, don't talk," she murmured, and pulled his mouth back to hers. It was his taste, and his taste only, that could satisfy her growing hunger. She was famished, only now aware that she had fasted all her life. For a soaring, blinding moment, his mouth bruised hers; then he wrenched away. He held her shoulders in a crushing grip, but Gwen felt no pain as his eyes met hers. She could only stare. Her confusion, her need, her willingness, were plain on her face. Luke's oath was savage and swift as he turned away.

"You should know better than to look at a man like that."

Gwen heard the harsh journey of air in and out of his lungs. Her fingers shook as she ran them nervously through her hair. "I—I don't know how I looked."

"Malleable," Luke muttered. He stared down at the sluggish river before turning back to her. "Pliant, willing and outrageously innocent. Do you know how difficult it is to resist the untouched, the uncorrupted?"

Helplessly, Gwen shook her head. "No, I...."

"Of course you don't," Luke cut in sharply. She winced at his tone, and he let out a long breath. "Good heavens, how easy it is to forget what a child you are."

"I'm not, I..." Gwen shook her head in mute denial. "It happened so fast, I didn't think. I just..."

"I can hardly deny that it's my fault." His tone had cooled, and its marked disinterest had the edge of a knife. "You'rc an extraordinary creature, part will-o'-the-wisp, part Amazon, and I have a problem keeping my hands off you. Knowing I can have you is not exactly an incentive to restrain myself."

His matter-of-fact tone scraped at Gwen's raw pride, even as it tripped her temper. "You're hateful."

"Agreed," Luke said with a brief nod. "But still, I think, civilized enough not to take advantage of an innocent girl."

"I am not..." Gwen managed before she felt the need to swallow. "I am not an innocent girl, I'm a grown woman!"

"As you wish. Do you still want me to takc advantage of you?" Luke's tone was agreeable now.

"No!" Impatiently, she brushed at the hair on her forehead. "I mean, it wouldn't be... Certainly not!"

"In that case..." Taking her arm, Luke firmly guided Gwen inside Malon's cabin.

Chapter 10

Knocking on Luke's door was not the easiest thing Gwen had ever done, but it was necessary. She felt it necessary to prove to herself that she would not succumb to a newly discovered weakness again. She was a grown woman, capable of handling herself. She had asked to read Luke's manuscript, had agreed to proof it. She would not back down because of a kiss or a moment of madness. Still, Gwen braced herself as she lifted her knuckles to the wood. She held her breath.

"Come in."

These simple, ordinary words from inside the room caught at her heart. Letting out her breath slowly, she arranged her features in casual, almost indifferent lines and opened the door. Luke did not even bother to look up.

Reference books were piled on the table and scattered over the floor. Papers—typewritten, handwritten, crumpled and smooth—were strewn everywhere. On the table in the midst of the chaos was a battered portable typewriter. There sat the creator of the havoc, frowning at the keys while he pounded on them. The curtains were still drawn, closing out the late-morning sun, and the bed was a tangle of sheets. Everywhere were books, papers, folders.

"What a mess," Gwen murmured involuntarily. At her voice, Luke glanced up. There was at first a crease of annoyance between his brows, then a look of mild surprise before all was smoothed away.

"Hello," he said easily. He did not rise, but leaned back in his chair to look at her.

Gwen advanced, stepping over books and around papers on the journey. "This is incredible." She lifted her hand to gesture around the room, then dropped it to her side. "How do you live like this?"

Luke looked around, shrugged and met the curiosity in her eyes. "I don't, I work like this. If you've come to tidy up, I'll tell you the same thing I told the girl Anabelle used to send up here. Mess with my papers, and I'll toss you out the window."

Amused, Gwen stuck her hands in her pockets

and nudged a book out of her way with her toe. "So, you're temperamental after all." This, she felt, was a trait she could understand and deal with.

"If you like," he agreed. "This way, if I lose something, I can only swear at myself, not at some hapless maid or well-meaning secretary. I have an aversion for well-meaning secretaries. What can I do for you? I'm afraid the coffee's cold."

The formality in his tone made it clear this was his domain. Gwen schooled her voice to sound briskly professional. "You said yesterday you'd like me to proof your manuscript. I'd be glad to do it. If," she added with a glance around the room, "you can find it."

He smiled his charming, irresistible smile. Gwen hardened herself against it. "Are you an organized soul, Gwenivere? I've always admired organization as long as it doesn't infringe on my habits. Sit," he invited with a gesture of his hand.

Gwen stepped over two dictionaries and an encyclopedia. "Would you mind if I opened the drapes first?" she asked.

"If you wish," he answered as he reached for a pile of typewritten pages. "Just don't get domestic."

"Nothing could be further from my mind," she assured him, and had the pleasure of seeing him wince at the brilliance of the sunlight that streamed into the room. "There," she said, adopting the tone of a nursery school teacher, "isn't that better?"

"Sit."

Gwen did so after removing a pile of magazines from the chair across from him.

"You look older with your hair up," Luke commented mildly. "Nearly sixteen."

A fire lit in her eyes, but she managed to keep her voice cool. "Do you mind if I get started?"

"Not at all." Luke handed her a stack of typewritten material. "You'll find a pencil and a dictionary somewhere. Do as much as you like, just be quiet about it."

Gwen's mouth opened to retort, but as he was typing again, she closed it. After locating a pencil under a pile of discarded magazines, she picked up the first page. She refused to admit that the project excited her, that she wanted the job because it meant sharing something with him. Dismissing such thoughts, she resolved to read with objective professionalism. Minutes later, her pencil was forgotten—she was enthralled.

Time passed. Gwen no longer heard the clicking of the typewriter. Dust motes danced in the insistent sunlight, but Gwen was unaware of them. Luke's characters were flesh and blood to her. She felt she knew them, cared about them. She was even unaware that her eyes had filled with tears. She felt as the woman in Luke's story felt; desperately in love, confused, proud, vulnerable. She wept for the beauty of the words and the despair of the heroine. Suddenly, she lifted her eyes.

Luke had stopped typing, but for how long, she did not know. She blinked to clear her vision. He was watching her. His eyes were intent and searching, his mouth unsmiling. Helplessly Gwen stared back, letting the tears fall freely. Her weakness frightened her. He was not touching her, not speaking to her, yet her whole body felt attuned to him. She opened her mouth, but no words came. She shook her head, but he neither moved nor spoke. Knowing her only defense was escape, Gwen stood and darted from the room.

The bayou offered a haven, so she abandoned the house and fled toward it. She had calmed herself considerably by the time she neared Malon's cabin. Taking long, deep breaths, Gwen slowed her steps. It would not do to have Malon see her out of breath and distressed. As she rounded the last bend in the path, she saw Malon stepping from his pirogue onto the dock. Already, she felt reason returning.

"A good catch?" she asked, grateful she could smile at him without effort.

"Not bad," he answered with typical understatement. "Did you come for dinner?"

"Dinner?" Gwen repeated, glancing automatically at the sun. ''Is it so late?'' Could the afternoon have gone so swiftly? she wondered.

''It is late enough because I'm hungry,'' Malon replied. ''We'll cook up some shrimp and eat, then you can take your mama her share. Can you still make coffee?''

''Of course I can still make coffee—just don't tell Tillie.'' Gwen followed him inside, letting the screen door slam behind them.

Before long the cabin was filled with the pungent scent of shrimp gumbo cooking and the quiet strains of Chopin. Raphael sunned on the windowsill, leaving the humans to deal with the domestic chores. Gwen felt the tension draining from her system. She ate, surprised at her appetite until she recalled she had eaten nothing since breakfast.

''You still like my cooking, *hein?*'' Pleased, Malon spooned more gumbo onto her plate.

''I just didn't want to hurt your feelings,'' Gwen told him between bites. Malon watched her clean her plate and chuckled. With a contented sigh, Gwen sat back. ''I haven't eaten that much in two years.''

''That's why you're skinny.'' Malon leaned back, too, and lit a strong French cigarette. Gwen remembered the scent as well as she remembered the tastes. She had been twelve—curious and ultimately sick—when she persuaded Malon to let her try one. He had offered no sympathy and no lecture. Grinning at the memory, Gwen watched the thin column of smoke rise.

"Now you feel better," Malon commented. At his statement, she shifted her eyes back to his. Instantly, she saw he was not referring to her hunger. Her shoulders lifted and then fell with her sigh.

"Some. I needed to come here—it's helped. I'm having trouble understanding myself, and there's... well, there's this man."

"There is bound to be," Malon agreed, blowing a series of smoke rings. "You are a woman."

"Yes, but not a very smart one. I don't know very much about men. And he's nothing like the men I've known in any case." She turned to Malon. "The trouble is..." She made a small, frustrated sound and walked to the window. "The trouble is, I'm becoming more involved, more emotionally involved with...this man than I can afford to."

"'Afford to,'" he repeated with a snort. "What do you mean, 'afford to'? Emotions cost you nothing."

"Oh, Malon." When she turned back to him, her eyes were unhappy. "Sometimes they cost everything. I'm beginning to need him, beginning to feel an—an attachment that can lead nowhere."

"And why can it lead nowhere?"

"Because I need love." After running a hand through her hair, Gwen paced the width of the cabin.

"So does everyone," Malon told her, carefully crushing out his cigarette.

"But he doesn't love me," she said miserably. Her hands made a futile gesture. "He doesn't love me, yet I can't stop thinking about him. When I'm with him I forget everything else. It's wrong, he's involved with someone else, and... Oh, Malon, it's so complicated." Her voice faltered away.

"Life is not simple, little girl," he said, reverting to her childhood title, "but we live it." Rising, he moved toward her, then patted her cheek. "Complications provide spice."

"Right now," she said with a small smile, "I'd rather be bland."

"Did you come for advice or for sympathy?" His eyes were small and sharp, his palm rough. He smelled of fish and tobacco. Gwen felt the ground was more solid where he stood.

"I came to be with you," she told him softly, "because you are the only father I have." Slipping her arms around his waist, she rested her head on one of his powerful shoulders. She felt his wide hand stroke her hair. "Malon," she murmured. "I don't want to be in love with him."

"So, do you come for an antilove potion? Do you want a snakeskin for his pillow?"

Gwen laughed and tilted back her head. "No."

"Good. I like him. I would feel bad putting a hex on him."

She realized Malon had known all along she had been speaking of Luke. Always she had been as clear as a piece of glass to him. Still, she was more comfortable with him than with anyone else. Gwen studied him, wondering what secrets he held behind the small blue eyes. "Malon, you never told me you'd been to Budapest."

"You never asked."

She smiled and relaxed. "If I asked now, would you tell me?"

"I'll tell you while you do the dishes."

Bradley frowned at his canvas, then at his model. "You're not giving me the spark," he complained as he pushed the fisherman's cap further back on his head.

Three nights of fitful sleep had dimmed Gwen's spark considerably. She sat, as Bradley had directed her, in the smoothly worn U formed by two branches of an ancient oak. She wore the robe he had chosen, with a magnolia tucked behind her ear. Following his instructions, she had left her hair free and kept her makeup light. Because of their size and color, her eyes dominated the picture. But they did not, as Bradley had anticipated, hold the light he had seen before. There was a listlessness in the set of her shoulders, a moodiness in the set of her mouth.

"Gwen," Bradley said with exaggerated patience, "depression is not the mood we're seeking."

"I'm sorry, Bradley." Gwen shrugged and sent him a weary smile. "I haven't been sleeping well."

"Warm milk," Monica Wilkins stated from her perch on a three-legged stool. She was painting, with quiet diligence, a tidy clump of asters. "Always helps me."

Gwen wanted to wrinkle her nose at the thought, but instead she answered politely. "Maybe I'll try that next time."

"Don't scald it, though," Monica warned as she perfected her image of a petal.

"No, I won't," Gwen assured her with equal gravity.

"Now that we've got that settled...." Bradley began, in such a martyrlike voice that Gwen laughed.

"I'm sorry, Bradley, I'm afraid I'm a terrible model."

"Nonsense," Bradley said. "You've just got to relax."

"Wine," Monica announced, still peering critically at her asters.

"I beg your pardon?" Bradley turned his head and frowned.

"Wine," Monica repeated. "A nice glass of wine would relax her beautifully."

"Yes, I suppose it might, if we had any." Bradley adjusted the brim of his cap and studied the tip of his brush.

"I have," Monica told him in her wispy voice.

"Have what?"

Gwen's eyes went back to Bradley. I'm beginning to feel as though I was at a tennis match, she thought, lifting a hand to the base of her neck.

"Wine," Monica answered, carefully adding a vein to a pale green leaf. "I have a thermos of white wine in my bag. It's nicely chilled."

"How clever of you," Bradley told her admiringly.

"Thank you." Monica blushed. "You're certainly welcome to it, if you think it might help." Carefully she opened a bulky macramé sack and pulled out a red thermos.

"Monica, I'm in your debt." Gallantly, Bradley bowed over the thermos. Monica let out what sounded suspiciously like a giggle before she went back to her asters.

"Bradley, I really don't think this is necessary," Gwen began.

"Just the thing to put you into the mood," he disagreed as he unscrewed the thermos lid. Wine poured, light and golden, into the plastic cup.

"But Bradley, I hardly drink at all."

"Glad to hear it." He held out the cup. "Bad for your health."

"Bradley," Gwen began again, trying to keep her voice firm. "It's barely ten o'clock in the morning."

"Yes, drink up, the light will be wrong soon."

"Oh, good grief." Defeated, Gwen lifted the plastic cup to her lips and sipped. With a sigh, she sipped again. "This is crazy," she muttered into the wine.

"What's that, Gwen?" Monica called out.

"I said this is lovely," Gwen amended. "Thank you, Monica."

"Glad to help." As the women exchanged smiles, Bradley tipped more wine into the cup.

"Drink it up," he ordered, like a parent urging medicine on a child. "We don't want to lose the light."

Obediently, Gwen tilted the cup. When she handed it back to Bradley, she heaved a huge sigh. "Am I relaxed?" she asked. There was a pleasant lightness near the top of her head. "My, it's gotten warm, hasn't it?" She smiled at no one in particular as Bradley replaced the lid on the thermos.

"I hope I haven't overdone it," he muttered to Monica.

"One never knows about people's metabolisms,"

Monica said. With a noncommittal grunt, Bradley returned to his canvas.

"Now look this way, love," he ordered as Gwen's attention wandered. "Remember, I want contrasts. I see the delicacy of your bone structure, the femininity in the pose, but I want to see character in your face. I want spirit—no, more—I want challenge in your eyes. Dare the onlooker to touch the untouched."

"Untouched," Gwen murmured as her memory stirred. "I'm not a child," she asserted, and straightened her shoulders.

"No," Bradley agreed as he studied her closely. "Yes, yes, that's perfect!" He grabbed his brush. Glancing over his shoulder, he caught sight of Luke approaching, and then he gave his full attention to his work. "Ah, the mouth's perfect," he muttered, "just between sulky and a pout. Don't change it, don't change a thing. Bless you, Monica!"

Bradley worked feverishly, unaware that the wine was a far less potent stimulant to his model than the man who now stood beside him. It was his presence that brought the rush of color to her cheeks, that brightened her eyes with challenge and made her mouth grow soft, sulky and inviting. Luke's own face was inscrutable as he watched. Though he stood in quiet observation, there was an air of alertness about him. Bradley muttered as he worked. A crow cawed monotonously in the distance.

A myriad of thoughts and feelings rushed through Gwen's mind. Longing warred fiercely with pride. Luke had infuriated her, charmed her, laughed at her, rejected her. I will not fall in love with him, she told herself. I will not allow it to happen. *He won't make a fool of me again.*

"Magnificent," Bradley murmured.

"Yes, it is." Luke slipped his hands into his pockets as he studied the portrait. "You've caught her."

"It's rare," Bradley muttered, touching up the shadows of Gwen's cheeks in the portrait. "Her looks are just a bonus. It's that aura of innocence mixed with the hint of banked fires. Incredible combination. Every man who sees this portrait will want her."

A flash of irritation crossed Luke's face as he lifted his eyes to Gwen's. "Yes, I imagine so."

"I'm calling it *The Virgin Temptress.* It suits, don't you think?"

"Hmm."

Taking this as full agreement, Bradley lapsed back into unintelligible mutters. Abruptly, he put down his brush and began packing his equipment. "You did beautifully," he told Gwen. "We're losing the morning light. We should start a bit earlier, I think. Three more good sittings should do it now.''

''I'll walk back with you, Bradley.'' Monica rose. ''I've done about all I can do on this one.'' Gathering up her paints, easel and stool, she started after Bradley.

Gwen slipped down from her seat in the fork of the tree with a quick flutter of white. As her bare feet touched the grass, the wine spun dizzily in her head. Instinctively she rested her hand against the tree for support. Watching her, Luke lifted a brow in speculation. With exaggerated care, she straightened, swallowed the odd dryness in her throat and started to walk. Her legs felt strangely weak. It was her intention to walk past Luke with icy dignity, but he stopped her easily with a hand on her arm.

''Are you all right?''

The sun had the wine bubbling inside her. Clearing her throat, Gwen spoke distinctly. ''Of course. I am just fine.''

Luke placed two fingers under her chin and lifted it. He studied her upturned face. Humor leaped into his eyes. ''Why, Gwenivere, you're sloshed.''

Knowing the truth of his statement only stiffened her dignity. ''I have no idea what you are talking about. If you would kindly remove your hand from my face, I would greatly appreciate it.''

''Sure. But don't blame me if you fall on it once

the support's gone.'' Luke dropped his hand, and Gwen swayed dangerously. She gripped Luke's shirt to right herself.

''If you will excuse me,'' she said regally, but neither moved nor dropped her hand. Heaving a deep sigh, Gwen raised her face again and frowned. ''I'm waiting for you to stand still.''

''Oh. Sorry. May one ask how you came to be in this condition?''

''Relaxed,'' Gwen corrected.

''I beg your pardon?''

''That's what I am. It was either wine or warm milk. Monica's a whiz at these things. I'm not too fond of warm milk, and there wasn't any handy in any case.''

''No, I can see it might be difficult to come by,'' Luke agreed, slipping a supporting arm around her waist as she began to weave her way across the lawn.

''I only had a topful, you know.''

''That should do it.''

''Oh, dear.'' Gwen stopped abruptly. ''I've stepped on a bee.'' She sat down in a floating film of white. ''I suppose the poor little thing will go off and die.'' Lifting her foot, she frowned at the small welt on the ball of her foot.

''Happily bombed, I should think.'' Luke sat

down and took her foot in his hand. "Hurt?" he asked as he drew out the stinger.

"No, I don't feel anything."

"Small wonder. I think it might be wise to tell Bradley you don't want to be quite so relaxed at ten in the morning."

"He's very serious about his art," Gwen said confidentially. "He believes I'll become immoral."

"A distinct possibility if you continue to relax before noon," Luke agreed dryly. "But I believe you mean 'immortal.'"

"Do you think so, too?" Gwen lifted her face to the sun. "I really thought he and Monica were macadamias."

"What?"

"Nuts." Gwen lay back in the grass and shut her eyes. "I think it would be rather sweet if they fell in love, don't you?"

"Adorable."

"You're just cynical because you've been in love so many times."

"Have I?" He traced a finger over her ankle as he watched the sun highlight her hair. "Why do you say that?"

"Your books. You know how women think, how they feel. When I was reading yesterday, I hurt because it was too real, too personal." The robe shifted lightly with her sigh. ''I imagine you've made love with dozens of women.''

''Making love and being in love are entirely separate things.''

Gwen opened her eyes. ''Sometimes,'' she agreed. ''For some people.''

''You're a romantic,'' Luke told her with a shrug. ''Only a romantic can wear floating white or toss flowers to the stars or believe a magician's illusions.''

''How odd.'' Gwen's voice was genuinely puzzled as she closed her eyes again. ''I've never thought of myself as a romantic. Is it wrong?''

''No.'' The word was quick and faintly annoyed. Luke rose and stared down at her. Her hair was spread out under her, glinting with golden lights. The robe crossed lightly over her breasts, making an inviting shadow. Swearing under his breath, he bent and scooped her into his arms.

''Mmm, you're very strong.'' Her head spun gently, so she rested it against his shoulder. ''I noticed that the first day, when I watched you chop down the tree. Michael lifts weights.''

''Good for Michael.''

''No, actually, he strained his back.'' With a giggle, Gwen snuggled deeper into the curve of his shoulder. ''Michael isn't very physical, you see. He plays bridge.'' Gwen lifted her face and smiled cheerfully. "I'm quite hopeless at bridge. Michael says my mind needs discipline."

"I simply must meet this Michael."

"He has fifty-seven ties, you know."

"Yes, I imagine he does."

"His shoes are always shined," Gwen added wistfully, and traced Luke's jawline with her fingertip. "I really must try to be more tidy. He tells me continually that the image a person projects is important, but I tend to forget. Feeding pigeons in the park isn't good for a corporate image."

"What is?"

"Opera," she said instantly. "German opera particularly, but I fall asleep. I like to watch murder mysteries on the late-night TV."

"Philistine," Luke concluded as his mouth twitched into a smile.

"Exactly," Gwen agreed, feeling more cheerful than she had in weeks. "Your face is leaner than his, too, and he never forgets to shave."

"Good for Michael," Luke mumbled again as he mounted the porch steps.

"He never made me feel the way you do." At these words Luke stopped and stared down into Gwen's eyes. Cushioned by the wine, Gwen met his look with a gentle smile. "Why do you suppose that is?"

Luke's voice was edged with roughness. ''Can you really be so utterly guileless?''

She considered the question, then shrugged. ''I don't know. I suppose so. Do you want me to be?''

For a moment, Luke's arms tightened, shifting her closer against him. In immediate response, Gwen closed her eyes and offered her mouth. When his lips brushed over her brow, she sighed and cuddled closer. ''Sometimes you're a very nice man,'' she murmured.

''Am I?'' He frowned down at her. ''Let's say sometimes I remember there are a few basic rules. At the moment, I'm finding my memory unfortunately clear.''

''A very nice man,'' Gwen repeated, and kissed a spot under his jaw. With a yawn, she settled comfortably against him. ''But I won't fall in love with you.''

Luke looked down at her quiet face with its aureole of soft curls. ''A wise decision,'' he said softly, and carried her into the house.

Chapter 11

It was dark when Gwen awoke. Disoriented, she stared at the dim shapes of furniture and the pale silver moonlight. It was a knock at the door that had awakened her, and it came again, soft and insistent. Brushing her hair from her face, she sat up. The room spun once, then settled. Gwen moaned quietly and swallowed before she rose to answer the knock. In the hallway the light was bright. She put her hand over her eyes to shield them.

''Oh, darling, I'm sorry to wake you.'' Anabelle gave a sympathetic sigh. ''I know how these headaches are.''

''Headaches?'' Gwen repeated, gingerly uncovering her eyes.

"Yes, Luke told me all about it. Did you take some aspirin?"

"Aspirin?" Gwen searched her memory. Abruptly, color rushed to her cheeks. "Oh!"

Taking this as an affirmative response, Anabelle smiled. "Are you feeling better now?"

"I haven't got a headache," Gwen murmured.

"Oh, I'm so glad, because you have a phone call." Anabelle smiled more brightly. "It's from New York, so I really thought it best to wake you. It's that Michael of yours. He has a lovely voice."

"Michael," Gwen echoed softly. She sighed, wishing she could return to the comforting darkness of her room. She felt only weariness at the sound of his name. Glancing down, she saw she still wore the white robe. She could clearly remember her conversation with Luke and, more disturbing, the feel of his arms as he carried her.

"You really shouldn't keep him waiting, darling." Anabelle interrupted Gwen's thoughts with gentle prompting. "It's long-distance."

"No, of course not." Gwen followed her mother to the foot of the stairs.

"I'll just run along and have Tillie warm up some dinner for you." Anabelle retreated tactfully, leaving Gwen staring down at the waiting receiver. She took a deep breath, blew it out and picked up the phone.

"Hello, Michael."

"Gwen—I was beginning to think I'd been left on hold." His voice was even, well pitched and annoyed.

"I'm sorry." The apology was automatic, and immediately, she swore at herself for giving it. Why does he always intimidate me? she demanded silently of herself. "I was busy," she added in a firmer voice. "I wasn't expecting to hear from you."

"I hope it's a pleasant surprise," he replied. From the tone of his voice, Gwen knew he had already concluded it was. "I've been busy myself," he went on without bothering to hear her answer. "Right up to my chin in a lawsuit against Delron Corporation. Tricky business. It's had me chained to my desk."

"I'm sorry to hear that, Michael," Gwen said. Glancing up, she saw Luke coming down the steps. *Oh, perfect,* she thought in despair. She feigned unconcern with a faint nod of greeting, but when he stopped and leaned against the newel post, she frowned. "Do you mind?" she whispered sharply to Luke.

"No, not a bit." He smiled but made no effort to move. "Say hello for me."

Her eyes narrowed into furious slits. "You're horrible, absolutely horrible."

"What?" came Michael's puzzled voice. "What did you say?"

"Oh, nothing," Gwen said sharply.

"For heaven's sake, Gwen, I'm simply trying to tell you about the Delron case. You needn't get testy."

"I am not testy. Why did you call, Michael?"

"To see when you'd be coming home, sweetheart. I miss you." He was using his quiet, persuasive tone, and Gwen sighed. Closing her eyes, she rested the receiver against her forehead a moment.

"Does he always make you feel guilty?" Luke asked conversationally. Gwen jerked up her chin and glared.

"Shut up," she ordered, furious that he could read her so accurately.

"What?" Michael's voice shouted through the receiver. Luke gave a quick laugh at the outraged voice. "We must have a bad connection," he concluded.

"Must have," Gwen muttered. Taking a deep breath, Gwen decided to clear the air once and for all. "Michael, I…"

"I thought I'd given you enough time to cool off," Michael said pleasantly.

"Cool off?"

"It was foolish of us to fight that way, sweetheart.

Of course I know you didn't mean the things you said."

"I didn't?"

"You know you have a tendency to say rash things when you're in a temper," Michael reminded her in a patient, forgiving tone. "Of course," he went on, "I suppose I was partially to blame."

"You were?" Gwen struggled to keep her voice quiet and reasonable. "How could you be partially to blame for my temper?" Glancing up, she saw Luke still watching her.

"I'm afraid I rushed you. You simply weren't ready for a sudden proposal."

"Michael, we've been seeing each other for nearly a year," Gwen reminded him, pushing her fingers through her hair in irritation. The gesture caused the V of her bodice to widen enticingly.

"Of course, sweetheart," he said soothingly. "But I should have prepared you."

"*Prepared me?* I don't want to be prepared, Michael, do you understand? I want to be surprised. And if you call me sweetheart again in that patronizing voice, I'm going to scream."

"Now, now, Gwen, don't get upset. I'm more than willing to forgive and forget."

"Oh." Gwen swallowed her rage. "Oh, that's generous of you, Michael. I don't know what to say."

''Just say when you'll be back, sweetheart. We'll have a nice celebration dinner and set the date. Tiffany's has some lovely rings. You can take your pick.''

''Michael,'' Gwen said, ''please listen to me. Really listen this time. I'm not what you want.... I can't be what you want. If I tried, I'd shrivel up inside. Please, I do care about you, but don't ask me to be someone I'm not.''

''I don't know what you're talking about, Gwen,'' he interrupted. ''I'm not asking you—''

''Michael,'' Gwen said, cutting him off. ''I just can't go through all this again. I did mean the things I said, but I don't want to have to say them all again. I'm not good for you, Michael. Find someone who knows how to fix vodka martinis for twenty.''

''You're talking nonsense.'' It was his cool attorney's voice, and Gwen closed her eyes, knowing arguments were futile. ''We'll straighten all this out when you get home.''

''No, Michael,'' she said, knowing he wouldn't hear.

''Give me a call and I'll meet your plane. Goodbye, Gwen.''

''Goodbye, Michael,'' she murmured, even while she replaced the receiver. She felt a wave of sorrow and guilt. Lifting her eyes, she met Luke's. There was no amusement in them now, only understanding. She felt that amusement would have been easier to handle. "I'd appreciate it very much," she said quietly, "if you wouldn't say anything just now." She walked past him and up the stairs while he looked after her.

Gwen stood on her balcony under a moonlit sky. Moss-draped cypress trees appeared ghostly and tipped with silver. There was a bird singing in a sweet, clear voice, and she wondered if it was a nightingale. The time seemed right for nightingales. She sighed, remembering that Luke had called her a romantic. Perhaps he was right. But it was not the soft night or the song of a bird that kept her out of bed and on the balcony.

Of course you can't sleep, she berated herself silently. How can you expect to sleep at night when you slept all afternoon? Color rushed to her cheeks as she recalled the reason for her peaceful midday nap. I certainly managed to make a first-class fool of myself. Did he have to be there? Couldn't I have stumbled into the house without an audience? Why can I never be cool and dignified around him?

And then the call from Michael. Gwen lifted her hand to the base of her neck and tried to massage away the tension. Again she played over the telephone conversation in her mind, attempting to find some way she could have made her feelings clearer.

It's all been said before, she reminded herself, but he doesn't listen. *He forgives me.* With a quiet laugh, Gwen pressed her fingers to her eyes. He forgives me but thinks nothing of the cruel things he said. He doesn't even love me. He loves the woman he'd like me to be.

As she watched, a star shivered and fell in a speeding arc of light. Gwen caught her breath at the fleeting flash from heaven. Abruptly her thoughts centered on Luke. With him, she had felt a meteoric intensity, a brilliant heat. But she knew she could not hold him any more than the night sky could hold the trailing shimmer of light. Feeling a sudden chill, Gwen slipped back into her room. The middle of the night's a bad time for thinking, she decided. I'd be much better off if I went downstairs and tried some of Monica's detestable warm milk.

Gwen moved quickly down the hall, not bothering to switch on a light. She knew her way, just as she knew which steps creaked and which boards moaned. An unexpected sound made her whirl around as she reached the head of the stairs.

"Mama!" Stunned, Gwen watched her mother creep down the third-floor staircase. Anabelle started at Gwen's voice, and her hand fluttered to her heart.

"Gwenivere, you scared the wits out of me!" Anabelle's soft bosom rose with her breath. Her hair was charmingly disordered around her face. The robe she wore was frilly, pink and feminine. "What-ever are you doing out here in the dark?"

"I couldn't sleep." Gwen moved closer and caught the familiar scent of lilac. "Mama...."

"Of course, you're probably starving." Anabelle gave a sympathetic cluck. "It doesn't do to miss meals, you know."

"Mama, what were you doing upstairs?"

"Upstairs?" Anabelle repeated, then glanced back over her shoulder. "Oh, why, I was just up with Luke." She smiled, not noticing Gwen's draining color.

"W-with Luke?"

"Yes." She made a token gesture of tidying her hair. "He's such a marvelous, generous man."

Gwen gently took her mother's hand. "Mama." She bit her lip to steady her voice and took a deep breath. "Are you certain this is what you want?"

"Is what what I want, darling?"

"This—this relationship with Luke," Gwen managed to get out, although the words hurt her throat.

"Oh, Gwen, I simply couldn't get along without Luke." She gave Gwen's icy hand a squeeze. "Goodness, you're cold. You'd best get back to bed, dear. Is there anything I can get for you?"

"No," Gwen answered quietly. "No, there's nothing." She gave Anabelle a quick, desperate hug. "Please, you go back to bed, I'll be fine."

"All right, dear." Anabelle kissed her brow in a way Gwen recognized from childhood. Satisfied that there was no fever, Anabelle patted her cheek. "Good night, Gwen."

"Good night, Mama," Gwen murmured, watching her disappear down the hall.

Gwen waited until the sound of the closing door had echoed into silence before she let out a shuddering breath. Face it, Gwen, you've been falling for your mother's man. For a moment, she merely stared down at her empty hands. Doing nothing wasn't enough, she reflected. I could have stopped it.... I didn't want to stop it. There's nothing to do now but get untangled while I still can. It's time to face things head-on. Lifting her chin, she began to climb the stairs to the third floor.

Without giving herself a chance to think any further, she knocked at Luke's door.

"Yes?" The reply was curt and immediate.

Refusing to give in to the urge to turn and run, Gwen twisted the knob and pushed open Luke's door. He was, as he had been before, seated in the midst of his own disorder. He was hitting the keys of the typewriter in a quick, staccato rhythm, and his eyes were intent and concentrated. Faded, low-slung jeans were his only concession to modesty. The faintest hint of lilac drifted through the air.

Moistening her lips, Gwen kept her eyes from the tousled sheets of the bed.

I am in love with him, she realized suddenly, and simultaneously remembered it was impossible for her to be so. I'll have to find a way to fall out of love with him, she told herself, warding off a brief stab of misery. I'll have to start now. Keeping her head high, she closed the door behind her and leaned against it.

"Luke?"

"Hmm?" He glanced up absently, his fingers still working the keys. His expression altered as he focused on her. His hands lay still. "What are you doing here?" There was such sharp impatience in his voice that Gwen bit her lip.

"I'm sorry to interrupt your work. I need to talk to you."

"At this hour of the night?" His tone was politely incredulous. "Run along, Gwen, I'm busy."

Gwen swallowed her pride. "Luke, please. It's important."

"So's my sanity," he muttered, without changing rhythm.

She ran a hand through her hair. *Sanity,* she thought desperately, I must have lost mine the moment he put down that ax and walked toward me. "You're making this very difficult."

"I?" he tossed back furiously. "I make it difficult? Do you know how you look at me? Do you know how many times I've found myself alone with you when you're half-dressed?'' Instinctively, Gwen reached for the low neckline of her robe. ''Contrary to popular opinion,'' he continued as he rose and strode to a small table across the room, ''I am a mortal man given to normal instincts.'' There was a decanter of brandy on the table, and he poured himself a hefty glass. ''Damn it, I want you. Haven't I made that clear enough?''

His tone was rough. Gwen felt the tears burn in her throat. When she spoke, her voice was thick with them. ''I'm sorry, I didn't mean...'' She broke off with a helpless shrug.

''For God's sake, don't cry,'' he said impatiently. ''I'm in no mood to give you a few comforting kisses and send you along. If I touch you now, you won't leave here tonight.'' His eyes met hers. She swallowed even the thought of tears. ''I'm not in a civilized mood, Gwen. I told you once that I know my limit. Well, I've reached it.'' He lifted the decanter and poured again.

Temptation fluttered along her skin. He wanted her, she could almost taste his desire. How easy it would be to take just one small step...to steal a night, a moment. The night would be full and rich. *But the morning would be empty.* Gwen's eyes dropped, and she struggled with her own heart.

When his passion was spent, she knew her love would starve. Love has found another fool, she thought resignedly. It's best to do this quickly.

"This isn't easy for me," Gwen told him quietly. Though she fought for calm, her eyes were tragic as they met his. "I need to talk to you about Mama."

Luke turned and walked to the French doors. Tossing them open, he stared out into the night. "What about her?"

"I was wrong to interfere." Gwen shut her eyes tight and struggled to strengthen her voice. "It was wrong of me to come here thinking I had any say in whom my mother becomes involved with."

Luke swore and whirled back to face her. She watched him struggle with temper. "You are an idiot. Anabelle is a beautiful woman—"

"Please," Gwen interrupted swiftly, "let me finish. I need to say this, and it's so difficult. I'd like to say it all at once." She still stood with her back to the door, poised for escape. Luke shrugged, dropped back into his chair and signaled for her to continue. "It isn't up to me to decide what's right for my mother, it's not my right to interfere. You're good for her, I can't deny it." Gwen's breath trembled before she could steady it. "And I can't deny I'm attracted to you, but it's nothing that can't be resolved by a bit of distance. I think—I think if you and I just stay out of each other's way for the rest of my visit, everything will work out.''

''Oh, do you?'' Luke gave a quick laugh as he set down his glass. ''That's an amazing piece of logic.'' He rubbed the bridge of his nose between his thumb and forefinger. Gwen frowned at the action, finding it somehow out of character.

''I'm leaving next week,'' Gwen told him. ''There's no need for me to stay, and I've left several things undone back in New York.'' Hurriedly, she turned to the door.

''Gwen.'' Luke's voice stopped her, but she could not bear to turn and face him again. ''Don't waste yourself on Michael.''

''I don't intend to,'' she answered in a choked voice. Blind with tears, she opened the door and plunged into the darkness.

Chapter 12

Gwen dressed with care. She stretched out the process, dawdling over the buttons of her pale lavender blouse. After another sleepless night, Gwen knew she could not survive even a few more days in the same house with Luke. She could not be sophisticated, mature or philosophical about love. She went to her closet and pulled out her suitcase.

When two women love the same man, she mused, one of them has to lose. If it were anyone else, I could fight her. She opened the first case. How does a daughter fight her own mother? Even if she wins, she loses. I haven't really lost, she reflected as she moved to her dresser and pulled open a drawer. You have to have something first to lose it. I never had Luke.

Gwen packed methodically, using the task as a diversion. She refused to speculate on what she would do when she returned to New York. While packing, she had no past and no future, only the present. She would have to face the shambles of her life soon enough.

"Gwen." Anabelle knocked quickly and stuck her head into the room. "I wonder if you've seen… Oh!" She opened the door all the way when she saw Gwen's half-packed cases. "What's this?"

Gwen moistened her lips and strove for casualness. "I've got to get back to New York."

"Oh." There was disappointment in the single syllable. "But you just got here. Are you going back to Michael?"

"No, Mama, I'm not going back to Michael."

"I see." She paused a moment. "Is there some trouble at your office?"

The excuse was so perfect, agreement trembled on Gwen's tongue. Regretably, the lie would not form on her lips. "No."

Anabelle tilted her head at her daughter's tone, then quietly closed the door at her back. "You know I don't like to pry, Gwen, and I know you're a very private person, but…" Anabelle sighed before she walked over to sit on Gwen's bed. "I really think you'd better tell me what this is all about."

"Oh, Mama." Gwen turned away and rested both palms on her dresser. "It's such an awful mess."

"It can't be as bad as all that." Anabelle folded her hands neatly in her lap. "Just tell me straight out, it's the best way."

Gwen took a breath and held it. "I'm in love with Luke," she said quickly, then expelled the breath in one swift whoosh.

"And..." Anabelle prompted.

Gwen's eyes flew to the mirror in search of her mother's. "Mama, I said I was in love with Luke."

"Yes, darling, I heard that part. I'm waiting for the part about the dreadful mess."

"Mama." Gingerly, Gwen turned around. Anabelle smiled patiently. "It's not just an infatuation or a crush, I'm really in love with him."

"Oh, yes, well, that's nice."

"I don't think you understand." Gwen covered her face with her hands for a moment and then dropped them. "I even wanted him to—to make love with me."

Anabelle blushed a soft, gentle pink and brushed at her skirts. "Yes, well...I'm sure that's quite natural. I don't believe you and I ever had a talk about...ah, the birds and the bees."

"Oh, good grief, Mama," Gwen said impatiently.

"I don't need a lecture on sex. I know all about that."

"Oh?" Anabelle lifted her brows in maternal censure. "I see."

"No, I don't mean..." Gwen stopped in frustration. How did this conversation get away from me? she wondered. "Mama, please, this is hard enough. I came home to get rid of the man, and before I knew it, I was involved with him. I didn't plan it, I didn't want it. I'd never, never do anything to hurt you, and I was wrong because years don't mean a thing, and no one has the right to choose for anyone else. Now I have to go away because I love you both so terribly, don't you see?" Gwen ended on a note of despair and dropped down at Anabelle's feet.

Anabelle stared down at the tragic face thoughtfully. "Perhaps I will in a minute," she answered, furrowing her brow. "No, actually, I don't think I will. Why don't you try again? Start with the part about your coming here to get rid of Luke. I believe that's where I got confused."

Gwen sniffled and accepted Anabelle's lace hankie. "I wanted to make him go away because I thought it was wrong for you to have an affair with him. But it was none of my—"

"A what?" Anabelle interrupted. Her hand paused on its journey to smooth Gwen's curls. *"An affair?"* she repeated, blinking rapidly. "An affair?

Luke and I?'' To Gwen's amazement, Anabelle tossed back her head and laughed. It was a young, gay sound. ''How delightful! Darling, darling, how flattering. My, my.'' She smiled into space, her cheeks rosy with pleasure. ''Such a handsome young man, too. He must be—'' she stopped and fluttered her lashes ''—well, a year or two younger than I.'' She laughed again and clapped her hands together as Gwen looked on. Bending down, she kissed her daughter soundly. ''Thank you, sweet, sweet child. I don't know when I've had a nicer present.''

''Now *I* don't understand.'' Gwen wiped a lingering tear from her lashes. ''Are you saying you and Luke aren't lovers?''

''Oh, my.'' Anabelle rolled her eyes. ''How very blunt you are.''

''Mama, please, I'll go mad in a moment.'' Briefly, Gwen pressed her fingers to her eyes. Rising, she began to pace the room. ''You talked and talked about him in all your letters. You said he'd changed your life. You said he was the most wonderful man you'd ever met. You couldn't get along without him. And just last night you were coming out of his room in the middle of the night. And you've been acting strangely.'' Gwen whirled around and paced in the other direction. ''You can't deny it. Locking your door and practically pushing me out of the house on the flimsiest of excuses.''

"Oh, dear." Anabelle clucked her tongue and touched a hand to her hair. "I begin to see. I suppose it was silly of me to keep it a secret." Standing, Anabelle took a blouse from Gwen's suitcase, shook it out and walked to the closet. "Yes, it's obviously my fault. But then, I wanted to surprise you. Poor darling, no wonder you've been so unhappy and confused. I'm afraid I thought you were brooding over Michael, but it wasn't him at all, was it? Luke makes much better sense, I'm sure." Carefully, Anabelle hung up the blouse. "Now, when I think back on it, I can see how you might think so." She moved back to the suitcase while Gwen prayed for patience. "Luke and I aren't having an affair, though I do thank you for the kind thought, dear. We are, however, collaborating in a sense. Why don't you sit down?"

"I think," Gwen said, "I'm going to scream any minute."

"Always so impatient," Anabelle sighed. "Well, this is a bit embarrassing. I feel so foolish." She placed her hands on her cheeks as they grew warm. "Oh, I do hope you won't laugh at me. I'm...I'm writing a book." The confession came out in a swift jumble of words.

"What?" Gwen exclaimed, touching her hand to her ear to check her hearing.

"I've always wanted to, but I never thought I

could until Luke encouraged me.'' Excitement joined the embarrassment in Anabelle's voice. ''I've always had such pretty stories in my head, but I never had the courage to write them down. Luke says—'' Anabelle lifted her chin and glowed proudly ''—he says I have a natural talent.''

''Talent?'' Gwen echoed as she sank onto the bed.

''Isn't that lovely of him?'' Anabelle enthused. She shook out one of Gwen's packed dresses and moved toward the closet. ''He's given me so much help, so much time and encouragement! He doesn't even mind if I pop up to his room and try out an idea! Why, just last night he stopped his own work to listen to me.''

Remembering the conclusions she had drawn, Gwen shut her eyes. ''Oh, good grief! Why didn't you tell me?''

''I wanted to surprise you. And to be honest, I felt you'd think I was being silly.'' She began neatly to put away Gwen's lingerie. ''My, what a pretty chemise. New York has such wonderful shops. Then there's the money.''

''Money,'' Gwen repeated. Opening her eyes, she tried valiantly to follow her mother's winding train of thought. ''What money?''

''Luke thinks I should sell the manuscript when

I'm finished. It's—well, it's a bit crass, don't you think?''

''Oh, Mama.'' Gwen could only close her eyes again.

''I am sorry about not telling you and about locking my door so you wouldn't catch me writing. And about shooing you out of the house so that I could finish up. You aren't angry with me, are you?''

''No, no, I'm not angry.'' Gwen stared up at Anabelle's glowing face and then buried her own in her hands and laughed. ''Oh, help! What a fool I've made of myself!'' She rose quickly and embraced her mother. ''I'm proud of you, Mama. Very proud.''

''You haven't read it yet,'' Anabelle reminded her.

''I don't have to read it to be proud of you. And I don't think you're silly, I think you're marvelous.'' Drawing away slightly, she studied Anabelle's face. ''Luke's right,'' she said, kissing both of her mother's cheeks. ''You are a beautiful woman.''

''Did he say that?'' Anabelle dimpled. ''How sweet.'' After patting Gwen's shoulder, she moved to the door. ''I think we've solved everything nicely. Come down after you're unpacked, and I'll let you read my first chapters.''

''Mama.'' Gwen shook her head. ''I can't stay....''

"Oh, Luke." Anabelle beamed as she opened the door. "How lucky. You'll never believe the mess Gwen and I have just straightened out."

"Oh?" Luke looked past Anabelle to Gwen, then studied the open cases on her bed. "Going somewhere?"

"Yes."

"No," Anabelle said simultaneously. "Not anymore. She was going back to New York, but we solved everything nicely."

"Mama," Gwen said warningly, and stepped forward.

"I've confessed all," she told Luke with a bright smile. "Gwen knows all about my secret hobby. The poor darling thought you and I were having a romance."

"Weren't we?" Luke lifted her hand to his lips.

"Oh, you devil." Anabelle patted his cheek, highly pleased. "I must get along now, but I'm sure Luke will want to hear what you told me about being in love with him."

"Mama!" The sharp retort emerged as a tragic whisper.

"I'd close the door," Anabelle suggested to Luke. "Gwen favors her privacy."

"I'll do that," Luke agreed, and kissed her hand again. With a delighted blush and flutter, she disappeared.

"A truly marvelous woman," Luke commented, quietly closing the door and turning the key. He turned it over in his palm a moment, studying it, then slipped it into his pocket. Gwen decided it was better strategy not to comment. "Now, suppose you tell me what you told Anabelle about being in love with me."

Looking into his calm eyes, Gwen knew it wasn't going to be easy. Temper would not work as long as he had the key. It was vital that she remain as calm as he. "I owe you an apology," she said as she casually moved to her closet. Taking the dress Anabelle had just replaced, Gwen folded it and laid it back in the suitcase.

Luke continued to stand by the door, watching her movements. "For what, precisely?"

Gwen bit the underside of her lip hard and moved back to the closet. "For the things I said about you and Mama."

"You're apologizing for believing we were having an affair?" Luke smiled at her for the first time, and although she heard it in his voice, she did not turn to see it. "I took it as a compliment."

Turning slowly, Gwen decided to brazen it out. It was impossible, she decided, to be any more humiliated than she already was. "I'm well aware that I've made a fool of myself. And I know that I deserve to feel every bit as ridiculous as I feel. As I look back, I believe that you decided on the very first day to teach me a lesson. You never admitted you were having an affair with my mother, you simply told me it was none of my business. I felt differently at the time.'' Gwen paused to catch her breath, and Luke moved into the room to lean comfortably on one of the bedposts. ''I was wrong and you were right. It wasn't any of my business, and you succeeded in teaching me a lesson just by letting me draw my own conclusions. These were helped along by Mama's unusual behavior and her affection for you. You could, of course, have saved me a great deal of anxiety and humiliation by explaining things, but you chose to make your point. Point taken, Mr. Powers,'' she continued as she worked herself up into a temper. ''I've been put in my place by an expert. Now, I'd like you to get out of here and leave me alone. If there's one thing I want above all else, it's never to see you again. I can only be thankful we live on opposite ends of the continent.''

Luke waited a moment while she tore two skirts out of her closet and heaved them into the case. ''Can I get a copy of that speech for my files?''

Gwen whirled, eyes flaming. ''You unfeeling, pompous boor! I've done all the groveling I'm going to do. What more do you want?''

''Was that groveling?'' he asked, lifting a brow in interest. ''Fascinating. What I want,'' he continued, ''is for you to elaborate on the statement Anabelle made before she left the room. I found it very interesting.''

''You want it all, don't you?'' Gwen snapped, slamming the lid on her first case. ''All right, then, I'll give it to you. It makes little difference at this point.'' She took a breath to help the words come quickly. ''I love you. What will you do now that you know?'' she demanded, keeping her head high. ''Write it into one of your books for comic relief?''

Luke considered a moment and then shrugged. ''No. I rather think I'll marry you.''

In stunned silence, Gwen stared at him. ''I don't think that's very funny.''

''No, I doubt marriage is a funny business. I'm sure it has its moments, though. We'll have to find out.'' Straightening, he walked over and put his hands on her shoulders. ''Soon.''

''Don't touch me,'' she whispered, and tried to jerk out of his hold.

''Oh, yes, I'll touch you.'' He turned Gwen to face him. ''I'll do much more than touch you. Idiot,'' he said roughly when he saw her tear-drenched eyes. ''Are you so blind you can't see what you've put me through? I wanted you from the first moment I saw you. You stood there smiling at me, and I felt as though someone had hit me with a blunt instrument. I wanted to teach you a lesson, all right, but

I didn't expect to learn one. I didn't expect some skinny kid to tangle herself up in my mind so that I couldn't get her out.'' He pulled her close as she stared up at him, dry-eyed and fascinated. ''I love you to the edge of madness,'' he murmured before his mouth crushed hers.

It's a dream, Gwen thought dazedly as his mouth roamed her face, teasing her skin. It must be a dream. She threw her arms around his neck and clung, praying never to wake up. ''Luke,'' she managed before her mouth was silenced again. ''Tell me you mean it,'' she begged as he tasted her neck. ''Please tell me you mean it.''

''Look at me,'' he ordered, taking her chin in his hand. She did, and found her answer. Joy bubbled inside her and escaped in laughter. Laughing with her, Luke rested his brow against hers. ''I believe I've surprised you.''

''Oh, Luke.'' She buried her face in his shoulder, holding him as if she would never let him go. ''I'm not surprised, I'm delirious.'' She sighed, weak from laughter, dizzy with love. ''How did this happen?''

''I haven't the faintest idea.'' He brushed his lips over the top of her head. ''Falling in love with you was not in my plans.''

''Why not?'' she demanded, rubbing her cheek against his. ''I'm a very nice person.''

''You're a child,'' he corrected, lost in the scent

of her hair. "Do you realize what we were doing when I was your age?" He gave a quick, mystified laugh. "I was working on my second novel, and you were drawing pictures with your Crayolas."

"It's twelve years, not twenty," Gwen countered, slipping her hands under his shirt to feel the warmth of his back. "And you can hardly make an issue out of an age difference, particularly a twelve-year age difference, after all this. You don't have any double standards, do you?" she asked, lifting a brow.

Luke gave her hair a brief tug. "It's not just the years. You're so innocent, so unspoiled. Wanting you was driving me mad, then loving you only made it worse." He kissed her lightly behind the ear, and she shivered with pleasure. "Even up to last night I was determined not to take advantage of that innocence. Part of me still wants to leave you that way."

"I hope the rest of you has more sense," Gwen tossed back her head to look up at him.

"I'm serious."

"So am I." She ran a fingertip along his jawline. "Buy Bradley's portrait, if you want an image."

"I already have." He smiled, caught her fingers in his and kissed them. "You don't think I'd let anyone else have it, do you?"

"Have me, too." Amusement vanished from his face as she pressed against him. "I'm a woman, Luke, not a child or an image. I love you, and I want you.'' Rising on her toes, she met his mouth. His hands sought her, possessed her, while she trembled with excitement. Her love seemed to expand, surrounding her until there was nothing else. She pressed closer, offering everything. It was he who drew away.

''Gwen.'' Luke let out a long breath and shook his head. ''It's difficult to remember that you're Anabelle's daughter and that she trusts me.''

''I'm trying to make it impossible,'' she countered. She could feel the speed of his heartbeat against hers, and reveled in a new sense of power. ''Aren't you going to corrupt me?''

''Undoubtedly,'' he agreed. Framing her face with his hands, he kissed her nose. ''After we're married.''

''Oh.'' Gwen pouted a moment, then shrugged. ''That's sensible, I suppose. Michael was always sensible, too.''

Luke's eyes narrowed at the mischief in hers. ''That,'' he said distinctly, ''was a low blow. Do you know how very near I came to pulling the phone out of the wall last night when I heard you talking to him?''

''Did you?'' Gwen's face illuminated at the thought. ''Were you jealous?''

''That's one way of putting it,'' Luke agreed.

''Well,'' Gwen considered carefully, trying not to

smile, “I suppose I can understand that. As I said, he’s a very sensible man. It’s all right, though, I’m sure you’re every bit as sensible as Michael.”

Luke studied her carefully, but Gwen managed to keep the smile a mere hint on her lips. “Are you challenging me to kiss you into insensibility?”

“Oh, yes,” she agreed, and closed her eyes. “Please do.”

“I never could resist a dare,” Luke murmured, drawing her into his arms.

* * * * *